HIGHLAND QUEST

B.J. SCOTT

SOUL MATE PUBLISHING

New York

HIGHLAND QUEST
Copyright©2012
B.J. SCOTT

Cover Design by Rae Monet, Inc.

This book is a work of fiction. The names, characters, places, and incidents are the products of the author's imagination or are used fictitiously. Any resemblance to actual events, business establishments, locales, or persons, living or dead, is entirely coincidental.

All rights reserved. No part of this publication may be reproduced, stored in a retrieval system, or transmitted in any form or by any means (electronic, mechanical, photocopying, recording, or otherwise) without the priority written permission of both the copyright owner and the publisher. The only exception is brief quotations in printed reviews.

The scanning, uploading, and distribution of this book via the Internet or via any other means without the permission of the publisher is illegal and punishable by law. Please purchase only authorized electronic editions, and do not participate in or encourage electronic piracy of copyrighted materials. Your support of the author's rights is appreciated.

Published in the United States of America by
Soul Mate Publishing
P.O. Box 24
Macedon, New York, 14502

ISBN: 978-1-61935-318-3
eBook ISBN: 978-1-61935-166-0

www.SoulMatePublishing.com
The publisher does not have any control over and does not assume any responsibility for author or third-party websites or their content.

To my husband Steve,

for your continued support and faith in my dream.

To my family

for their continued love and encouragement.

Acknowledgements

As always there are so many people who touch our lives and influence our success. People who with their acts of kindness or support make our lives a little easier and lot more pleasant.

My husband and soul mate, Steve, who has put up with my hectic schedule, a messy house, less one on one time when I need to write and for buying me take out so I could get this book finished.

To my three fab critique partners. Marie, Jennifer, and Colleen aka (Ann, Meggan and Callie) Without your excellent input, eyes for details and encouragement, this book would never have been written. I cherish your friendships more than words can express. Thank you from the bottom of my heart.

As always a huge thank you to the readers who supported my first book and asked for a second. The Fraser saga continues because of you.

To the staff at Soul Mate Publishing for helping to make the book shine.

Finally, kudos to my fellow authors who have enriched my life and dazzle the world with their words and wonderful stories.

Chapter 1

Loch Ryan Scotland, 1307

"Wa . . . water," Bryce mumbled, but there was no one there to listen.

His throat was parched and he ran his tongue over dry, cracked lips, but his action offered no relief. An entire loch lay only a few feet away, but he couldn't muster the strength to drag himself to the bank and quench his thirst.

"Cold . . . so cold."

Despite the sun beating down on him, he'd swear he was encased in ice. His life's blood seeped from his wounds, soaking the ground beneath him. He tried to raise his head, but the excruciating pain radiating across his chest stole his breath away.

Was this what it felt like to die? If so, he prayed the Almighty would be merciful and take him now.

Bryce moaned, a shift in his position bringing on another nauseating wave of agony. He sucked in a short, sharp, gulp of air and stretched his arm out as far as he could, his fingers grappling in the dirt.

If only I could reach my sword.

Beads of perspiration dampened his brow. As the strength slowly drained from his body, drawing a simple breath became more difficult. The end grew near. No time to make amends for sins of the past, and he had committed his share.

Regrets? He had those, too. "Fallon." He whispered her name then heaved a ragged sigh. He could see her beautiful face, her soft, porcelain-like skin with just a sprinkling of freckles across her nose. Raven tresses hanging loose in a riot of curls down her back. Her petite, slender body had just the right curves to drive a man wild with desire. Mysterious sapphire eyes that held him captive and a heart-shaped mouth he'd never tire of kissing. If he had one wish before he died, it would be to hold her in his arms one more time, to find himself nestled between her thighs, making love until neither of them could take anymore.

But he'd missed his chance when she left Fraser Castle after his brother's wedding, returning with her clan to their home in the borderlands. Determined not to allow Fallon, or any woman, to breach the protective wall he'd built around his heart, he'd let her go.

A restless spirit, he longed for adventure. While he admired his two older brothers, he was tired of living in their shadows. Alasdair had turned down the position of Laird when their father and older brother were killed at Berwick on Tweed. Connor, the next in line, had accepted the responsibility and did the Clan proud. He was happily married and Bryce was certain his wee son, Andrew, would be raised to follow in his father's footsteps.

Bryce held no land or title. Until he had made a name for himself and earned these things, he had nothing to offer a wife. But marriage and family were not part of his immediate plans. He loved women, all women. Be they large, small, short, tall, fair, or plain, it made no difference as long as they were willing to warm his bed, and expected no long-term commitment in return.

A rogue many would say, but he made no secret of his intentions. So far, this way of life had served him well, and should he die in battle, he'd leave no one behind to mourn his loss.

When he was a lad of sixteen, he'd made the mistake of falling for the daughter of the village smithy. Totally enamored with each other, they'd vowed their eternal love and he believed they'd marry some day.

He swallowed hard at the ball of emotion rising in his throat, and clenched his teeth against the sudden ache gripping his heart. He'd heard when a man is about to die, his life experiences flash before his eyes. But some memories were far too painful to revisit.

He balled his fists at his sides, his nails digging into his palms. He didn't want to think about the past and didn't want a woman in his life. While Fallon was the only lass who had tempted him to stray from his chosen path, she was better off without him. Or so he'd told himself when he returned from a morning ride to learn she'd left Fraser Castle without saying goodbye.

Clinging to the memory of their brief time together, Bryce closed his eyes and waited for death to take him. But distant voices and the sound of approaching footfall alerted him to the fact that he was no longer alone.

"Over here," a man shouted. "I think this one is still breathing."

"Aye, he's alive, but for how long? The lad has lost a lot of blood," another man commented and clucked his tongue.

Hovering on the edge of consciousness, Bryce heard the conversation going on between two men, maybe more. He tried to open his eyes, but the lids proved too heavy.

Judging by the familiar burr, these men were Scottish, but so were the traitorous bastards who had attacked them.

For a sennight, he'd ridden day and night. However in the end, he was too late to warn the Bruce's brothers and their small group of Irish and Scottish islanders of the impending threat. Rushing headlong into an ambush and outnumbered four to one, their fate was sealed.

This wasn't the first time the MacDougall Clan sided with the English. Staunch supporters of John Comyn's bid for the Scottish crown, they'd turned their swords and their loyalty against their countrymen when Comyn was murdered at Grey Fryer's Abbey and Robert the Bruce was accused of the deed.

After the massacre at Methven—the last major battle fought between the English and the Bruce before he went into hiding—the buggers lay in wait, attacking the Scottish survivors as they tried to make their way to the Argyle Mountains to regroup. The battle of *Dail Righ* would forever be a stain on the MacDougall clan's name, and a battle Bryce would long remember.

Nor would he forget their leader. Today he'd had the long-awaited chance to make good on his oath to see the blackguard pay for his treasonous acts, but he'd failed. Instead, he'd found himself on the receiving end of Dungal's sword.

"I canna believe Scots would kill Scots. These poor fellows dinna have a prayer of making it to shore unharmed," the first man said.

"Aye, the ship was run aground and there must be at least fifty dead men on the bank of the loch. There appears to be a mix of Irish and Scots, but nary an English soldier or a MacDougall plaid among them." The man speaking nudged Bryce's shoulder with the toe of his boot. "This appears to be the only one alive."

A dizzying wave of excruciating pain shot through Bryce's chest as he was rolled onto to his side.

"What do you plan to do with this fellow, Donald?" the second man asked. "We canna just leave him here to bleed to death."

"We'll take him with us. My niece has some knowledge of healing. She cared for my wife when she had the pox . . . rest her soul." Donald paused for a moment before he continued. "After Mairi died, the lass decided to stay on for a while. Mayhap there is something she can do for him. Best we make haste. I dinna want to be here if the bastards return."

"I'll be surprised if he survives the journey. But we can always bury him along the way if need be," the second man responded.

Strong hands slid beneath Bryce's shoulders, raising him to a sitting position, then someone grabbed his legs. A few garbled words of protest were all he could manage before darkness closed around him.

"Fallon! Are you here, lass?" her Uncle Donald shouted. "I need your help. Where are you hiding?"

"I'm here, Uncle," she called, unnerved by his anxious tone. "I was out back tending to the herb garden." She came into the shadow of the doorway, wiping the dirt from her hands on her apron. "What's all the *palver* about?"

"We came across a group of men on the bank of Loch Ryan. They were ambushed by traitors."

Fallon wrapped her arms around her waist and shuddered at his words. "The attack happened as I predicted?"

Donald nodded. "Aye. Exactly the way you saw it in your vision."

"Where is the man who survived? Take me to him."

Donald blinked several times and his mouth dropped open at her question. "He's outside in the cart. How did you—"

"Please, take me to him at once." She lifted her skirt and headed for the door. "We must hurry, his time grows short."

Her uncle led the way to where his two friends waited by the cart.

"Let me through." She pushed past the two burly men, but stopped dead in her tracks when she saw the wounded man.

Bryce!

"He's hurt verra badly. We dinna think he'd survive the trip." Angus shook his head and crossed himself.

Her pulse racing, Fallon struggled to maintain her composure. It had been several months since she'd seen Bryce. To be honest, she believed the day she left Fraser Castle and returned to the borderlands would be their last encounter. Leaving without saying goodbye had to have been one of the most difficult things she had ever done. Purging him from her mind proved a challenge, but getting him out of her heart completely was impossible.

Bryce's home was in the Highlands. What was he doing in Galloway? Was he alone, or were Connor and Alasdair with him and lost in the battle? Her heart sank at the thought. Despite their constant banter and bickering, Bryce was close to his two older brothers. If they'd perished in the raid, he'd be devastated by their loss.

While their so-called lawless deeds against the English crown were justified, she knew the Fraser brothers were wanted by Longshanks for murder and treason. Her uncle, a supporter of Robert the Bruce's efforts to regain his royal position of power in Scotland, would not hesitate to help Bryce, but she didn't know if his friends could be trusted to do the same. Would they betray him and turn him in if they knew there was a price on his head?

Erring on the side of caution, she decided it best to keep his identity a secret until she could speak to him.

She moved to Bryce's side. Her heart twisted in her chest as she surveyed his injuries. There was so much blood. If not for his slow uneven breathing, she would have believed he was dead.

Squaring her shoulders, she faced Angus. "Bring him inside so I can tend to his wounds. Please be gentle." Turning on her heel, she hurried back to the croft.

Angus, a strapping man at least six-foot-four, lifted Bryce from the cart and carried him into the wattle and daub hut as if he weighed no more than a bairn. "Where do you want him?"

"Put him on the raised pallet near the hearth. Once he's settled, could you fetch me a bucket of water from the well?" As she doled out orders, her eyes never left her patient. She still could not believe he was here and feared if she turned away, even for a second, he'd disappear. "I'll also need some more wood and peat for the fire."

"Aye." Angus rushed out the door to do her bidding.

After gathering the supplies needed to tend Bryce's wounds, she removed his bloody, dirt-encrusted tunic and tossed it on the floor.

Donald leaned over her shoulder and exhaled sharply. "It's just as I thought. The sword went clear through. The lad is lucky to be alive."

"Aye, but if I tarry any longer, he'll bleed to death." Without hesitation, she took two dirks from her basket of herbs, placed them amidst the hot coals in the hearth, and waited until the blades glowed red.

"I'll need you and Ian to hold him down." She plucked a dirk from the fire and approached the pallet.

"What are you planning to do?" her uncle asked.

"There is no time to try and staunch the bleeding or to stitch the wound. I'll have to seal it." Tears welled in her eyes, but she blinked them away. Adding to Bryce's pain was the last thing she wanted, but she pushed her emotions aside and prepared do what was necessary to save his life.

Donald and Ian looked at each other, the color draining from their faces as they moved into position—one holding Bryce's feet, the other his shoulders.

"Are you sure there is no other way?" Donald asked and then turned his head when she brought the hot steel closer to Bryce's chest.

"If I dinna do this, he will die." She wiped the perspiration from her brow with the back of her hand and said a quick prayer before plunging the dirk into the wound.

Bryce's eyes flew open, his body jerking and bucking the instant the molten metal made contact. He thrashed about wildly, lashing out with his fists, and shouted in pain.

"We canna hold him much longer!" Ian widened his stance and tightened his grip on Bryce's shoulders.

"You must keep him still. I'm almost through." The acrid odor of burning chest hair and charred flesh stung her nostrils and sickened her stomach, but this had to be done.

"He's too strong." Donald sprawled across Bryce's legs, using his body weight to keep them on the pallet.

Satisfied that the wound was sealed, Fallon motioned for her uncle to stand up. "Please turn him to his side while I retrieve the other dirk." Once Bryce was positioned to her satisfaction, she repeated the process. But this time he offered no resistance.

The ordeal over, she stepped away from the pallet, drew in a slow, deep breath, and choked down the bile rising from her stomach. Her hands trembled as she repeatedly slid them down the front of her apron. Once her heart had settled and the strength retuned to her wobbly legs, she moved to Bryce's side.

"Are you all right, lass?" Donald inquired. "You were looking so pale I thought you might faint."

"I'm fine. Best you worry about Ian." She pointed to the man as he rushed outside with his hand cupped over his mouth. "Once Angus returns with the water and I've washed away the blood, I'll apply some salve to his burns." She lifted Bryce's hand and absently stroked her fingers across the back of it. "I'll also need some whiskey to dull the pain when he awakens."

"Do you honestly think that's going to happen?" Angus crossed the room carrying a wooden bucket, water sloshing over the rim and onto the rush-covered dirt floor. "I just saw Ian outside. He was pretty green about the gills, and I'm guessing he lost his last meal while bending over a rock."

"I've done all I can for him. It's up to the Almighty to decide if he lives or dies." Fallon swept her fingertips across Bryce's sweat-soaked brow and released a shuddering breath. "I will pray that he lives."

"He's a strapping lad. Judging by the scars on his chest and arms, this isn't his first battle." Donald placed his hand on her shoulder. "It is going to be a long night. Mayhap you should have a wee bite to eat and try to get some rest. I can sit with him for a while."

"Nay. I want to be here if he wakes up." She placed a small wooden stool beside the pallet and sat down.

Time passed slowly and other than a few moments of fitful sleep and mumbled words in Gaelic she could not decipher, Bryce didn't stir. His breathing remained labored. His cheeks were flushed, heat radiated from his body, and a fine sheen of sweat covered his chest and limbs. Yet he began to shiver if she removed any of the covers.

As his condition weakened, her concern grew. She rose, but left him only long enough to retrieve some willow bark tea from a pot simmering on the hearth. Gently sliding her hand behind his head, she raised it a little, and brought a wooden cup to his lips.

"Drink," she urged, even though she doubted he could hear her. Despite her efforts, the herbal brew, meant to ease his pain and combat fever, was impossible to administer in his unconscious state, most of it dribbling down his chin.

She placed the cup on the table beside the pallet then took a few minutes to stretch her legs and to work out the stiffness in her back before continuing her vigil. An attempt to busy herself with needlework proved futile, her mind constantly wandering back to Bryce. As each hour passed, the fever burned hotter, and she was more convinced he'd not survive the night.

"Och, Bryce, what evil twist of fate has brought you back into my life? A woman's heart can only take so much torture." She lightly stroked his cheek, but he did not respond. "When last we parted, I never thought I would see you again. And now—"

She choked back a sob. The last few days they'd spent together at Fraser Castle were bittersweet. True, the joy of seeing Connor and Cailin united in marriage had made her heart soar, and Andrew's birth was a time for celebration. But she also remembered standing outside the great hall while the bride and groom took part in their wedding dance, wishing for one brief moment it were her and Bryce who had just exchanged their vows.

A beautiful bride, Cailin stared up at her husband with such love and devotion. Judging by the way Connor returned her moonstruck gaze and possessively held her close, it was obvious he shared her sentiment.

Would a man ever look at her with such adoration? The fact that she might never experience such a moment was almost too much to endure. She wrapped her arms around her waist and turned, only to find Bryce standing directly behind her.

"Bryce," she whispered his name when their eyes met. Her stomach did a nervous flip. She fisted her hands in her skirt to keep them from trembling and glanced at the floor.

Undeniably a handsome man, she'd found him appealing from the moment he arrived at the Scott's Castle, but there was something more than mere physical attraction that drew her to him.

While they'd met in passing, and in actuality had spent very little time alone together, it felt as if she'd known him for years. There was something familiar about him and a level of comfort she experienced when in his presence, a sense of calm and acceptance that had eluded her when in the company of most people she encountered.

While her unwelcome premonitions focused primarily on death and illness, she had experienced the odd vision of happy events yet to take place. On more than one occasion she'd seen a brown-haired man walking toward her, which according to Scottish lore was a good sign. A dark-haired woman kept pace at his left side and if the legend held true, she was likely the lass he was meant to marry.

When the woman inclined her head, Fallon saw her own image. But when her suitor grasped her hand and brought it to his lips, he disappeared in a wisp of smoke before she could see his face.

Was the mysterious man in her dream Bryce?

She shook her head. While she wanted to believe they were destined for each other, the fact she'd never seen her intended's features could only mean one thing. She would never find her true love.

Mayhap a life of solitude was for the best. From the time she was a wee lass, she believed herself cursed. Everyone she dared to love had died. Seeing their demise and being helpless to stop it weighed heavy on her mind and heart.

The first visions of pending death and misfortune occurred when she had barely seen four summers. Aside from her parents, most people kept their distance. An only child, she'd spent the better part of her life alone, an outcast because people feared what they didn't understand. *Taibhsearchd* was deemed a gift by some. Her mother thought second sight was a blessing, one passed down from mother to daughter and a reason to rejoice. But Fallon considered herself very unlucky.

Then again, mayhap she didn't want to find a mate. Aside from her father, her uncle, Laird Scott, and a few others she respected, she found most men to be domineering brutes. They expected their women to subserviently await their orders and held little or no revere for their wives, beyond what they could offer between the plaids. If a woman dared to speak her mind or show any initiative, they were quickly put in their place. If given a choice between an oppressive, loveless marriage and a life alone, she'd pick the latter.

She shuddered at the thought of daughters being used as pawns, a means to gain land, alliances, and chattel. She thanked the Almighty on a daily basis that her parents had gone against tradition and raised her to be a strong, independent woman.

While she'd had many suitors express an interest, once they learned of her unwillingness to comply with the old ways and her so-called gift, they abandoned her as if she had a plague. But when she met Bryce, she sensed he was different. In addition to the fact he made her heart race and her stomach flutter with excitement, he claimed to set no store in her ability to see the future and accepted her for who she was. They'd connected on more than one level, or so she'd thought.

The fierce loyalty Bryce showed for his brothers and his willingness to kill the enemy was a stark contrast to the gentleness and concern he showed for his sister-by-marriage when he'd brought her to Buccleuch seeking refuge.

Bryce put on a bold front and professed he wanted no woman in his life, but he'd revealed his sensitive, caring side. He did not chastise her for her temerity and spirit. Nor did he shy away from her because of her gift of second sight. Yet, in spite of his debonair demeanor, there was something that tortured his soul. If only he would open up to her and share his inner thoughts. Mayhap they could have . . .

Fallon gave her head a shake and straightened her spine. What was she thinking? She'd spent the last few months trying to forget Bryce and she refused to allow herself to be swayed by emotion. Again. He had made his choice when he'd allowed her to leave Fraser Castle without protest. He was not here by choice and would surely depart to rejoin the cause as soon as he was able. She didn't need him in her life. She didn't need anyone.

Fallon could not deny she'd had strong feelings for Bryce, but that was in the past. She'd put it behind her and meant to keep it there. A life of solitude was for the best.

Exhausted, she laid her head on the edge of the pallet. "A short rest is all I need." Her eyes drifted shut, but Bryce's face filled her mind.

Waking with a start a short time later, she glanced around the dark croft. The tallow candles had burned down to a snub and the remnants of a fire smoldering in the hearth offered the only source of light. Her uncle had added more wood and peat before retiring, but the room had grown chilly. She wrapped a length of plaid around her shoulders and huddled beneath it for warmth. Before long, her heavy-lidded eyes closed again, and she surrendered to sleep.

Chapter 2

He made his way through a dense forest that seemed to go on forever, stumbled over rocks and fallen logs, but somehow managing to stay on his feet. Sweat soaked his brow and tunic. His chest tightened and his leg muscles cramped from the exertion. The stitch in his side caused him to double over in pain more than once, but he had to keep going. He paused for a moment to catch his breath then continued to run as if the Devil were dancing on his heels.

The sound of a waterfall echoed in the distance. He envisioned a stream rushing over a bed of smooth stones, prisms of sunlight dancing across the cool, clear surface. He could almost taste the icy liquid sliding across his tongue and down his desiccated throat.

"Only a wee bit farther." Those words became his mantra.

When he finally broke free of the woods, he came to an abrupt halt. His mouth gaped open at the sight, his thundering heart drowning out the noise around him.

A meadow, dotted with fragrant heather, stretched in all directions, as far as the eye could see. The sweet floral scent reminded him of his childhood, of carefree days romping and wrestling in the grass with his brothers, and the familiar aroma of his mother's hair.

Tears ran down his cheek, and he scrubbed them away with the sleeve of his tunic. Cupping his hand over his eyes, he peered up at a cloudless azure sky. A hawk circled above him, looking for prey. A rabbit scurried by, brushing his leg as if he were not even there.

He caught sight of his goal. A mountain stream cascading over a cliff and emptying into a loch. "A wee bit farther," he shouted and took off running again.

The distance grew shorter, but a sense of urgency increased with each of his strides. Something was amiss. He could feel it in his bones.

"Where do you think you're going?" A man stepped from the shadow of a lone pine in the middle of the field, blocking his path.

Blinded by the sun, Bryce narrowed his eyes until his foe's features came into view. He would never forget his face or the cadence of the man's voice. Both had haunted his dreams for almost a year. "Dungal MacDougall," he hissed through clenched teeth.

Instinctively, Bryce reached for his sword, but the baldric on his back was empty. "This canna be." He glanced down and found the sheath at his side held no weapon.

He looked over Dungal's shoulder and spotted a ship on the loch. The vessel was headed into an ambush—hundreds of men lying in wait along the shore. Those on the water didn't stand a chance.

Bryce tried to shout out a warning, but had no voice. He tried to run forward, but his legs were like anvils.

He watched in horror as the unsuspecting men disembarked, only to be slaughtered when they reached the shore. The once pristine sand turned red with their blood, but their comrades kept coming.

It was over so fast. Too late to warn them, Bryce hung his head in shame, his heart torn asunder by grief.

Anger welled in his chest and a knot formed in his belly. With his hands fisted at his sides, he met Dungal's smug expression with a scowl. "I'll see you rot in Hell for your acts of treason against Scotland."

Dungal threw back his head and laughed. "And how

do you intend to make that happen? You are but one man." With his sword raised in the air, he shouted, "BUAIDH NO BAS!"

His clan members answered with the same MacDougall war cry. "Victory or death!"

Bryce had to do something. He'd not give up without a fight. He lunged forward, his only thought to subdue Dungal and relieve him of his weapon. The sharp pain as his enemy's blade pierced his chest was the last thing he'd anticipated.

Staggering backward, Bryce looked down at the hand he clutched to his chest. Blood oozed between his fingers and drenched the front of his shirt. He dropped to his knees, his breath coming in short, sharp pants.

Dungal circled around behind him, placed his boot between his shoulders, and shoved him to the ground.

Sputtering and spitting the dirt from his mouth, Bryce rolled to his back, staring up into the face of his nemesis.

Dungal laughed again and arched his sword in the air, prepared to deliver the final blow, when a young woman strolled out of the woods.

Bryce tried to call out, to warn her to run, but she kept walking in their direction.

Dungal's mouth drew into an evil grin as the lass approached. "Now, that is what I call a lovely prize. When I am finished with you, I will claim her as a spoil of war."

Powerless to stop him, Bryce groaned and turned his head to the side. There was something familiar about the lass. As she stepped out of shadows and into the light, his heart clenched and his breath caught.

"Fallon!"

"Aye, Bryce." She ran her hand over his brow. "I'm here. You must rest. We can speak when you are stronger."

He thrashed about, but never opened his eyes. He called out her name again, babbled in a mix of Scots and Gaelic, and tossed his head from side-to-side.

"How fares the lad? I heard him shouting." Donald strode across the room.

She glanced down at Bryce and touched his face. "The fever has not broken. He's restless and very weak." She swallowed against the knot of emotion in her throat, but could not stay the tears sliding down her cheeks. She turned her head and quickly scrubbed them away with the heel of her hand.

Donald moved to the other side of the pallet, leaving her no choice but to face him. His frown deepened. "You seem overly concerned about a stranger. Is there something I should know?"

Fallon shifted in her seat then dragged her hand across the back of her neck. She trusted Donald, but was concerned for Bryce's safety.

He would be in grave danger if the English learned he'd survived the attack and discovered his whereabouts. On the other hand, if her uncle were found guilty of harboring a fugitive, he would be hanged for treason.

What to do?

"You are not my daughter, but while you are living under my roof, I am responsible for your welfare. Your aunt would come back to haunt me if I dinna look out for your best interests. Do you know this man?" His tone hardened.

Fallon inclined her chin and met her uncle's discerning stare. She'd never been a good liar, and he did have a right to know Bryce was a wanted man.

Donald crossed his arms over his chest and glared at her. "I'll ask you again. Do you know this man?"

Fallon gave a hesitant nod. "Aye. We've met before."

"Judging by your moonstruck expression when you look

at the lad, I'd say there was a lot more between you than a simple meeting. Should I be fetching the priest?"

Fallon shook her head. "Nay. It was not like that."

While they had never joined their bodies in the physical sense, she did feel a powerful bond to Bryce. Unlike anything she had ever known. Whenever she looked at his handsome face, fine, chiseled features, and muscular physique her breath caught and her heart raced like a runaway horse.

Despite the obvious attraction between them, Bryce had made it clear on more than one occasion that he had no desire for a wife, and she refused to beg for any man's affection. She regretted leaving Fraser Castle without saying goodbye, but at the time believed it was for the best. But seeing him again rekindled feelings she'd believed were buried and forgotten. She closed her eyes, her mind wandering back to the first time they'd kissed.

His breath was sweetened with mint and fennel. The press of his mouth, a light brush across her lips, was almost reverent in the beginning, as if murmuring a prayer. But as she relaxed, giving in to temptation, his advances became more passionate, more intense. To surrender to this willful behavior was wrong and could only lead to heartache, but instead of resisting, she opened her mouth to his sweet invasion.

The first time he slid his tongue across the seam of her lips she was certain her bones would melt. When he pulled her against his broad chest and muscular thighs, she felt the proof of his arousal. Her knees buckled, and she thought she might perish, the need to be with this man so strong and intense.

"Did he dishonor you?" Donald asked bluntly.

The heat of a blush rose in her cheeks and she turned her head. "Nay. We are just friends. There is nothing between us and never will be." There was a time when she'd thought things might be different with Bryce. She'd actually found herself hoping the stubborn fool would find his senses, realize they were meant to be together, and come after her. But then quickly resolved herself to the fact it would be a mistake.

"When we brought him to the croft, you gave no indication that you were acquainted. If you have nothing to hide, why did you keep his identity a secret?" Donald wandered halfway across the room, paused, and then turned to face her. "What is his name? I have the right to know."

"Bryce Fraser."

"Fraser, you say?" Donald cut her off before she could finish. "Kin to the patriot Sir Simon Fraser?"

"Aye, he was his father's cousin. Bryce and his two older brothers, Connor and Alasdair, spent time at Oliver Castle after their parents were killed in raids by the English. He was like their surrogate father. They fought side-by-side at the battle of Methven, Dail Righ, and Kirkenclif, but were helpless to do anything to stop Simon's brutal execution." Fallon crossed herself and muttered a quick prayer.

"His brother is also the man whose wife was to be hanged for murdering one of Edward's officers. And a wanted man," Donald quickly added.

"Aye, but his wife, Cailin, was innocent. Two soldiers attacked her then tried to have their way with her. Connor came to her aid and killed the officer while defending her honor."

She continued before her uncle had a chance to respond. "The scoundrel was the brother of the lord of Carlisle Castle and he demanded justice be served. When Bryce and his brothers rescued Cailin from Lord Borden's clutches, she was with child, and had been severely flogged."

She paused, remembering the brutal wounds slashing across Cailin's back. But for the grace of God they could have killed her. She licked her dry lips and continued.

"They brought her to the Scott's castle, knowing Laird Scott would grant them sanctuary. She was placed in my care. When Cailin was well enough to travel, Borden attacked them on their journey and tried to take her prisoner. Connor intervened and demanded her release, but Borden threatened to throw her off a cliff. Bryce killed him as he was about to make good on his threat."

Donald raked his fingers through his hair and began to pace. "The English defile our women all too often these days and need to be stopped. However—"

"I'm sorry for not telling you the truth sooner, Uncle, but I felt it was my duty to keep Bryce's secret. At least until he had a chance to explain how he came to be at Loch Ryan." She dropped her head, cradling it in her hands. Had she said too much?

Donald coughed to clear his throat. "Dinna *fash* over this, lass. I'll not give his secret away. Simon Fraser's bravery and that of his cousins has been heralded throughout Scotland. They are considered heroes and honored by Robert the Bruce as such. The lad is welcome to stay as long as necessary."

When Donald gently slid his fingers over her shoulder and gave her a comforting squeeze, Fallon leaned into his touch, then clutched his palm and curled her head to the side to press her lips against the back of his hand. "Thank you, Uncle."

Redirecting her attention to Bryce, she dipped a linen rag into a bowl of cold water, willow bark, and comfrey. After ringing the cloth out, she laid it across his fevered brow. "What about Angus and Ian? Can they be trusted not to say anything?"

"Like your friends, they are both sympathetic to the cause. I'd trust them with my life. Neither is the sort to betray me or mine. But you can rest assured, I will speak to them and emphasize the need for silence." Donald paused. "Will you be needin' anything more?"

She shook her head. "Nay."

"Then I'll be off to find Angus and Ian." Donald turned and left the croft.

Fallon waited for her uncle to close the door before lifting Bryce's hand and clutching it to her breast. While he had never opened his eyes, he'd called her name several times in his delirium. Mayhap he harbored feelings for her after all.

Nay, she refused to let him into her heart again.

You're a fool, Fallon MacCrery. He doesna even know you're here. Besides, he has no use for a wife. He longs for adventure and plans to remain focused on Scotland's fight for independence or to die trying.

Afraid of having her hopes dashed again, she chastised herself for being vulnerable to the ranting of a sick man.

The fact that she found herself attracted to Bryce was of no importance. Until now, she had managed to live without him and would continue to do so. She didn't need a man to complete her life. She'd tend to his injuries, but the rest of the time would keep her distance.

Hovering on the edge of the abyss between life and death, Bryce struggled to open his eyes. He was so hot, his body a blazing inferno, yet he shivered uncontrollably when a sudden burst of cool air, followed by something wet and cool, caressed his skin.

Where am I?

Panic twisted his gut and squeezed his chest. The last thing he remembered, aside from the excruciating pain, was lying in a pool of blood near the bank of the loch, waiting for death to take him. The ambush, the battle, his confrontation with Dungal MacDougall, came flooding back.

He couldn't stay here. He had to get away before the blackguards returned.

Fallon's face flashed before his mind's eye. She was in danger and he had to warn her. "Dear, Lord, this canna be happening again. Fallon," he managed to mumble amidst a strangled breath.

He tried to move, but the effort drained what little strength he could muster. He tried to speak once more, but to no avail. Fingers gently pressed to his lips muffled the attempt.

"Shhh. It's all right, Bryce. You're safe." She lightly stroked his cheek.

The familiar lilt of her voice struck a cord in his heart. Since the day she'd left Fraser Castle, it had haunted his dreams. He inhaled the memorable scent of heather and a hint of lavender then released a soft sigh.

Fallon.

But how could this be? She's miles away at Buccleuch, the Scott's castle in the Borderlands. He groaned when his head was lifted, then he sputtered when a cup was brought to his lips. Blade-sharp pain sliced through his chest, and he fought to catch a breath.

"You must try to take some of this brew, Bryce. The herbs will ease your discomfort and the fluids will help to replenish your body. Please try."

He heard the frustration and concern in her voice. He wished he could do as she asked. His tongue felt thick and tasted like dry wood. His throat was parched, but he could not manage the simple task of taking a drink. He wanted to reach out and tell her everything would be fine, but he could not raise his arms from the pallet.

Another attempt to open his eyes caused the room to spin and nausea tugged at his belly. He struggled to focus on the face of the woman sitting at his bedside, but felt himself losing the battle as darkness closed in around the edges of his vision.

He had no idea how much time had passed when he finally awoke, but the sound of a woman humming a Celtic tune caused him to stir. "Have I died and gone to Heaven?" Bryce forced his eyes open, thankful the dreadful spinning had stopped. His vision blurred, then cleared and he found himself gazing at Fallon in disbelief. "What are you doing here, lass? I must be dreaming. If not, the Almighty is playing a cruel jest."

She put aside her needlework and leaned over the pallet. "Nay, you're not dreaming. You gave me quite a scare, but you're very much alive."

"Where am I?"

"This croft belongs to my uncle. He bid me care for my sick aunt when she came down with the pox. Sadly, she passed. Uncle Donald was lost without her, so I decided to stay on for a while."

"How long have I been here?" Bryce ran his tongue over his dry, cracked lips.

"Three days have passed since you were found on the bank of Loch Ryan following a battle with the Clan MacDougall. My uncle and two of his friends brought you here and placed you in my care."

"Did anyone else survive the slaughter?" Bryce brought a shaky hand to his forehead, shading his eyes from the light streaming through the window.

"I fear there were no others. At least none that were still alive." She bowed her head and started to pray.

Bryce eased two fingers under her chin and lifted. "Are you sure no one else got away? What of Robert's brothers, Alexander and Thomas? Where they killed?"

She shook her head. "We've heard tell the Bruce's brothers were taken to Carlisle Castle to stand trial. There may have been a few who escaped, but my uncle fears most were slain as they left the ship."

Bryce dragged his arm over his eyes and moaned. "Their deaths are on my head. I hoped to warn them, but arrived too late." An unsavory mix of guilt and remorse washed over him. Why hadn't moved more swiftly?

"You did your best. From what I was told, they never stood a chance. You are lucky to be alive." She lifted his head and brought the tea to his lips again. "Take a drink."

As the warm liquid splashed across his tongue, he grasped the cup with both hands, holding it steady while he drained the contents.

"Enough for now." She placed the cup on a small wooden table beside the pallet and lowered his head. "You need to get some sleep. I'll close the shutters and see that you are not disturbed."

"I've been asleep for three days."

"And you need more." She prepared to leave, but he grasped her wrist, holding her in place. "Dinna go. Let me look at you. I'd forgotten just how breathtaking you are."

Fallon shifted in her chair and smiled. "I'll not be falling for your sweet talk, Bryce Fraser. You need your rest if you want to regain your strength." She stood, quickly moving out of his reach. "Sleep now. I'll make some broth. Mayhap after a nap, you will feel up to eating something." She turned and walked toward the hearth.

"Wait. If the English or the MacDougalls find me, you and your uncle will be punished for offering aid to a fugitive. I won't have that on my head as well. Where are my clothes?" He swung his legs off the side of the pallet and tried to sit, but a wave of dizziness overwhelmed him. He gasped, the pain hitting him like a horse kick to his chest.

"Foolish man. You're not going anywhere." She eased him back down and covered him with a pelt. "My uncle knows who you are and he told me you are welcome to stay until your wounds have healed. I've spent the last three days tending you, and you'll not be getting off that pallet until I say so."

"But, Fallon, you don't understand. I'm a fugitive and am—"

"I understand you are a *thrawn*, head-strong man. You are as weak as a newly born colt and would not make it to the door without collapsing. Since I dinna fancy hauling you back to bed, I'd suggest you stay put and do as you are told." She planted her hands on her hips and tapped her toe on the floor.

He could not help smiling at her candor and the air of authority with which she spoke. Her spirit and temerity were two of the things he found appealing. He'd seen it in the way she challenged him the day they met, and he could see it now. The fire in her eyes, her furrowed brow, and expression of determination on her face were all indications she'd not back down.

He'd been intrigued by Fallon from the moment she walked into Cailin's chamber at the Scott stronghold and took charge of her care. A man would have to be blind or a eunuch not to notice her attractive features and slender figure. But there was more to Fallon than met the eye. She possessed an inner radiance and spirit that far exceeded her external beauty. Were he looking for a wife, which he wasn't, Fallon would be his choice.

"If you move about too soon, you'll reopen those wounds. You need to rest. Do I make myself clear?"

"Aye, perfectly clear." He bit his lower lip to hide a smirk. "Could you do one thing for me?" He coughed, his voice becoming raspy and quiet.

"What is it you need?" Fallon took a step in his direction.

"Come closer, I'm suddenly feeling very—" He sucked in a sharp breath and squeezed his eyes shut.

Fallon hurried to his side and leaned over him. "Has the pain gotten worse? What can I do to help?" Concern returned to her voice as she examined the dressing, then ran her hand over his brow.

"I . . . I need . . ." His voice trailed off to barely a whisper. He grasped her shoulders and jerked her toward him. "A kiss." He pressed his lips to hers, despite the hands she'd planted on his chest in an effort to break free.

She tasted sweet, like the ripe red berries she'd had to break her fast, and even better than he remembered. It had been several months since he'd felt the tug of desire in his stomach, the tightness in his loins. Her velvet soft lips quivered, then parted, allowing him to sample the mysteries of her mouth. Yet when she finally wiggled free of his grasp, the glower on her face spoke volumes.

"Bryce Fraser, you are an incorrigible man." She brought her hand to her lips and backed away.

"Aye. But now if I perish in my sleep, I'll die happy." He smiled and closed his eyes.

Chapter 3

Fallon fought the temptation to run her fingers through the coarse, black hair dusting Bryce's chest. Her desire to caress the broad span of muscles beneath sun-bronzed skin was almost too much to bear. While they had never completed the deed, they'd come very close to joining on at least one occasion in the past. She could not help wondering what it would be like to have him take her naked body in his arms, flesh to flesh, hearts beating in unison as he made her his own. She nibbled on her lower lip.

"Are you feeling well, lass? You suddenly look flushed." Bryce lifted his hand and stroked her cheek with his knuckles.

"I'm fine," she answered abruptly. She peeled back the linen-wrapped poultice, exposing Bryce's wound. "You're healing nicely. I'm pleased to see that the area around the burn has not festered." She applied a thin layer of salve over the puckered skin, then covered it with a clean dressing. She repeated the procedure with the wound on his back.

"You did a fine job of sealing the wounds. Most women would not have known what to do, nor had the courage to do what was necessary. I've seen hardened warriors shy away from the task." Bryce sat, slid to the edge of the raised pallet, and dropped his feet to the floor. "I owe you my life. Thank you."

"I had no other options. You would have bled to death otherwise." Her eyes trailed the floor as she wiped her hands on her apron. "You grow stronger every day. How long before you leave?" Her stomach plummeted at the thought of his imminent departure.

"Are you trying to get rid of me?" he asked in a teasing tone. "Other than bringing me meals and caring for my injuries, I have seen very little of you during my convalescence. If I dinna know better, I'd say you were afraid to be alone with me."

She glanced up to find him grinning, his head cocked to one side. "You flatter yourself, Bryce. I have other things to do besides sitting by your side all day. Now if there is nothing more you need, I will get back to my chores in the garden."

Fallon turned, unable to look him in the eye, for fear he'd know she was lying. His stolen kiss the day he'd first regained consciousness had left her longing for things that could never be and she needed to remain focused. The less time they spent together, the easier it would be when he left.

"I'll be leaving soon. I've already tarried longer than I should."

"You are welcome to stay as long as you want." She spun around to face him. "But I know you, Bryce, and foolish man that you are, I'm sure you are anxious to be up and on your way . . . even if you are not yet ready to travel. There must be a dragon to slay, a village to save, or a damsel to rescue." She didn't bother to hide the sarcasm in her voice.

"Each day, every hour I stay, puts you and your uncle in peril." After securing a length of plaid around his waist, Bryce braced his hands on the edge of the pallet, and slowly raised himself to a wobbly stance.

Fighting the urge to offer support, she stood her ground. "That was a risk we were willing to accept and our decision to make. I would not hesitate to do it again, but hope the need never arises."

"And I'm grateful for everything you've done for me. But you're right. There is something of importance that I must do. I've been laid up for over a sennight and fear I may already be too late." His brow furrowed.

She turned her back to him again, hiding her disappointment. "You'll always have something pressing to do, something that involves a dangerous task," she replied sharply, then released a shuddering breath. When he didn't comment, she continued. "You are not well enough to travel."

Bryce slid his muscular arms around her waist and drew her close, her back resting against his chest. "I'm a lot stronger than you think," he whispered in her ear. "If only you'd let me show you."

She stiffened her spine at first, but melted against his muscular form when he nuzzled the side of her neck.

"You smell so good. Like a field of heather on a spring morning after a rain. The scent of you makes me dizzy."

She wanted him to stay, but refused to share her thoughts. From the time she was able to talk, her mother had instilled in her a fierce independence, and for that she'd be eternally grateful.

Unlike most women of the day, she did not cater to a man's every whim or wait to be told what to do. She'd always chosen her own path and made her own decisions. She'd not plead for any man's affection. If he chose to stay, it had to be of his own accord. If he wished to leave, then so be it. But she'd not waste her time or her breath on something that could never be.

She held no claim on him, and had no right to expect him to choose between her and his duty to the Scottish cause. But she could not understand why he had to repeatedly risk his life?

He nipped at her ear lobe, and waves of want spread throughout her body like a wildfire out of control. Determined to resist, she struggled to twist free of his grasp, but he tightened his hold and turned her around to face him.

"If I could stay with you, I would." He dipped his head and feathered light kisses across her cheek and the tip of her nose. "But I am a wanted man, and have pledged my sword to the Bruce. I canna rest until the English are driven from Scottish soil and Robert sits on the throne where he belongs. Too many have already perished at the hands of those Saxon blackguards." He slid two fingers beneath her chin, brushed his lips across her mouth, then gazed into her eyes. "Will you give me a memory to carry into battle?"

She placed her hands against his shoulders and tried to push him away. "Release me at once," she demanded, but instead, he lowered his head and captured her lips with a kiss that under normal circumstances would curl her toes and leave her begging for more.

But she was not about to give in, would not allow herself to be manipulated. "I said let me go. I wish my uncle had never brought you here." She shoved him again, but he held her even tighter.

"Am I interrupting something?" Donald cleared his throat and slammed the door behind him. "The offer to fetch a priest still stands," he said in a tone that reflected his disapproval.

Bryce immediately released Fallon and sat hard on the edge of the pallet.

"That won't be necessary, Uncle. Bryce will be leaving soon. He has pressing things to attend to." Fallon smoothed her hands down the front of her skirt, but did not look at either of the two men.

"Is he well enough to make this journey?" Donald asked sternly.

"Nay. But that dinna seem to matter," Fallon snapped. "He is determined to be on his way."

"I appreciate your concern and your kindness, Donald, but what Fallon says is true. I have a matter of grave importance that must be taken care of. I am—"

"Mayhap it is for the best." Donald cut in before Bryce could finish.

"Uncle, what are you saying?" Fallon placed her hand on Donald's forearm. "You told me he could stay until his wounds were healed."

"Given what I've just witnessed, I'd say he has regained sufficient strength to do many things. Besides, when I was in the village today, I heard rumors that the MacDougalls are on their way back from Carlisle Castle. They should arrive in the next day or so, and it would be better if Bryce is not here when they return."

Fallon studied her uncle's downtrodden expression then asked, "There is something else troubling you besides the return of the MacDougalls. What is it?"

"The Bruce's brothers were tried and executed for treason. If they find out that Bryce is still alive, I am sure they will show him no quarter."

Bryce's face drained of color, his expression tightening to one of anger. "Your uncle is right. I will ready myself and leave as soon as you bring me something to wear. I'll not put you in jeopardy. My mission is now more important than ever."

Fallon offered no argument. While they'd only spent a short time together at Buccleuch and later at Fraser Castles, she'd learned that once Bryce made up his mind, he was not easily swayed. She moved to a shelf near the door and picked up his tunic and trews. "I washed and mended these for you. Please try not to get any more holes in them." She handed him the clothes he'd been wearing the day he was brought to her uncle's croft.

"I'll do my best to keep them in one piece." After pulling the shirt over his head, he tugged on his trews, then stood and tied the drawstring at his waist. "Have you my boots?" he asked while holding onto the table for support.

"They are by the door." Fallon retrieved them and slid out a chair for him to sit upon. "I wish you would at least wait until morning to leave. Your face has paled and you're sweating."

"I'm fine." He snatched a boot from her hand, slid his foot in, then quickly donned the other one. "Have you a horse I can borrow, Donald?"

"Aye. I have several fine mounts in the field. The bay is the fastest, but *the dubh* has more stamina."

"I've no coin, but will return the horse and pay for the use of it when I come back this way." He looked at Fallon and winked. "I'll take the black."

If he was trying to ease her mind, it didn't work. She was not fooled by his brave front, or his promise to return. Her heart clenched at the thought of never seeing him again.

"Fix him some provisions, Fallon, while I go and fetch the horse. When you are ready to leave, Bryce, I'll meet you in the stable." Donald gave them both a wary glance before he left the croft.

Fallon removed a canvas sack from the shelf then began to fill it with dried fruit, cheese, and oatcakes.

"That won't be necessary. You have already done enough."

"It's no trouble. I may not be able to convince you to wait, but won't have you starving along the way." She kept her back to him as she worked.

Bryce closed the gap between them. She heard his footsteps, felt his warm breath on the back of her neck as he spoke, but didn't turn around.

"Please dinna be angry with me, Fallon. I could not bear to think you held me any ill will. This is for the best." He gently touched her shoulder.

"Dinna leave." She dropped the sack and whipped around to face him, the words escaping before she could stop them. "Why must you go? Why must you risk your life?"

"You know why." He yanked her against his chest and captured her mouth.

But this time she did not fight his advances. She wrapped her arms around his neck, responding with equal enthusiasm to his kiss. Her lips parted, welcoming the sweep of his tongue. As he deepened the exploration, her knees buckled, and she clung to his tunic as if her life depended on it.

Unshed tears stung her eyes, but she managed to blink them away. This might be the last time they would see each other and she suddenly found herself wanting a memory that would last forever. What she was about to ask was wrong, and could only lead to heartache. While she knew she should fight temptation with her last breath, she was only human.

"Join with me, Bryce," she whispered against his lips.

He drew his head back and stared at her in disbelief. "Do you have any idea what you are saying? What about your uncle?" he asked on a strangled breath. "He'll see me drawn and quartered if he finds us together. I canna say I would blame him if he chose to run me through."

"He's gone to fetch the horse. The field is at the top of the hill and by the time he grooms the beast and readies the saddle, we'll—"

He muffled her words with a kiss and at the same time fumbled to open the laces of her gown. "I want you, Fallon." His hands slid along the swell of her breasts and cupped them gently. "You're so beautiful."

When he pressed his lips to the base of her throat, she closed her eyes and dropped her head back, giving him better access. The hot trail of kisses branded her flesh as he moved ever closer to his prize.

Her breasts grew heavier with each stroke of his thumbs, straining to be released from the confines of fabric. Taut nipples ached to be suckled. He ignited a passion she had never known and an urgent need that threatened to consume her body and soul. To give in to her fervent desires was a sin, but she no longer cared about the consequences.

The sound of her uncle's voice coming from just outside the croft not only brought her crashing back to reality, but to her senses as well. She clutched the neck of her gown and backed away. "I'm sorry. We canna. Not now. Not like this." She turned and ran toward the back door.

"Fallon wait. Please let me—"

Bryce called after her, but whatever else he wanted to say became muffled when she closed the door behind her.

When he didn't follow, she heaved a sigh of relief. With her back resting on the door, she closed her eyes.

How could she have allowed things to get so out of hand? Did she honestly think that offering herself to him like a brazen harlot would make him stay? Until now, she didn't realize to what length she'd go to keep him by her side. Ashamed of her wanton behavior, she vowed never to give in to desire again. Bryce was leaving and there was nothing she could do to stop him. She had but two choices to make. Either she saw him away and wished him God spede, or repeated the same mistake she'd made when she left Fraser Castle and allow him to go without saying goodbye.

Her decision swift, she fisted her skirt and ran toward the stable. If anything were to happen to him . . . She paused, quickly crossed her heart, then darted forward. She'd never forgive herself for letting him leave without a proper send off.

As she rounded the front of the croft, she slowed her pace to a brisk walk. Saying goodbye was one thing, but appearing a desperate fool entirely another.

Bryce led the black gelding from the stable. His movements were guarded, but he appeared far more able-bodied than she'd anticipated. Still, if he pushed himself too hard or met up with an enemy along the way, he'd certainly be at a disadvantage.

By the grace of the Almighty, the sword had missed his heart and lungs. However, it would take a bit of time before he regained the strength and full use of his arm. Being left handed was not only a curse according to Scottish superstition, but also a disadvantage with such an injury.

"Take this with you." Donald handed Bryce a claymore and the baldric he'd been wearing when they found him on the bank of the loch. "You might have need of them."

"Thank you." Bryce secured the weapon on his back. "I am grateful for your help," he said as the two men grasped forearms and exchanged a hardy shake.

"Do you have everything you need?" Donald asked.

"Aye. Fallon packed me a satchel of food, I have a wineskin of ale that I can later fill with water, and this sound horse." He tied the supplies and a length of plaid to the back of the saddle and prepared to mount. "Please say goodbye to Fallon for me and thank her for the wonderful care."

"Women can be a peculiar lot. They often have trouble saying farewell, so mayhap it is better you depart this way."

"Do I mean so little that you would leave a missive with my uncle rather than say goodbye in person?" Fallon sauntered toward him with her head held high. Spying her herb basket on a stump beside the garden, she quickly retrieved it, and reached inside. "Take this with you as well." She handed him the same dirk she'd used to cauterize his wound. "It saved your life once. Mayhap it will prove to be lucky in future."

Bryce glanced at the fire-blackened blade. "I'm sure it will be." He tucked her knife in his boot.

"Do you have far to go?" She took a step closer and gazed up at him.

"A day's hard ride, two at best, but I dare not tell you any more. The less you know the safer you will be."

"A wise decision, lad." Donald thumped Bryce on the back. "Safe journey and take care. I'll leave the two of you to say farewell." With a curt nod, he disappeared into the croft.

"He's a good man." Bryce closed the distance between them. "Most would have turned me over to the authorities and collected the price on my head."

"Aye, he is a wonderful man, and I love him dearly. He has been like a father to me."

"Where are your parents, Fallon?" he asked softly.

She blew out a trembling breath. Funny how in all the times they'd talked, she'd never shared that tidbit of information. "My mother died in childbirth when I was ten, and my father was killed at the battle of Falkirk."

His eyes shadowed. "I'm sorry."

She swallowed the knot in her throat at the thought of her beloved parents and continued. "Though she knew it was dangerous for her to have more children, my mother was willing to risk all to give my da a son. She and the babe both died that night." She closed her eyes briefly at the image of the blood-soaked sheets, the blood covering her arms to her elbows, the cord wrapped tightly around the infant's neck.

"My da was away that night. You see, he was a strong supporter of William Wallace. They were engaged in a battle and he couldn't be there. I tried to save my mam and brother, but I failed. Both my parents died doing what they believed was their destiny."

Bryce tucked a loose strand of hair behind her ear. "You don't know how to fail, Fallon. God's plan is mysterious to all of us. You were but a wee bairn with adult responsibilities."

She shook her head. "Nay. You are a kind man, Bryce Fraser, but I saw the blood, in a vision, and I did naught to warm my mother."

He caught her face between his firm hands, forcing her to meet his sympathetic gaze. "Do you really believe you could have changed what had happened?"

"Mayhap." She lowered her gaze. She couldn't stand the pity and understanding in his eyes.

"Nay. But you are one remarkable woman, Fallon. I'll miss that."

She couldn't respond to the kindness and warmth in his voice. How could she risk her heart?

"I dinna think you wanted to bid me farewell, or I'd have come looking for you." He brushed her ear with a kiss.

The simple gesture sent a shiver of desire racing to her very core. She inhaled slowly and waited for her pulse to stop pounding before she spoke. "I made that mistake once and dinna intend to do it again. While I wish you would stay and allow your wounds to heal fully, I understand how important duty and honor are to you."

"About what almost happened between us in the croft. I dinna mean to take advantage of the situation. Nor did I wish to lead you astray. I—"

She placed her fingers against his lips. "Please. I was as much to blame and would really like to forget it ever happened."

"Consider it forgotten." Bryce clutched her hand and kissed her fingertips, but she pulled out of his grasp and backed away.

She unfastened a pendant from around her neck and placed it in his palm. "My mother gave this to me when I was only a sprout. She bid me wear it always and promised it would protect me."

Bryce studied the silver star-shaped talisman suspended on a length of leather. A brilliant emerald sat in the center. She didn't dare voice her belief that the precious gem held protective powers. Though Bryce accepted much about her, she feared that would be too much for him to believe.

"I canna take this. It means too much to you." Bryce tried to give it back, but she closed his fist around the gift.

"You will take it and keep it with you. Promise me you'll wear it." She peered up at him through tearful eyes and smiled. "Now be off." She turned to walk away, but he grasped her elbow and drew her into an embrace.

"Not without a goodbye kiss." He lowered his head and their lips were about to touch when he hesitated.

Fallon closed her eyes and waited, but when the kiss did not come she looked at him in disbelief. "What's wrong?"

"Your uncle is staring out the window, watching my every move," he whispered. "He has been so kind, I dinna want to show him any disrespect by making improper advances."

Fallon glanced over her shoulder, and spotted Donald as he disappeared behind the curtain.

Once again Fate had stepped in when they were about to share an intimate moment. Mayhap it was sign. Standing on tiptoe, she kissed him soundly, then moved away. "Take that with you, Bryce, and be careful. She turned and scurried into the croft.

Chapter 4

"No! Dinna go. Please come back," Fallon called out to the brown-haired man, but he paid her no mind.

Wrapped in a shroud, he walked with stealth away from her. According to Scottish lore, this was a very bad omen to be sure.

Her breath caught and her chest tightened when a woman with fiery red hair came into view and blocked his path.

Desperate to keep them apart, Fallon tried to hurry forward, but she couldn't will her legs to move. She called out again, but this time she had no voice.

It was too late to intervene.

The red-haired beauty flashed the man a smile and beckoned him to her side with a wave of her hand.

The man quickened his pace, closing the distance between them. He pulled the woman into his arms and buried his face in the curve of her neck.

Fallon gasped. With her hand clutched to her throat, she watched in horror as the woman's once comely features transformed into those of a wrinkled old hag.

The man raised his head and glanced over his shoulder, revealing his identity as the woman prepared to claim his soul.

"Bryce. No!"

Fallon's head snapped back and her eyes flew open. Her heart hammered against her ribs, her stomach twisted with fear, and her chest constricted. She couldn't breathe. While she was aware the events in her vision were symbolic and not real, they still unnerved her greatly.

The Scots were deep-rooted in their mythical heritage and belief in the power of magic, both good and evil, especially the Highlanders. Unwelcome visits from the *taibhs*, spirits who resembled those about to die, haunted her dreams.

While she should be accustomed to the premonitions by now, they never failed to catch her off guard, leaving her physically and emotionally drained. Especially when they showed the possible demise of someone she cared about.

Fallon shuddered at the thought of her most recent vision. She had to warn Bryce, to do something to intervene or he'd die at the hands of his enemy.

"Where is he?"

The gruff male voice caused the hairs on the back of Fallon's neck to bristle. She spun around, her eyes locking with the hostile gaze of a robust warrior dressed in a heavy linen gambeson, a tunic of mail and brandishing a claymore. She immediately recognized the plaid often worn by the Clan MacDougall draped over his shoulder. A few feet behind him stood two of his burly clansmen, one on either side of her uncle. She sucked in a short, sharp breath and averted her eyes, trying not to stare at Donald's disheveled appearance, the bruises on his face, or the jagged cut above his left eye. There was no doubt in her mind he'd suffered a brutal beating at the hand of these scoundrels.

"I told you she just arrived and knows nothing about the man you seek. She—"

The warrior to Donald's left delivered a punishing blow to Donald's stomach, silencing his slurred words.

"Who are you? Why do you hold my uncle in chains?" Fallon raised her chin and glared at the MacDougall leader. She already knew the answer, but had caught her uncle's discerning stare and the quick shake of his head before he doubled over in pain.

"My name is Dungal MacDougall." He widened his stance and crossed his arms over his muscular chest, an act that made him look even more imposing. He took a menacing step forward and studied Fallon like he was judging a prize horse at an auction. "Mayhap the old man is telling the truth. I would have remembered one so fair." He stroked her cheek then lifted a lock of her hair.

To keep from reacting to his vile touch, Fallon stared straight ahead and clenched her fists in her skirt. She wanted to swat his paw away, to tell him how disgusting she found his uninvited advances, but feared the repercussions would fall squarely on Donald's shoulders.

Dungal's lips curled in an evil grin. "You are a coy little minx, but I tire of this game. The man I seek is an enemy of the English crown. He is a fugitive from justice. We have reason to believe your uncle offered him refuge—a treasonable offence. Tell me where Bryce Fraser is or your uncle will suffer for your insolence."

"She knows nothing," Donald sputtered.

"My uncle speaks the truth. You are welcome to search the croft and the grounds if you wish, but you'll find no one." She stepped aside, giving him access.

Dungal inclined his head in the direction of the hut. "Take a look." On his orders, two of his clansmen moved forward to check it out.

The minutes seemed like hours until the men returned. "There is no one inside, but it has been over a sennight since the battle. He could have come and gone."

"Fraser was badly injured when I left him to die on the beach. I should have beheaded him and made sure he dinna live. The next time we meet, he willna be so lucky." Dungal returned his attention to Fallon and moved to within inches of where she stood. "I will ask you again. Did you and your uncle tend to Bryce Fraser's wounds and help him to escape?"

Dungal dragged his calloused finger along her chin, down her neck, and across her shoulder, before grabbing her upper arm with a crushing force. "Tell me where I can find Fraser and I may show mercy. Lie to me, and you will join your uncle on the gallows. It would be a shame to see such a pretty neck stretched and snapped by the hangman's noose."

Fallon nibbled on her lower lip. She had no idea what to do. Telling Dungal what he wanted to hear might save her uncle's life, or mayhap could buy him more time. However, there were no guarantees when dealing with the Devil. How could she betray Bryce?

She swallowed the bile rising in her throat. Her eyes remained focused on her uncle. "I dinna know the man you are looking for. I was summoned to care for my sick aunt. But I arrived too late. She died of the pox shortly after I got here." She bowed her head and crossed herself.

After a few minutes of silent deliberation, Dungal faced his men. "Take the old man to the village, where he will be tried and punished for treason."

"Nay!" Fallon lunged forward and clutched Dungal's forearm. "You canna arrest and execute an innocent man."

Dungal tossed his head back, a cruel laugh resonating from his chest. But just as quickly, his cynical smirk changed to a threatening scowl. "On King Edward's orders, I can and will do as I see fit. I have every reason to believe he aided a fugitive wanted for murder, concealed his whereabouts, and allowed him to escape. For those crimes, he will pay. As for you . . ." He paused, then wrenched his arm free of Fallon's grasp. "I have yet to decide your fate." He stomped toward his men. "Let's go."

"Please, you must listen to me."

When Dungal failed to acknowledge her plea, she ran to Donald and threw her arms around his neck. "I'm so sorry. If only there was something I could do."

"Hush, Fallon, there is nothing you can say to change things," her uncle whispered. "Be a good lass and stay here. Once I've cleared my name, I'll be home."

Fallon tried to hold onto her uncle, but one of the guards grabbed her from behind and tugged them apart.

Donald's attempt to reassure did little to stay her apprehension. Fallon wrapped her arms around her middle in a protective embrace as she watched them lead her uncle away. Despite his promise, she knew he would never return. He'd be tried and executed, to set an example if nothing more. Tears welled in her eyes and she blinked them away.

Wailing and pleading would do no good. A heartless man like Dungal would view it as a sign of weakness and use it to his advantage. She'd be of no aid to Donald if they arrested her as well. Guilt twisted her gut. In protecting Bryce, had she betrayed her family?

Fallon crumpled to her knees as the horses thundered away from the croft. "I must do something to help my uncle, but what?" She dropped her head into her hands and prayed for answers that never came.

The gelding spent, Bryce slowed the beast to a walk. He patted the horse's sweat-soaked neck and spoke softly. "You've done yourself proud. Once we arrive at our destination, I'll see you're given a generous portion of oats and are put to pasture in a lush field."

The horse snorted and whinnied as if he understood, then trotted toward the gates of Turnberry. While the rendezvous point with Robert and Alasdair was in an undisclosed area outside the village proper, Bryce had arranged to meet with one of the Bruce's men in the local tavern. In turn, he'd be escorted to the Bruce's hiding spot. They expected him to arrive a fortnight ago and he hoped they'd not given up on him.

The bustling seaside village was a flurry of activity. Wares were offered from carts lining the streets. Holding bolts of fabric, iron pots, and finely forged weapons in the air, peddlers called out as he passed. When one item in particular caught Bryce's eye, he reined in his mount and slid from the saddle. He leaned over the array of broaches, pendants, and hair accessories, plucking a carved wooden horse from the pile.

"Do you have a wee one at home?" the peddler asked.

"Nay, but my brother and his wife have a new babe." The image of the chubby-cheeked cherub was still fresh in his mind and, the Almighty willing, he intended to be there to watch his nephew grow to manhood. He reached into his pouch, took out a silver coin, and paid the merchant.

Bryce held the toy in his hand and closed his eyes, remembering the last time he spoke with his brother Connor.

"What's this nonsense I've heard about you leaving?" Connor slammed the door and stormed across the chamber.

"It's a fact." Bryce glanced over his shoulder in his brother's direction then returned his attention to the task of packing his clothes.

"You canna go. I'll not allow it."

"How do you mean to stop me? I'm a grown man, and you'll not be dictating what I can do. I've lived in your shadow long enough. The time has come for me to strike out on my own." Rather than meet Connor's stare of disapproval, Bryce picked up a pair of trews and shoved them into the canvas sack.

"Damnation, Bryce, I care what happens to you. We've already lost our parents and two of our brothers to the English. I'll not have you traipsing off on some fool's errand the way Alasdair did. Your place is here, at Fraser Castle."

"Has Hell frozen over then?"

"What's that supposed to mean?" Connor grabbed Bryce by the shoulder and spun him around.

Bryce shrugged out of his brother's grasp and looked him in the eye. "I never thought I would see the day that you, of all people, would question my decision to rejoin the cause. You've been hell-bent to rid Scotland of the English as long as I can remember. You were with us at Methven, Dahl Righ, and Kirkenclif, witnessing the carnage. I swore on all that is holy to seek restitution. Robert the Bruce is returning to Scotland. I intend to join him and will finally have my chance to make good on those promises."

"*What makes you think the outcome will be any different this time around?" Connor glared at Bryce. "As laird of Clan Fraser, I forbid you to go."*

Bryce refused to back down. If pushed too far, he could be every bit as obstinate as both his older brothers combined. "This time, we intend to win." He slammed his balled fist on a wooden table beside him, the vibration sending a tankard of ale to the floor. "Nothing you can do or say is going to change my mind."

"*You're a* thrawn *man." Connor threw his hands into the air and began to pace the length of Bryce's chamber.*

"*It's a family trait." Connor stopped short, his expression less threatening than before. He drew in a slow, deep breath, pinched the bridge of his nose, and gave his head a shake. "You always were a hard-headed fool. Mayhap, I should go with you and see that you stay out of trouble. Besides, if Robert hopes to drive de Valance out of Scotland, he'll need every able-bodied man he can get."*

"*One man willna make a difference. You have honored your oath to Robert many times over. Your place is here with Cailin and the babe."*

"*That may be, but Alasdair is already with the Bruce on the* Eilean Arainn*. Duty dictates that I accompany you and do what I can. Cailin will be safe here."*

"*Have you forgotten what happened the last time you left your wife and ran off to do battle? You thought she was securely sequestered at the priory, but it didn't take long for the English to find her. Falsely accused of murdering a man you killed in her defense, she was tried, flogged, and slated for execution."*

"I dinna need any reminders." Connor dropped his head forward and rubbed his hand over the back of his neck.

"Mayhap you do." Bryce hated to be blunt, but would use whatever he could to keep his brother from following. "She is still a fugitive and is wanted by the English. Will you risk her life again?"

"We are all fugitives according to Longshanks, yet you risk yours. If captured, they'll hang you," Connor pointed out.

"It's a chance I'm willing to take." Bryce raised a brow and smiled. "Besides, they'll have to catch me first."

Connor exhaled sharply and shook his head. "When do you leave?"

"I plan to head for Loch Ryan at daybreak. If I make haste, I should arrive in just shy of a sennight."

"I thought you were meeting Robert and Alasdair near Turnberry."

"I did, but the Bruce's brothers, Alex and Thomas, are preparing to cross into Galloway at Loch Ryan as part of a diversion to keep the English busy."

"Why not wait for Robert and Alasdair?" Connor asked.

"My gut tells me the MacDougalls of Lorn will be lying in wait and I fancy the chance to face the traitorous bastards again. Dungal will rue the day he decided to side with the English and betray his Scottish roots." When Connor did not offer a response, Bryce picked up a tunic and stuffed it into the sack then pulled the drawstring closed. "This is something I need to do, but would rather leave on good terms and with your blessing."

"If I canna convince you to stay, I have no choice but to wish you God's spede." Connor yanked Bryce into a tight *embrace. "Believe it or not, I understand. Be careful, little brother, and watch your back. If you run off and get yourself killed, I will never forgive you."*

"I'll do my best to return in one piece. I plan to watch Andrew grow to be as fine a man as his da. It will take more than the English army to keep me from returning."

The peddler coughed to clear his throat. He picked up the sapphire-encrusted comb and held it in Bryce's direction.

Bryce took the piece and turned it over in his hand. The gems sparkled in the sunlight, reminding him of Fallon's eyes.

Fallon. He cursed under his breath and tossed the comb onto the peddler's cart. Why had she come into his life again? Now, of all times, when he needed to remain focused on the cause, needed his wits about him.

"I have no woman in my life." Bryce tucked the wooden toy into his *sporran*, grasped the horse's mane, and ascended into the saddle. "Where might I find The Skull and Bucket Inn?"

"The alehouse is a large stone building near the peer. You canna miss it." The peddler pointed toward the waterfront then tipped his cap. "Good day, m'lord."

"And to you, my good man." Bryce pressed his heels into the horse's flanks, urging him forward. As they rounded the corner, he spied the inn, just as the merchant described.

After entrusting his mount to an eager stable boy, and giving the lad a coin for feed and water, Bryce entered the establishment. He ducked his head before stepping through the low-hung doorframe, then narrowed his eyes in an attempt to acclimate to the dim light and haze of peat smoke. The stench of stale ale and roasting meat assaulted his nostrils as he scanned the premises, searching for his contact man.

In the corner by the rear exit sat a patron he recognized immediately. Bryce strode with purpose across the room, arriving at the table with his hand outstretched.

"Gordon, it's good to see you."

Gordon jumped to his feet and after they exchanged greetings, he ushered Bryce to the table. "What kept you? The missive that you would be joining the Bruce came well over a fortnight ago. When you dinna show up as planned, Alasdair feared the worst. He has accompanied me daily, but Robert had need of him today."

"I had a run in with Dungal MacDougall at Loch Ryan." Bryce pressed his hand to the wound on his chest. While on the mend, he still had not completely regained his strength.

"You were with Thomas and Alex when they landed? Where are they? Have they gone on to Carrick?" Gordon asked his questions in rapid succession then paused. "Are you ailing, man? You suddenly look pale."

"I arrived too late and was unable to warn them of an ambush." Bryce lowered his head and rubbed his forehead. The news of the massacre and execution of his brothers had obviously not yet reached Robert. "The MacDougalls were waiting for them when they arrived. They dinna stand a chance. Those that were not killed or left for dead were taken prisoner. Thomas and Alexander stood trial at Carlisle Castle and were hanged for treason."

"How did you manage to escape in one piece?"

"Dungal thought me as good as dead or I'd not be here to bear witness. The last I heard, the MacDougalls were back in Scotland and plan to rejoin Aymer de Valance. I'd suggest we make haste and let Robert know. I've no doubt the spineless bastards are on their way as we speak."

Gordon nodded and downed his ale in one gulp. He dragged his hand across his mouth and belched loudly. "Best we leave through the rear entrance."

Chapter 5

"The Bruce has hidden his presence well. The entrance to his encampment is perilous at best." Bryce shifted in the saddle and glanced around at steep rock cliffs, surrounded by dense forest and treacherous ravines.

"Aye. After the defeat at Methven and near annihilation of the Scottish army, the Bruce vowed he would never be caught off guard again. He abandoned many of the old ways of warfare in favor of the covert tactics used by William Wallace." Gordon pointed to a path between two boulders. "From his vantage point, he can see the enemy coming from all directions."

"It appears he has taken all the necessary precautions." Bryce pressed his heels into the horse's side.

"Halt!"

Both men reined in their horses and peered skyward when a deep voice echoed from a ledge above them.

"State your business or die where you are."

"We're here to see Robert the Bruce. He is expecting us," Gordon shouted in response.

A tall warrior stepped out of the shadows. "Och, Gordon. I dinna recognize you, man. Go on ahead."

Gordon nodded and nudged his mount forward. Bryce followed.

They traveled through a long, narrow passageway leading to a small clearing.

"Bryce! It's high time you arrived."

The familiar, deep rumble of Alasdair's voice immediately caught Bryce' attention. He dismounted, handed his horse over to a squire, then spun around to greet his eldest brother.

When together, they quarreled often, but as he lumbered toward him, Bryce realized just how much he'd missed their banter. But the sentiment changed when Alasdair entrapped him in his heavily muscled arms and hoisted him off the ground.

"Put me down. I canna breathe, you big ox." Bryce gasped for air and stumbled when Alasdair released him, but quickly recovered his balance.

"I'm glad to see you, little brother." Alasdair took a step back and frowned. "Mind, you do look thin and pale. What ails you?" His jovial tone shifted to one of concern.

"I'm fine. A wee bit tired from the journey is all." Rather than explain about his encounter with the MacDougalls, Bryce decided to wait and do so when he met with Robert. The last thing he needed was his brother hovering over him like a mother hen.

"If what you claim is true, then tell me why you are so late in arriving. We were expecting you almost a fortnight ago. When you dinna arrive as planned, I was certain you met with foul play."

"I'm sorry for any concern my delay has caused, but it could not be helped.

"Now there is a sight for sore eyes."

Another familiar voice prompted Bryce to turn around. "Cameron! It is so good to see you." He moved in the older man's direction.

Cameron was Bryce's cousin, Sir Simon Fraser's, closest friend and the captain of the guard at Oliver Castle—the Fraser stronghold in the borderlands. He strode toward Bryce with his arm outstretched. "I'm relieved to see you, too. Alasdair has liked to have gone out of his mind with worry. I told him there was no reason to *fash*. You have always been a clever lad." He thumped Bryce on the back and gave his forearm a shake.

Bryce returned the greeting. "How do you fare these days? I have not seen you since the English bastards executed Simon." He lowered his head and crossed his chest.

"Aye. That was a dark day in Scottish history to be sure." Cameron mimicked Bryce's gesture of respect for his friend.

"I'm surprised to see you here. Where have you been keeping yourself?" Bryce asked.

"Once I heard you and your brothers made it safely back to Fraser Castle, I stayed on Oliver Castle with Simon's wife and daughters. Mary returned from the priory to be with her mam. It has been bandied about the keep she is to marry soon. One of the suitors her father chose for the lass before his untimely death offered a fine price for her hand. From what I'm told, she is quite taken with him. Joan is expecting a wee one in the spring, but visits her mam when she can."

The news that his cousin's widow and daughters were safe and doing well came as a welcomed relief. He owed so much to Simon and his family's welfare crossed his mind often. "What brings you here?" Bryce asked Cameron.

"When I heard the Bruce was returning to Scotland, I arranged to meet him at Turnberry." He patted the sword at his side. "I may be getting a little long in the tooth, but can still outride and outfight a young pup like you."

Bryce laughed. "I'm sure you can, my friend, and I dinna plan to challenge you and find out."

"I was just asking Bryce what took him so long to arrive. As usual, he is giving me a runaround," Alasdair interjected.

Cameron frowned. "Aye. I was wondering what kept you myself."

Bryce shrugged. "Sometimes things arise you canna foresee. Do either of you know where I can find Robert? I need to speak to him." Bryce preferred to change the subject.

"I'm here." Robert the Bruce approached them with all the pride and authority befitting the King of Scotland. While he was leaner than Bryce remembered, he still presented a formidable image.

"Robert, it's good to see you." Bryce nodded out of respect then offered his hand.

"I'm glad you arrived unscathed. Come with me." Robert motioned for Bryce and Alasdair to follow him. They entered a cave lit by tallow candles and the glow of a cookfire set amidst a pile of stones. "What tidings do you bring?"

Bryce kicked at a rock and hesitated before answering. His gut twisted. He hated being the bearer of bad news, but Robert had a right to know the fate of his brothers.

"I wish I had better news to share." Bryce cleared his throat and continued. "As you are aware, I was supposed to arrive in Turnberry a fortnight ago, but went to Loch Ryan instead."

Robert's posture stiffened. "Go on."

"I had my suspicions that your brothers were in danger of an ambush, so went to warn them." Bryce shifted his weight from one foot to the other as he searched for the right words. "I was too late."

"My brothers?" Robert's voice wavered.

"The MacDougalls lay in wait and showed no quarter. All were killed as they left the ship, except for your brothers. They were captured and taken to Carlisle Castle, tried, and executed for treason." Bryce laid his hand on Robert's shoulder and gave it a squeeze. "I'm sorry. They offered their lives so you could return to Scotland unimpeded, rebuild your forces, and drive de Valance out once and for all. Don't let their sacrifice be in vain."

Robert's face blanched, but as if it were carved in stone, his expression never changed. "They knew the risk and died for something they believed in. How is it you escape unharmed?"

Bryce absently rubbed his injury before peeling off his tunic to reveal the blackened wound. "I didn't. Everything was over by the time I arrived. But the blackguards had yet to leave. I confronted Dungal, but things dinna go as I intended. Instead of finding my revenge, I met with his sword instead."

"And he let you live? That doesna sound like Dungal."

"He made the mistake of leaving me for dead on the shore of the loch. I was certain he was right, but as luck would have it, several men from a nearby village came along and took me with them. The niece of one of these men is a healer. She sealed the wound with a hot blade and cared for me until I was strong enough to sit a horse."

"You were fortunate." Robert turned and began to warm his hand over the fire.

"You are a fool to endanger your life by coming here." Alasdair grabbed Bryce by the upper arm and yanked him around to face him. "You should have sent word and returned to Fraser Castle."

"I'm a grown man and dinna need to be coddled. Besides, I have more information to share with Robert, and am determined to do my part to see that MacDougall pays for his treacherous acts," Bryce countered.

"There's more?" Robert asked and raised a brow.

"Aye. I fear Aymer de Valance knows of your return and will try to stop you from reaching Carrick."

Robert nodded. "He chased me halfway across Scotland after the battle of Methven, and even when I was on the Isle of Arran, but I managed to stay one step ahead of him. He has already challenged us once since our return to the mainland, but failed. I'm not surprised he has devised a plot to intervene."

"Mayhap we should leave right away," Alasdair suggested. "Get out of the area before de Valance arrives and put as much distance between us and the coast as possible.

Once we are settled in Carrick, he'll be hard-pressed to touch us."

"We will leave in good time. I spent many months preparing my strategy and won't let this turn of events sway my agenda." Robert stroked his bearded chin and shook his head. "Nay, my brothers did not give their lives so I could turn tail and run. I am more determined now than ever to drive the English and their miscreants out of Scotland, but I still intend to stick to my original agenda. We leave two days hence. MacDougall will rue the day he chose to betray his countrymen."

Robert stormed off, but before he exited the cave, he stopped, then glanced over his shoulder. "Rest, Bryce. Alasdair, have the cook fix him something to eat. He must be famished after his journey. We will talk again later."

"Robert is right. You need to have something to eat and a good night's sleep before you leave on the morrow." Alasdair patted Bryce on the back before ushering him toward the entrance of the cave.

"Leave? What are you talking about? Robert said it would be a while before we move out." Bryce refused to budge. He shook his head and raked his fingers through his hair. "I'm not going anywhere until Robert gives the word."

"We will be moving deeper into Carrick in a few days, but you will be departing for Fraser Castle on the morrow. You've delivered your missives and need to go home to recuperate from your injury."

"I have no intention of going anywhere," Bryce replied adamantly. He knew this would happen when his brother found out he'd been injured. Ever since their father and oldest brother were killed, Alasdair had taken it upon himself to protect his remaining brothers. Sometimes he took that self-appointed responsibility to excess and this was obviously going to be one of those times.

Bryce squared his shoulders and met his brother's stare. "I will accompany Robert and see justice served. You'll not sway me on this."

"I'll not hear of it." Alasdair slammed his balled fist against the stone wall of the cave, the blow causing his knuckles to crack and bleed.

"You'll not tell me what to do," Bryce countered. "I'm a grown man and dinna need my brother giving me orders. I've been through all of this with Connor and I—"

"Connor allowed you to come? What is wrong with the man? Is he daft?" Alasdair threw his hands into the air.

"Connor has no say in what I do, any more than you do. I am not going to discuss this any further. My wound is on the mend, and I plan to honor my oath to Robert."

"Robert will understand," Alasdair growled.

"He won't have to since I'm not leaving. Besides which, if I was going to stay anywhere it would have been with . . ." He glanced away. He'd said too much.

"With who?" Alasdair's eyebrows lifted and a slight smile curled his upper lip. "Nay . . . Wait, dinna tell me. You met a comely lass who caught your fancy and was willing to lift her skirt. I suppose you found it near to impossible to leave her bed. When will you learn women are nothing but trouble?"

"Fallon."

"What's that you say?" Alasdair asked.

"It was Fallon's uncle who found me on the bank of the loch and she nursed me back to health." Even he could hear the way his voice mellowed when he spoke her name.

"Bah! I dinna care who she was. I still say women are more problems than they're worth. Look what happened to Connor. Once smitten, there was no turning back. I thought you had more sense. Mayhap I was wrong."

"I am as dedicated to the cause as you, and I dinna have room for a woman in my life. Nothing happened between us. I left as soon as I was well enough to travel, but I am concerned about her safety and that of her uncle. Should the English discover she tended my wounds, it could put them in danger."

"That may be, but you wouldn't be the first man to have his head turned by a comely lass. Given your bonny face and carefree way with the lassies, I always thought you would be the first to fall in love or forced to take a wife, not Connor." Alasdair patted his belly. "If you know what I mean?"

Anger churned in his gut as he tamped down the urge to strike out and silence his brother once and for all. He'd listened to quite enough. While Alasdair meant well, he had a tendency to interfere far too much in his private life.

"What does a buffoon like you know about love? Unless of course you are referring to your passion for a leg of mutton or a flagon of whiskey."

"You seem to forget, I've seen you and Fallon together. I've also witnessed the way you look at her. It put me in mind of a lovesick hound. When we were at the Scott's castle and again at Fraser Castle, you couldn't keep your eyes off her. A man would have to be blind not to notice," Alasdair countered.

Bryce shook his head and raised his hand in protest. "I refuse to continue this conversation. There is no telling how this confrontation with the English will unfold and I'll not have Fallon pining for something that will never be. Once this is over, I intend to travel, and to make a name for myself. Mayhap I'll journey to Europe and offer my sword for hire."

"I'm glad to see that you're thinking with your head and not your . . ." Alasdair glanced down at Bryce's lap, laughed, then slapped him on the back. "Let's go and see about some food. I'm starving."

"When aren't you hungry?" Bryce grumbled and shook his head. "From the time we were lads, I've never known you to miss a meal."

"Once we've eaten, you can get some rest. It is a long journey to Fraser Castle."

Bryce stared at Alasdair in disbelief. "You really dinna listen to what I said. After we eat, I'd like to meet with Robert again and discuss his plan of attack."

Fallon leaned with her back pressed against the curtain wall, contemplating her next move. She'd spoken with Donald's friends, but neither Angus nor Ian could offer a solution to the problem. Were they to stand up on Donald's behalf, they'd implicate themselves and be arrested.

Both men had families to consider, so she really could not blame them for holding their tongues. Nothing would be gained in the senseless execution of anyone else. Feeling very much alone, she blew out a ragged breath. Dungal had wasted no time putting together a tribunal. By the time she arrived in the village, Donald's fate had already been decided.

The outcome of the mock trial was predictable, the execution set for sunrise. Given Dungal's determination to see Donald punished, Fallon was actually surprised her uncle been given that much time to live. She nervously twisted the corner of the plaid brat she wore about her head and shoulders and watched as Donald was led from the church to a stone croft at the edge of town. There, he'd be held until morning.

Fallon searched the area for Dungal and when she was certain he was not around, she squared her shoulders and approached the croft. But as she reached for the latch, the door swung open, and a guard blocked her path.

"What are you doing here? Be off with you." The mountain of a man widened his stance and crossed his thick arms over his broad chest.

"Please. I only wish a few minutes to speak to my uncle." She chewed on her lower lip, waiting for a reply.

"He's to have no visitors. Leave now before Dungal finds you here." His voice was cold and held no hint of emotion.

"I'll be but a minute. I'm sure if your da or uncle were imprisoned, you'd do what ever you could to see him."

"It is my duty to see Dungal's instructions are carried out, not to question them. Leave."

"I understand you are charged with standing watch, but surely you must have a heart. I only wish to speak with him, to offer comfort. I lost my parents when I was very young and he's been like my father." A few tears slid down her cheeks despite her efforts to keep them at bay.

"Dungal will have me flayed if I disobey his orders."

"You'd merely be showing compassion to a fellow Scot. A man who has but a few hours to live. Surely the Almighty will reward you for such kindness."

The guard's harsh expression softened. Had she managed to weaken his resolve?

"I wish there was something I could do for you, lass, but I was given my orders. If it were up to me, I'd grant your request, but—"

"Please. I only wish to speak to him." Choked with emotion, the words caught in her throat. "I give you my oath to leave before anyone knows I've been. I want to tell him I love him and to say . . . to say goodbye." Hands clasped tightly together, she prayed the sentry would change his mind.

The guard dragged his hand across his brow, then to her relief he stepped aside. "Very well. I'll grant you a moment to say farewell. But only for a moment and then you must be away and not come back."

Fallon brushed the tears from her cheeks with the back of her hand. "Thank you. I promise to be brief. You are most kind." She bobbed a curtsy and rushed past him. Her heart sank when she spied Donald standing by the window, watching as the gallows were tested.

"Uncle." She touched his arm.

Donald turned and immediately wrapped his arms around her shoulders. "I told you to stay at the croft. Why did you disobey me and come to town? If Dungal sees you, he may decide to arrest you as well." He whispered in her ear so the guard would not hear.

"I could not remain behind when you were to be punished. It is my fault you're here." She fought back the sob rising in her throat.

"Hush now, dinna cry. You are not to blame for any of this. I knew when I brought Bryce to the croft the consequences would be severe if anyone found out. But I could not leave him to die. I may be too old to fight for the cause, but I am a Scot. By offering him refuge, I feel in some way that I have done my part."

"But if I'd told you from the beginning I knew him and he was a fugitive, things might have been—"

"The fact you knew Bryce, or that he was wanted by Longshanks was of no importance in my decision to offer him sanctuary. I would have taken him in regardless of his past." Donald brushed a tear from her cheek with his knuckles.

"I wish there was something I could do to help, a way to stop the execution from happening. It is so unfair." Her heart was breaking. The thought of Donald being executed for helping Bryce tore at her soul.

"There is one thing you can do. But it is very dangerous." Donald kept his voice low.

"Anything. Tell me what." She clung to his arms in desperation.

"While I was waiting for the trial to begin, I overheard some of Dungal's men talking. Apparently they have gotten word the Bruce has returned to Scotland. He crossed near Turnberry while his brothers created the diversion at Loch Ryan. Dungal is leaving on the morrow, after the execution, to meet with Aymer de Valance. They will then try to intercept the Bruce before he can establish a stronghold in Carrick. By doing so, they hope to squelch his attempt to regain his throne."

"Do you think that is where Bryce was headed?"

"Aye. I'm certain of it, but he dinna say anything for fear it would put you in danger."

"What can I do to help?"

"You must leave at once for Turnberry. Warn the Bruce that de Valance knows of his plans and give them a chance to escape before it is too late."

"I canna leave you." Fallon fisted her fingers in the fabric of his tunic. "I'll not have you die alone."

Donald hugged her before he continued. "You must do this. I will die a better death knowing it had not been in vain. There is nothing you can do to stop the hanging, but you can save many lives, including Bryce's, if you leave now."

"But how will I find the Bruce? Surely his camp will be well hidden." Her pulse sped up in anticipation of her impending journey, but her heart clenched at the thought of leaving Donald behind.

"I also heard mention of an inn, The Skull and Bucket. Apparently the innkeeper knows how to find the Bruce. Seek him out and be careful, lass." Donald pressed a kiss to her forehead and before she could protest any further, called out to the guard. "See my niece out. Thank you for giving us a moment of privacy to say goodbye."

"I canna leave you. Please." Fallon sobbed. "There must be something we can do to stop this injustice. You canna just give up and allow Dungal to win."

The guard lumbered forward and grasped Fallon's upper arm. "You must be on your way, m'lady. There is no telling when Dungal might come by. Should he find you here, he'll stretch both our necks."

"Release her, and she'll leave peacefully," Donald demanded. "Be a brave lass and do as he says." He gently grasped her shoulders and tried to push her away.

Fallon refused to budge. "You canna die, Uncle. I won't—"

"You gave me your word, m'lady. You must leave now." The guard's tone hardened, but she held tighter.

"Fallon, listen to me." Donald slid his finger beneath her chin, forcing her to look at him. "The guard is right. If you wish to honor me, grant my last request. Go, before Dungal finds you. Please do as I ask and dinna come back. Promise me."

Fallon unfurled her fingers and bobbed her head.

"It's time, m'lady." The guard grasped her elbow and led her toward the door.

"Wait!" Fallon dug her heels in and wrenched her arm free of the man's grasp. She rushed back toward Donald and kissed him on the cheek. "I love you. Thank you for everything you have done for me."

"I love you too, lass," he whispered as the sentry yanked them apart.

The guard towed Fallon across the room and when they reached the door, he opened it a crack and peered out. "No sign of Dungal. Be off with you now and dinna return." He placed his hand on the small of her back and shoved her out the door, just as a man rounded the corner.

"What in damnation do you think you are doing here?"

Fallon's heart lodged in her throat. Dungal.

Chapter 6

"What is this woman doing here?" Dungal pointed at Fallon. "I thought I made myself clear when I told you the prisoner is to have no visitors." His words were sharp, his face threatening.

The sentry averted his eyes and studied the ground. "Um . . . well . . . well, you see—"

"He dinna let me see my uncle," Fallon cut him off, before his stammering gave them away. "I begged him to grant my request, but he wouldn't budge." She twisted the edge of her brat around her finger and glanced at her feet.

"Is that so?" Dungal snapped.

"Aye." The guard shifted his weight from one foot to the other. "I was telling the lass to be off when you came along."

Dungal stepped forward, glared at the guard for a moment, then dismissed him with a curt wave of his hand. "That will be all for now. We will discuss this later." He waited for the man to slam the outer door before confronting Fallon.

"You're a disobedient little chit, aren't you?" Dungal moved to within inches of where she stood.

His menacing form towered over her, hovering so close she could feel his ale-tainted breath on her cheek. His words sent a shudder of trepidation skittering along her spine and her heart hammered in her chest, but she refused to show him any fear. When he positioned his hands on the doorframe, trapping her against the wall, Fallon stared straight ahead. "I dinna know what you mean."

He leaned in closer, his lips brushing her ear. "You know very well what I'm referring to. Your uncle told you to stay home, yet you showed up in the village despite his orders."

"I love my uncle and dinna want him to be alone during his last hours on earth. If that is a crime, so be it."

"You make it sound so noble. But it tells me one thing."

"And what would that be?" Fallon asked.

"Your refusal to do as you're instructed shows me that you are not to be trusted."

Fallon's stiffened her posture, but continued to stare over Dungal's shoulder. "I think it deplorable that you willna allow me to say goodbye to my uncle."

"I dinna care what you think." Dungal nipped at her neck, then drew his head back when he got no reaction. "You have roused my curiosity among other things. I may have to rethink my decision to let you go." He dragged his finger along her cheek. "Unless you see fit to warm my bed. Then mayhap I can be persuaded to look the other way. You're a feisty lass, and I must admit, women with spirit are more entertaining to break."

Fallon pressed her hands to his chest and shoved with all her strength. Caught unprepared, Dungal stumbled backward, but quickly regained his balance.

"You try my patience, lass. I've already told you what a shame it would be to see you swing from the gallows. But give me any more trouble and you will join your uncle." This time Dungal used his brawn to wedge her against the door. He dropped his head, and despite her attempts to break free, he captured her lips in a brutal kiss.

Trapped by the bulk of his weight, she found it difficult to draw a breath. Her heartbeat thundered in her ears. Her stomach roiled and her skin crawled when he tried to force his tongue past her pursed lips. While she was not experienced in the passionate exchanges between men and women, she knew what it was like to be kissed by a man she cared for, and how his touch had made her feel.

When she kissed Bryce, her heart fluttered like a bevy of butterflies were trapped in her chest. Her breath caught, but in a pleasant way. Her pulse raced with excitement, followed by a sense of pleasure and euphoria she didn't want to end.

The vile impact of Dungal's unwelcome advances was different on every level from her brief, but intimate, encounters with Bryce. She tried to resist, but the more she struggled to break free, the more persistent he became. Taking intimate liberties, his large calloused hands roamed her body.

Relief washed over her when he finally lifted his head, but she could not hold her tongue. "Execute me if you see fit, but I'll not go willingly to your bed. I'd rather die." When Dungal laughed, she wiggled her arm free and lashed out, her nails connecting with his cheek.

Dungal cursed, quickly covering the welts with his hand. His eyes darkened and his face contorted with anger as he reached for the dirk at his side. "You'll pay for your defiance."

Brandishing the weapon in one hand, he wrapped his fingers around her throat with the other and shoved her against the wall. Her head snapped back, striking the stone. For a moment everything went dark. When her vision cleared, she met his hostile glare. Certain her life was over, Fallon closed her eyes and awaited the final blow.

"The men are assembled and await your instructions," one of the MacDougall clansmen called out. "A messenger has arrived with word from the Earl of Pembroke. He wishes to meet with you as soon as possible."

"We are not through with this by any means," Dungal growled in Fallon's ear. He released her and took a step back, then slid his dirk into its sheath and approached the man. "What news is so important that it canna wait?"

"There has been a turn of events you need to know about. Mayhap we should discuss this in private." The man glared at Fallon.

Dungal nodded and the two men moved away from where she stood. But despite the effort to lower their voices, she could still hear their conversation.

"A few days ago, the Bruce launched an attacked against English cavalry near Clatteringshaw Loch with his small force of Western Islanders. Rumor has it he is returning to his earldom of Carrick and as he goes, he is amassing a large following of those sympathetic to his cause."

Dungal cursed. "Stopping him has become even more important than ever. Assemble the men."

Fallon inhaled sharply. Was Bryce involved in the battle? Was he injured? She'd given him her talisman and bid him wear it, but would it be enough to keep him safe? She craned her neck in an attempt to hear the rest of the information being shared.

"What of Aymer de Valance?" Dungal asked.

"His attempt to retaliate with a surprise attack on the Bruce's encampment at Glen Trool failed."

Dungal raked his fingers through his hair and cursed again. "We honored our part of the arrangement by thwarting the landing at Loch Ryan. Is it too much to ask that the English complete their end of the bargain?"

"Nay." Dungal's clansman shook his head.

Fallon slowly released the breath she'd been holding while warily watching both men.

If she were going to escape, she must do it quickly.

Using Dungal's temporary distraction, she inched her way toward the edge of the croft. She'd have but one chance and hoped they were so engrossed in their conversation that neither man would notice she'd slipped away until it was too late.

"Tell the messenger I will speak to him, cousin, but first I have business to complete here." Dungal inclined his head in Fallon's direction, but did not turn around.

"I understand your desire for a comely lass, Dungal, and canna say that I blame you. But I'd stay clear of that one. I heard tell she's a *taibhsear.* Sees spirits and death, she does." He crossed himself and mumbled a prayer under his breath.

"I set no store in magic or superstition. She can no more foresee death or conjure spirits than you or I." Dungal tossed his head back, a sinister laugh erupting from his chest.

"That may be, but—" His cousin began to speak and stopped abruptly. "She's slipped around the corner of the hut and is getting away."

Heart hammering against her ribs and without looking back, Fallon lifted her skirts and ran.

"When my men find you, I'll see you'll join your uncle on the gallows," Dungal shouted.

Winded and about to double over from the sprint, Fallon's breaths came in short, sharp pants. She had not gone far enough to be safe, but she could never outrun them. If she remained in the open, Dungal would be on her in seconds, so she ducked into a dense thicket at the edge of the forest. Her only hope was to stay hidden until he tired of the chase.

She waited, afraid to move, to breathe, for fear of rustling a branch and alerting them to her location. Judging by sound of their voices, they were closing in fast. Unable to stand the uncertainty, she carefully peered through gap in the bracken, but only far enough to determine their proximity. They'd stopped so close to her hiding place, if she reached out, she could touch them.

"Let her go, m'lord. We dinna need any bad luck," his cousin warned. "The messenger is waiting."

"Damn the messenger and damn you. I want that lass," Dungal snapped, then shrugged out of his cousin's grasp.

Fallon covered her mouth to suppress a gasp and drew her head back when he took a step closer.

Had Dungal seen her? Could he hear her heart pounding and sense her fear? She closed her eyes and waited for him to pounce.

"If you have your mind set on claiming the lass, there will be time to do so later. Right now, there are more pressing matters to attend. You know where she lives and can sate your needs after you've spoken to the messenger and briefed the men."

"You're right as always, cousin. But I will see her punished. You can be certain of that. Let's go."

After a few moments of silence, Fallon hazarded another look. Dungal and his kinsman were gone. Tears surged forth as she crumpled to the ground and wept. She agonized over the decision to leave her uncle to die alone, wrestled with the idea of staying, but in the end knew there was nothing she could do to stop the execution. Even if she admitted her part in saving Bryce, Dungal would not let Donald go in favor of hanging her in his stead. He now had a personal grudge he meant to settle with her as well.

Despite her anguish, she summoned the strength to move beyond the guilt and sorrow. Bryce was in danger and the Scottish king needed her help.

There was no time to tarry. She had to warn the Bruce.

Fallon wiped her cheeks with a brush of her hand then slowly climbed to her feet. Dungal might be busy with his men, but he'd not be occupied for long. She contemplated going to her uncle's croft for supplies, food, and a mount, but the venture was too risky. The horse she'd ridden to town was tied behind the stable, which by now would be heavily guarded. To try and retrieve the animal would be a fool's errand.

Asking one of the farmers for help would only put him

in jeopardy and was completely out of the question. With one plausible answer to her problem remaining, Fallon swept the dirt from her gown, secured the brat about her shoulders, and began the trek to Turnberry on foot.

Relying on memories of a single trip to the seaside town she'd taken with her uncle, Fallon trudged along the rugged hills of Galloway, stumbled over fallen trees, climbed steep slopes, and scaled rocky crags. She recalled that beyond the treacherous terrain lay lush, green valleys dotted with heather and other assorted wild flowers, misty moors, boggy marshland, overgrown forests, and miles of farmland leading to the coast.

At her current rate of speed, she feared she'd never arrive ahead of the MacDougalls. About to give up hope of ever reaching her destination, she remembered her uncle's sacrifice, how he'd given his life to help Bryce, and bid her warn the Bruce. She'd not let his death be for naught. Despite what appeared to be insurmountable odds, she would forge ahead and not let Donald down. This thought, these words, prompted her to continue on.

Her arduous journey began late morning, but by mid afternoon, her shoulders slumped and her legs cramped. Her feet ached from walking on stones and uneven ground in her soft-soled slippers. Each step became pure agony. When she paused to scan the area for a place to rest, the sound of rushing water beyond the next ridge caught her attention. A loch or river must be ahead.

Mayhap she'd traveled further than she thought.

She hurried along the overgrown path, crested a hill, and heaved a weary sigh of relief. A stream, babbling over smooth stones, was a welcome sight. As she approached the oasis, the anticipation of quenching her thirst increased with each bit of ground she covered.

Upon reaching the bank, she fell to her knees, and gave

thanks. She dipped her hand into the cool clear water before bringing it to her lips. She closed her eyes and moaned aloud as the liquid slid over her tongue. She scooped out more, drinking greedily before splashing some on her face. When she'd had her fill, she removed her slippers and eased her bruised feet into the stream. The cool surge brought immediate relief.

Exhausted, she lay back on a bed of soft grass and inhaled deeply, allowing the scent of heather and wild flowers to fill her senses. Savoring the moment, she stared up at the clear blue sky. Her body relaxed and her eyes grew heavy. The temptation to close them for just a few minutes was overwhelming.

She sat up with a start and rubbed her eyes with the heel of her hand. For a moment she forgot where she was, but her lapse in memory was short-lived. She withdrew her feet from the stream, dried them with the end of her brat, then gingerly eased them into her slippers.

How long had she slept?

She brought her hand to her mouth and yawned. Judging by the sun's placement in the sky, she'd dozed for an hour or more, stealing precious time from the journey. Time she didn't have to waste. She rose, twisted, and stretched before taking a wobbly step.

While she should not have napped, the brief rest rejuvenated her energy and spirit. Ready to tackle the next leg of her journey, Fallon pressed on.

She entered a dense forest a few hours later, but with daylight waning, finding her way became increasingly difficult. Surrounded by tall trees and with no familiar landmarks, she quickly became disoriented. Unsure if she was headed in the right direction, Fallon paused and turned full circle, even more confused than ever.

Northwest was the direction she needed to go, but which

way was north? Everything looked the same. She sat on a tree stump and dropped her head into her hands.

What should she do now? How could she find her way?

The answer came to her as if by divine intervention. *The thickest moss grows on the north side of a tree. If ever you're lost, knowing this will be help you to find your way.* Her uncle's words immediately came to mind.

Fallon scrambled to her feet and moved to a nearby pine. She ran her hand around the trunk, pausing when she felt the soft, moist lichen. She raced to the next tree and repeated the process as she moved deeper into the woods.

As the darkness and chill of night settled over the forest, Fallon knew she'd have to stop traveling until daybreak. Foggy mist swirled around her feet, adding to the eeriness of her surroundings. While she searched for a place to rest, her stomach growled. She'd been so preoccupied with finding her way that food had not been a priority and was now something that would have to wait until morning, along with finding another source of water.

Fallon crawled onto a pile of flat stones surrounding the base of a tree. At least she'd be off the dew-soaked ground. With her back resting against the gnarled trunk, she tugged her brat around her shoulders, trying to generate some warmth. But her body trembled and her teeth chattered as the temperature continued to drop.

What she would not give for a fire and loaf of bread.

When she closed her eyes, she could almost taste the baked treat. Too hot to handle as it came out of the stone oven and dripping with sweet, fresh honey. She shook her head, trying to clear her mind. Wishing for things she could not have only made the longing worse. But forgetting about the gnawing emptiness of her stomach was not that easy. The only thing surpassing her hunger was her thirst. Fallon slid her tongue across her dry lips, but the act provided little relief.

The hoot of an owl caused her to jump. Ominous shadows crept over the ground, consuming everything in their path. While she didn't frighten easily, she'd never spent the night in the forest alone. Her nerves on edge, she inched the length of plaid up over her head and squeezed her eyes shut. With any luck she'd be able to sleep and morning would arrive quickly.

Chapter 7

Bryce tossed another log onto the fire. As he stared into the glowing embers, he heaved a deep sigh. The cacophony of thoughts racing through his mind made sleep impossible. His decision to join the Bruce was the right one, but he couldn't stop thinking about Fallon. He reached for his throat and stroked the talisman she'd given him. Praying she was safe, and that no one found out she'd aided in his escape. If anything were to happen to her, he'd never forgive himself. Had he let her down the way he did—

"You're brooding, brother." Alasdair sat on the log beside him.

"I dinna brood," Bryce snapped. He picked up a stick and stirred the fire.

Alasdair laughed and thumped Bryce on the back. "You sound exactly like Connor did when he was pining for Cailin."

"This is different." Bryce countered. "I'm not in love. I don't want a woman in my life, and have no intention of settling down with a wife and family."

"Even if it meant being with Fallon?" Alasdair raised a brow. "A man canna always control what is in his heart."

"I have no heart. The English saw to that when they slaughtered our parents and two brothers. When they joined with the MacDougalls, ransacked our camp in Methven, and executed Simon, they crushed what was left of it. When the blackguards murdered—" Bryce rose and began to pace. "I willna rest until Scotland is free. I'm not worthy of a wife. Any woman who falls in love with me is a fool."

"You're not responsible for what happened to Ashlen." Alasdair moved to Bryce's side and slid his hand over his brother's shoulder. "When the blackguards raided the village, you were but a bairn. There was nothing you could have done, and you must stop blaming yourself."

Bryce shrugged away and continued to pace. "I'm not a bairn now and dinna want to talk about the past."

"Then you will never be able to put it behind you."

"There is no need for you to be concerned. Once Longshanks' forces are driven back, I plan to go to France and tender my sword for hire, earn a title and some land of my own."

"If it is land you desire, Connor will give you as much as you need. A castle and men to guard it are not a problem. Robert can grant you a title and holdings for service rendered."

"I intend to earn my fortune and title."

Robert the Bruce joined them. "Am I interrupting a private discussion?" He stretched his arms over the fire and rubbed his hands together.

"Nay, Alasdair was spouting nonsense as usual. He can prattle on more than an old woman. It gets to a point where it hurts my ears."

"After your long journey and recent injury, I'm surprised you're not asleep." Robert studied both men before taking a seat on a large boulder on the opposite side of the fire.

"It seems my little brother is smitten with a lass he met when we were holed up at the castle of Michael Scott. But for the life of me, I canna understand why a man who is right in the head would want to tie himself down to a woman." Alasdair spat on the ground.

Robert stroked his beard and cocked his head to one side. "Is that so?"

"Dinna pay Alasdair's ramblings any mind. I never sleep before a major battle—especially when I don't know the details. I'd hope to speak with you after the evening meal, but was told you had retired early."

"I was taken aback by the news about Alex and Thomas and needed some time alone. Like most Scots, this war has taken a huge toll on my family. In addition to losing three brothers—God bless them—" Obviously choked with emotion, Robert lowered his head and crossed his heart. "My sisters, wife, and daughter are being held prisoners by the English. Now that I'm back in Scotland, I'll not rest easy until they are released."

Bryce sat on the log beside Alasdair and lowered his voice as he addressed Robert. "Your return to the mainland was a supposed to be a secret, yet you attacked the English at Clatteringshaw, alerting Aymer de Valance to your presence. Would it not have been a better plan to sneak in unannounced, establish yourself in Carrick, and then launch your attack?"

"Mayhap. But after Methven, de Valance chased me across Scotland, then hounded me relentlessly on the Isle of Arran, boasting to all that he had me on the run like a frightened rabbit. By launching our attack, we showed those sympathetic to the cause that I am indeed ready to resume my role as king. His failed attempt to strike back at Glen Tool proved we'll not be easily defeated again. Offers of alliances and support from the clans are mounting."

"That may be, but do you think it wise to tarry in one spot for too long? The MacDougalls are no doubt headed to Turnberry as we speak, and the Earl of Pembroke canna be far behind." Bryce understood the reason Robert needed to make a stand, but he also knew first hand how determined his enemy was to stop him.

"Our departure must be timed perfectly or it will appear as though I am running scared and not prepared to fight. This camp is strategically situated and well guarded. There are spies in the village, along the routes leading to Turnberry, and the surrounding area."

"Robert spent many months preparing for his return," Alasdair interjected. "Given you'll be leaving for Fraser Castle in the morning, you've nothing to worry about."

Robert cocked a brow. "You are leaving?"

"Damnation, Alasdair. I'm not going anywhere." Bryce crossed his arms over his chest and glared at his brother. "Why is it you canna listen for once, instead of trying to dictate? I'll be joining Robert's forces when he confronts de Valance. My mind is set and I won't discuss this with you again."

Alasdair sprang to his feet and towered over Bryce. "You're injured. I'll not have time to watch your back or coddle you."

"My wound is almost healed." Frustrated beyond control, he lurched forward. As a show of strength, he shoved Alasdair, causing him to stumble backward. He glared down at his brother, sitting in the dirt with a look of shock on his face. "I dinna need a nursemaid, and if I do, I'll find one who is qualified."

Robert stepped between them. "Save your anger for the battlefield. Bryce is a grown man. Best you allow him to decide for himself, Alasdair. I need every able-bodied warrior I can get."

Bryce faced Robert. "When do we depart, and where will we make our stand?" The sooner he honored his commitment to the cause, the sooner he could check to make sure Fallon was safe. A mix of guilt and trepidation tugged at his belly. He had no solid reason to think otherwise, yet something in his gut told him she could be in danger.

While he did not want to lead her on or give her false hope that there could someday be a relationship between them, he'd never forgive himself if anything happened to her and he had not been there to stop it. Or mayhap he was destined to habitually let people down when they needed him the most?

"We leave two days hence. Loudon Hill is situated in the heart of my earldom, and the perfect place to wait for de Valance's attack. This time, he's in for a surprise." Robert paused. "Are you listening to me, Bryce, or woolgathering?"

Bryce shook his head, his thoughts returning to the issue at hand. "How do you know he'll fall for your trap?"

"He's too pompous to ignore an open invitation to fight. Longshanks charged de Valance with thwarting the Scottish rebellion. If he wishes to remain in good favor with his king, he'll not decline a challenge he believes he'll win. With any luck, the MacDougalls will join him. I'll have my revenge for Dahl Righ and the deaths of my brothers."

Alasdair stood, stretched, then yawned. "I'm on guard duty in a few hours so need to get some sleep. Best you do the same, little brother."

"I'm not tired." Bryce tossed more wood on the burning pile. He was still annoyed with Alasdair, but his temper had cooled to a simmer. "You get some rest, and I'll take your watch. There's no point in both of us being awake all night."

Alasdair nodded and left. Robert accompanied him.

Alone with his musings, Bryce tugged a length of plaid around his shoulders and moved closer to the fire. Like the Bruce, he relished the idea of facing Dungal MacDougall again. If only he could be certain Fallon was safe.

"Do you think she's a faerie? If we catch her, she must grant us a wish."

Fallon shifted her position, and struggled to open heavy-lidded eyes. She shivered, her clothes damp from the dense morning dew. Rays of sunlight filtered through the treetops, caressing her cheeks. She inclined her head toward the welcomed warmth.

"She moved," someone squealed.

Fallon sat up with a start. This was not a dream. Two young lads stood a few feet a way, the eldest wielding a wooden sword. Her heart in her throat from the sudden fright, she studied the two young men as they returned her questioning stare.

The older lad puffed out his chest and stepped forward, shielding his younger companion. "This is Kennedy land. You're trespassing. Dinna try any tricks, Faerie, or I'll not hesitate to run you through."

"I'll get Da." The younger lad raced off, disappearing over a nearby ridge.

"I was on my way to the coast, but got lost when night fell. I thought it best to wait until morning to resume my journey. I had no idea where I was, let alone on Kennedy land." Fallon stood and brushed the leaves from her skirt. "If you please, I'll be off."

"Stop, Faerie! You're not going anywhere until my brother returns with our da. I'll warn you, he dinna take kindly to uninvited visitors on our land." He pointed his toy weapon at her chest.

"I'm not a faerie." Fallon fought the urge to laugh at the lad's bravado, but she was not certain she relished the idea of meeting his father. What if he was an ally to the MacDougalls, or worse, a minion of the English king? Many of the borderland castles were now controlled by Edward's men. Would he hold her prisoner and wait for Dungal to come and claim her?

The lad quickly scanned the area. "Are you alone?"

"Aye." Fallon sat on a tree stump. "No one is with me." She warily watched the lad, waiting for him to drop his guard, at which point, she intended to make a dash for the woods. Surely she could outrun a bairn.

He studied her for a moment before he spoke again. "The coast is too far a venture on foot. Where's your horse?"

"I have no mount, so I must be off if I wish to reach my destination." Fallon rose.

"Over here!" The younger lad returned and stumbled to a halt beside his brother. Winded, he doubled over and gasped for air.

A robust man with pleasing features crested the hill and joined the lads. "Who are you, and how did you come to be in the forest without an escort?"

Too late to escape, but still uncertain if he was a friend to the MacDougalls or a supporter of the Bruce, Fallon chose not to answer. The burr in his voice was definitely Scottish, but that didn't mean anything in a country torn apart by war and upheaval.

He narrowed his eyes and planted his hands on his hips. "Well, what have you to say for yourself?"

Deciding it might be better to respond than to risk his wrath, she cleared her throat and answered. "As I explained to the lad, I was on my way to Turnberry, but when the sun set, I found myself disoriented, so decided to rest here." She pointed to the rocks where she'd spent the night. She provided no more information about herself or her destination than was necessary. Hopefully it was enough to satisfy his curiosity and he'd let her be on her way.

"The village is at least a full day's hard ride. To walk would take you a close to a sennight. In addition, for a lass to travel alone is far too dangerous. You're lucky my sons found you, and not thieves, scoundrels, or the English. I canna believe you slept in the woods alone."

"There was no choice." Fallon wrung her hands, her eyes downcast. "I have an important missive to deliver to a friend and there was no one to accompany me."

"I am heading to Turnberry today. If you wish, you may ride along with me and my men. Does this friend of yours have a name?"

Fallon shook her head and backed away. "I appreciate the generous offer, but I dinna know you, and it is best I travel alone. It would not be proper for me to be seen in the company of strangers." While it sounded like a weak excuse, especially since she was traveling unescorted, it was the first thing that came to mind.

"John Kennedy." He bowed. "I am laird of Clan Kennedy and father to these two fine lads." He placed a hand on each of the boys' shoulders and smiled. "I am more concerned about your welfare than I am appearances. I promise to escort you safely to your destination. You have nothing to fear."

"My uncle, Douglas MacCrery, has mentioned the Kennedy Clan's contributions to the Scottish cause."

"I know your uncle well, and am proud to call him a friend. I am surprised he allows you to make this journey alone."

Fallon lowered her head and crossed herself. "My uncle is dead." She choked back a sob.

John looked puzzled. "Dead? I saw him in Turnberry little more than a fortnight ago, and he was as spry and ornery as ever."

"He was branded a traitor for aiding a Scottish patriot following an attack at Loch Ryan and hanged by Dungal MacDougall."

John cursed and slammed his fist against a nearby tree trunk. "The day that bastard meets his end canna come too soon. It's bad enough he opposes the Bruce's claim to the throne, but his clan's traitorous acts of aggression against their fellow Scots and their affiliation with the English is inexcusable."

The older lad waved his wooden sword in the air. "Let me at him, Da. I'll teach the MacDougalls a lesson they'll not forget."

"I think your mam would have something to say about that idea. You've only seen ten summers and have more growing to do before you go off to do battle." He patted the pouting lad's head then looked at Fallon. "My offer to see you to Turnberry stands."

Judging by his comments, John's loyalty lay with Robert the Bruce. With his help, she might be able to reach Bryce and warn him before Dungal arrived. It was now clear that if she continued on foot, she didn't have a prayer. "I am grateful for your kindness and will accompany you."

"A wise decision. First, we must return to the castle." John turned and headed down the path.

Fallon followed. Finding it difficult to keep up with his long strides, she scrambled to stay in step. They exited the forest. In the distance stood the Kennedy stronghold, an impressive castle surrounded by a moat and high stone curtain wall.

John slowed, allowing Fallon to catch up. "This is one of only a few lowland castles that have not fallen under Longshanks' rule. The English took over most of the coastal holdings, including Turnberry Castle, the former home and birthplace of King Robert."

Her empty stomach rumbled and the heat of a blush rose in her cheeks.

"Along with your lack of a mount, I noticed you carry no supplies."

"I had no time to gather any. I left with the clothes on my back and nothing more." She glanced down at her wrinkled attire then ran her fingers through her windblown hair.

"We can break our fast before we depart, and I'll ask my wife to fetch you a clean gown. Are you able to ride?"

Fallon squared her shoulders and raised her chin. "Aye, I learned to sit a horse when I was but five summers and ride as well as any man. Some say I have a way with horses."

"Good. The journey takes us over some very rough terrain. To reach our destination before nightfall we must move quickly. While honorable, I have no doubt my men will find a comely lass distracting. I dinna want to contend with temptation if we are forced to make camp for the night." He resumed his trek toward the keep.

As they neared the drawbridge, a brawny warrior with graying hair stepped out of the shadows, blocking the entrance to the castle. "The wee laddie claimed he and his brother found a faerie in the woods." He peered at Fallon, then threw back his head and laughed. "Is this her? She dinna appear fae to me. With her dirt-smudged face and tattered clothes she looks more like a homeless waif."

Consumed by embarrassment, heat rose in her cheeks. She smoothed her hands down the front of her soiled skirt. "I must look a fright, but have been traveling since yesterday."

"The lass can wash up before we leave for Turnberry," John informed the sentry.

"You're not thinking of taking her along, are you? She will only slow us down. We are going to meet—" The older man stopped speaking when John raised his hand.

"Enough. She is welcome to go with us, but must keep up the pace. After we've eaten, we'll be on our way." John moved through the castle gate. Fallon tagged along.

They crossed the bailey and despite the murmurs and stares of the crofters milling about, Fallon held her head high. They entered the keep and a stunning woman with titian hair greeted them.

"This lovely lady is my wife, Lillian." John took the woman's hand and kissed it. "Fallon will be accompanying us to Turnberry. But she will need to change her clothes before we break our fast."

Lillian smiled. "I would be very happy to help." She placed her hand on Fallon's forearm. "Come with me, I'll show you where you can clean up. I'm sure I have something that will fit."

John gave a curt nod, turned, then left them alone so they could tend to Fallon's needs.

Grateful for their kindness, she welcomed the offer of a clean gown, the chance to wash her face, and to comb her hair. A bowl of porridge and tankard of ale never tasted so good. Refreshed and her needs sated, she anxiously awaited their departure. The quicker they got to Turnberry, the sooner she'd see Bryce.

Despite the grumbling and wayward glances, none of the Kennedy warriors openly voiced their objection to taking a woman on the trip. Astride a black destrier and looking every bit a leader, John wore a padded linen gambeson, leather gauntlets, and hauberk of mail.

"If you plan to join us, lass, best you mount." John pointed to a palfrey tethered to a post. "Her name is Sage and like most woman has a mind of her own and needs a firm hand."

Fallon pulled herself into the saddle with ease then dug in her heels, prompting the spirited animal to lunge forward.

They rode nonstop for hours, covering many grueling miles before the sun dropped to just above the horizon and twilight's shadows crept across the path.

John slowed his horse to a walk and twisted in his saddle to face her. "You've done well, Fallon, but you must be getting tired and hungry."

"I'm fine," she lied. Her legs were numb, her back ached, and her stomach had been growling for the last two hours. "Will we reach Turnberry before dark?" Her pulse sped up at the thought of seeing Bryce.

"If we maintain the pace, we should arrive within the hour. You failed to tell me the reason for this urgent trip. It must be very important to risk your life."

Fallon chewed on her bottom lip. "Why do you journey to the coast with one hundred heavy horse and armed men?" she countered.

"I'll be joining with other Scottish forces in an endeavor to drive out the English. We will take you to the edge of the village, but you must complete the last part of the journey alone."

"The Bruce is not in Turnberry?"

"I dinna mention King Robert." John frowned.

"There was no need to say his name. I am aware of his return to Scotland and need to speak with him on a matter of great importance."

"Is he the friend you spoke of?"

"Nay." Fallon shook her head. "But the missive I need to deliver involves the king."

John reined in his horse. With a wave of his arm, he motioned for the men to halt. "Mayhap you should explain yourself, m'lady. Out of respect for your uncle, I dinna push the issue, other than to ask your name, when we were at my keep. Mainly because I believed you were going to Turnberry to meet a friend and it had nothing to do with Robert. Now that you have revealed the reason you travel, I refuse to take you any further without full disclosure. I'll not put the king in jeopardy."

Fallon swallowed past the lump in her throat. Her heart pounded as she tried to decide what to do. She had already said too much.

Dare she tell him the rest?

Her uncle warned her that the MacDougalls were not the only Scottish clan who refused to endorse or accept Robert the Bruce's claim to the throne. For that reason, he told her to trust no one and not to reveal her secret to anyone but the King. True to his word, Laird Kennedy had seen her safely to Turnberry. He'd also declared his loyalty to the Bruce.

"I'm waiting." John drummed his fingers on the pommel of his saddle.

"Until recently, I lived with my uncle in his croft near Loch Ryan. While hunting, he and his companions found a wounded man following the MacDougall raid on the Bruce's brothers. Everyone else was dead. What he dinna know was that the man he rescued and I were acquainted. I'm a healer and he needed my help."

"I know about the attack on the loch, but how does this involve the Bruce?" John shifted in his saddle and waited for her reply.

"My uncle was arrested for offering aid to an enemy of King Edward. While being held prisoner, he overheard news of the Bruce's return and that Aymer de Valance, the MacDougalls, McCann's, and a few other clans who supported John Comyn were planning a surprise attack on the patriot's camp. He bid me leave before his execution and warn Bryce . . . warn the king." She averted her gaze in an attempt to hide her tears, the thought of Donald's sacrifice still too fresh in her mind.

John leaned forward and clamped a meaty hand on her shoulder. "You're a brave lass. Donald would be proud. I will arrange for you to speak to the Bruce and your friend." He raised his arm and shouted to his men. "We are almost there. Ride hard and fast."

Laughter, rancorous curses, and the sound of clashing swords grew louder as they wove their way through the trees and along a steep rocky cliff.

"Are you certain this is the way to the Bruce's encampment?" Fallon blew the hair from her face and urged her horse forward.

"The camp is well hidden. No one can enter or leave without his knowledge."

"Halt!" a man shouted from atop a ragged ledge. "State your business."

"I'm John Kennedy, laird of Clan Kennedy, and these are my men. We come to offer our swords to the Bruce."

"And what of the lass?"

"She has an important missive for the king and poses no threat," John replied.

After a moment of silent deliberation, the man allowed them to pass.

Following the interrogation of three more guards along the way, they entered a clearing. John quickly dismounted and circled Fallon's palfrey. Strong hands enveloped her waist and before she could protest, she found herself placed on the ground.

Her limbs weak from the lengthy ride, she stumbled when she took her first step. John's arm immediately encircled her shoulders to steady her.

"Easy. It will take a few minutes to regain the feeling in your legs," he cautioned.

"John! I'm glad to see you, my friend." Robert the Bruce approached with his arm outstretched. After exchanging greetings, he looked at Fallon. "This is not your lovely wife, Lillian. Who is this young woman, and why does she accompany you?"

"Fallon!"

She turned. Her heart soared when she spotted Bryce, but her relief quickly sank like a stone in a loch when he stomped across the clearing, the expression on his face as dark as a thundercloud.

Chapter 8

"What in damnation are you doing here, lass?" Bryce threw his hands in the air, then turned his attention to John. "Are you daft? A man with half a brain would never bring a maiden into a camp full of randy warriors, especially when the enemy might attack at any moment." Bryce balled his fists at his side, anger twisting his gut.

John slid his arm from around Fallon's shoulder and stepped forward. "She was traveling alone and hell-bent on reaching you. Would you rather I'd left her to fend for herself?"

"I'd rather you dinna bring her here at all. You should have sent her home." Standing toe-to-toe with John, Bryce didn't bother to hide his disapproval. It took every ounce of self-control not to throttle the man for putting Fallon is such danger. But what infuriated him even more, was the familiarity with which he wrapped his arm around her shoulders.

Fallon stepped between the two men and placed her hand on Bryce's chest. "Please dinna speak as if I'm not present. Laird Kennedy tried to help—"

"A respectable woman doesna travel unescorted with a band of strangers, nor does she allow them to take inappropriate liberties." Based on emotion rather than logic, the rancorous words left Bryce's lips before he could curb his tongue.

The color drained from Fallon's cheeks. She clutched her throat and gasped. "What are you suggesting?"

"John is a married man, yet he held you in his arms," Bryce snapped.

While he had no claim on Fallon, he could not abide another man touching her. His attempt to rationalize his reaction as one that a brother might feel for a sister failed miserably. Despite his effort to tamp down the ire churning in his belly, he wanted nothing more than to draw his sword and run Kennedy through.

"I showed her the utmost respect, as did my men." John's voice rumbled from deep in his chest as he reached for the dirk at his side. "I'll cut out the tongue of any man who implies otherwise."

"How dare you accuse me of indecent behavior?" Fallon stiffened her posture and planted her hands on her hips. "Laird Kennedy was kind enough to escort me here and nothing more. My uncle overheard the MacDougall's plan of attack and bid me warn you. They are aware the Bruce is in Scotland and Dungal is planning to join forces with Aymer de Valance. Together they intend to stop King Robert before he has a chance to reach his earldom. They—"

"We already know about their plans," Bryce interrupted. "I canna believe you were fool enough to make this journey alone, or that your uncle would allow it. I demand you go home. I'll ask Robert to arrange it at once."

Tears welled in her eyes and she lowered her head. "I canna go home. My uncle is dead. Dungal saw him hanged for helping you."

Her words hit him like a kick to the gut. "Fallon . . . I—" How could he be such a fool? Unable to find the words to express his sympathy, he reached out to her, but she backed away. His heart plummeted when he saw the tears in her eyes. He knew how much she loved her uncle. And he was to blame for Donald's death. Now that her entire family was gone, what would she do? Where would she go?

"I hoped you would be pleased to see me, but I was

mistaken. I delivered my missive and honored the promise I made to my uncle. But I willna stand here and have you make false accusations. Nor will I allow you to insult Laird Kennedy." Before he could respond or apologize for his behavior, she fisted her skirt and ran.

"You're the one who is daft." Alasdair shoved Bryce, knocking him off balance. "You may not want her here, you may not want her at all, but you dinna have to act like an arse. Go after her and tell her you're sorry."

"I've no reason to apologize," Bryce growled at his brother, but his eyes remained focused on Fallon's retreat.

"You're wrong. Dungal hanged her uncle for aiding in your escape and was about to arrest Fallon, unless she agreed to be his leman. True, she took a great risk coming here, but she obviously cares more about your sorry hide than she does her own life. Something I fail to understand, given the way you just treated her." John said, his palm still cupping the handle of his dagger.

Bryce blew out a sigh of frustration and gave his head a shake. What John said ran all too true. He'd allowed jealousy to rear its ugly head and said far more than he had a right to say. But the fact she'd put herself in danger made it difficult to remain calm. "I'm only concerned for her safety. I canna believe she risked her life to come here. It is too dangerous."

"That may be, but you best go after her before she wanders off or gets lost." Alasdair gestured in the direction where Fallon had disappeared into a dense copse of trees.

"Alasdair has a point. I chose this spot because of its strategic location. The terrain around the camp is treacherous in daylight, and almost impossible to navigate at night." Robert, who'd remained silent up until now, voiced his opinion. "Best you be off. The sun has almost set and it grows darker as we speak."

Bryce nodded then trotted after Fallon, uncertain how he'd make amends when he finally caught up. Mayhap he had jumped to conclusions when he saw her in John's embrace. But the sight of her with another man's arm around her caused his blood to boil.

He cursed and quickened his pace.

Overtaking Fallon was harder than he'd anticipated. He prided himself on being physically fit, but her determination to avoid him proved stronger.

Dry leaves crunched beneath his feet as he raced along the overgrown path. He dodged small boulders and leapt over fallen branches. Insidious shadows crept over the forest floor. Soon it would be too dark to see. He prayed she'd remain on the trail, or he might never find her.

The farther they got from camp, the more Bryce worried about Fallon's safety. His heart hammered in his chest and his breathing became labored, but he refused to give up the search.

"You're a damn fool!" he chastised himself out loud. "Fallon is the bravest, most amazing woman you have ever met. Yet, you doubted her honor? You've no one to blame but yourself if anything happens to her. Just like—"

Bryce stumbled to a halt at the edge of a small clearing, relief washing over him when he spotted Fallon standing where the trail branched off in two directions.

Not wanting to startle her, or to cause her to bolt, he moved with stealth, hoping to get within arm's length before making his presence known. "I fancy the path on the right, but the one to the left might be more to your liking."

Fallon spun around to face him, the beams of light from a full moon highlighting her delicate features. Wide sapphire eyes blinked several times, her mouth drawn in a straight line. He wanted to kiss those pouty lips, to lower her to a soft bed of moss, and make her his own. But he knew better than to try.

"What are you doing here, Bryce?"

"You ran off in such a hurry, I feared you might get lost."

He closed the gap between them, but Fallon countered by backing up until her spine rested on the trunk of a tree.

"I thought you had no use for a wanton woman. Please go back to the encampment and let me be. I dinna need your help. I dinna need any man." She made no attempt to hide the anger in her tone.

"My words were poorly chosen. Forgive me." Bryce softened his voice and lightly stroked her cheek. "You may not want my assistance, but along with the darkness comes many perils."

"I'm not afraid. Please leave."

"I care about what happens to you, Fallon." He slid two fingers under her chin and caressed her bottom lip with his thumb. "I'm sorry. Can you ever forgive me for being such a buffoon?"

He snaked his arm around her waist and pulled her against his chest. Before she could protest, his mouth brushed her lips. "You're so beautiful. No wonder I canna purge you from my thoughts." He kissed her again, this time with purpose, but to his surprise, rather than melting in his arms as she had in the past, she brought her hands up and pushed with all her strength.

"Let me go! Despite what you think, I'll not surrender to licentious advances. You canna speak to me as if I were a shameless chit, embarrass me before the king, and then expect me to fall into your arms. Go back to the Bruce's camp and let me be."

She struggled to break free, but he tightened his embrace. "I never meant to offend you and should have let you explain. When John touched you, rage consumed me. The thought that he might have taken advantage of you was all I could think about. I know now that I was wrong and beg your forgiveness. If I could take back what I said, I—"

"What is it?" Fallon glanced over her shoulder when Bryce abruptly stopped speaking.

"Shhhh. Dinna move," he whispered in her ear. He slowly moved so his back angled toward the woods. "Listen to me carefully. Beyond the trees on the north end of the clearing is a large rocky ledge and cave. Run when I tell you to. No matter what happens keep going and dinna look back."

"Why? Tell me what's amiss."

"A wild boar is rooting around in the thicket to our right. I heard him snorting and caught the reflection of the moonlight in his eyes." Bryce kept his voice low and slowly shuffled Fallon backward. "We canna both outrun the beast, so I will distract him while you seek refuge."

Fallon clutched his arms, her nails digging into his flesh. "I won't leave you. We can both get away."

"There isn't time to argue. I need you to do as I request now." He pushed her toward the edge of the clearing. "Go to the cave and stay there until I come for you." He hoped for once she'd listen. He could not confront the boar knowing she was at risk of being gored.

Relieved when she did as instructed, Bryce pulled the dirk from his boot and turned in time to see the feral beast charging toward him. Widening his stance, he prayed for strength, and raised the weapon above his head. He'd have but one chance to hit his mark.

His heart hammered against his ribs and baited breath lodged in his throat. Sweat beaded on his forehead as the animal lurched forward, his tusk catching his leg and sending him crashing to the ground.

Fallon reached the perimeter of the clearing, then plowed through the thorny bracken and brush. Using the moonlight to guide her steps, she broke free of the trees, immediately catching sight of a stony incline and at the top she spied the opening to a cave. She hesitated for a moment and considered going back. But Bryce had been adamant she flee while he dealt with the boar. What if he was injured and needed his help? Her mind raced with questions. In the end, despite strong reservations, she decided to do as he asked.

She wasted no time climbing the weatherworn boulders, her fingers grasping jagged ridges to aid her grip. Her toes dug into loose dirt and gravel as she attempted to secure solid footing. The first few rocks were relatively flat and easy to scale, but the final two required her to climb them on hands and knees.

Grappling for the final ledge, Fallon pulled herself atop, and collapsed in a trembling heap.

An ear-piercing squeal broke the eerie silence.

"Bryce!" She rose to her feet and called out his name. Panic squeezed her chest, stealing her breath. Where was he? Had he defeated the animal or, Heaven forbid, had he lost the battle?

Nausea twisted her stomach as she contemplated possible scenarios. Overwhelmed by the urge to return to the clearing and render her assistance, she teetered at the lip of a rocky crag, coming dangerously close to toppling over the edge. Realizing her perilous position, she backed away. Bryce had stayed behind, allowing her time to escape. She honored his wishes and had fled. Now, despite her need to go to him, she had to stay put.

She narrowed her eyes, trying to see beyond the trees and through the darkness that shrouded her surroundings. Her efforts were useless.

She refused to believe he was dead, but where was he? What was taking him so long?

Her anger with Bryce had dissipated the moment he kissed her. Now she might never have a chance to tell him. She blinked away the tears, dropped her chin, and prayed. "Please, see him safely back to me. I beg of you. Dinna let him die."

"It's all over. We're safe."

Fallon's head snapped back at the sound of Bryce's voice. Caught up in her anguish, she didn't hear him approach. Her heart leapt at the sight of him. Without hesitation, she climbed to her feet, threw herself at the shadowy silhouette, and released a sob. "I feared you dead."

"Feared or wished." Bryce chuckled as he dragged her against his chest and tucked her head beneath his chin.

Fallon struggled to break free, but he tightened his hold. "How can you say such a thing?"

"You were very upset when I found you. But I'm glad you put your anger aside and did as I asked."

"What makes you think I've forgiven you?" Fallon pressed her hands to his chest and tried to break free of his grasp. "You were a fool for staying behind to face the boar. The beast could have killed you." She did her best to remain focused, to tamp down the urge to kiss him repeatedly, to hold him, and never let him go. He'd risked his life to save her and could have died.

"And you find my demise an upsetting prospect?" He cocked his head to the side and smiled. "Not long ago you were cursing me."

"I'm a healer. It is not in me to wish anyone harm. Even a *thrawn* fool like you." She drew in a deep breath and continued. "Your cruel words and accusations hurt me deeply. But I should be accustomed to that by now." She lowered her eyes and stared at her feet.

"You always put on such a brave front, Fallon, but something tells me you are not as strong as you appear." Bryce grazed her brow with a kiss.

"I dinna know what you're talking about." She scrubbed a tear from her cheek with the back of her hand. Aware of his scrutiny, she turned her head and tried again to wriggle free. But he'd not allow it.

"What happened to you in the past? You are a spirited, independent woman, unlike anyone I have ever known, yet I sense an underlying sadness. Tell me. I'm willing to listen if you wish to share."

"Why do you persist in badgering me? I—I don't want to discuss my past. It is not important." Fallon moved away when he dropped his arms, giving her some space. The sudden emptiness and sense of loss when he released her took her by surprise. She turned her back and blinked away the tears welling in her eyes.

He moved up behind her and slid his arms around her waist. "You're trembling. Come here." He tugged her against a solid wall of muscle. "Talk to me, Fallon. Why are you so determined to push people away? Why do you feel the need to do things alone?"

"Because, I have always been alone."

She turned in his arms and choked back a sob. "When I was a babe of four summers, I woke from a nightmare, a vision so powerful I could not stop shaking. I saw a banshee wailing outside the croft of our neighbor, my father's closest friend. I will never forget her face or her ear-piercing cry. I saw the image of my father's friend standing in the window, a shroud wrapped about his head and chest." She paused and released a shuddered breath. "When I told my mam, she insisted my da go to check on him."

"What did he find when he arrived?" Bryce asked softly.

"His friend was hail and hardy. He asked what possessed Da to visit him in the middle of the night and my father told him about my dream. The man laughed and said he dinna believe in superstition. The next day, my parents were told his heart gave out while he was milking his cows."

She bowed her head and mumbled a brief prayer.

"From that moment on, people avoided me. Feared me. They were certain if they even spoke to me, their fate would be sealed and they would die in agony. When I was a wee bit older, the bairns in our village mocked me and threw stones. Some called me a witch, and they placed *Rudha-an* branches in my path or over their doors to ward off evil. Other called me demon or the daughter of Satan. Do you have any idea how it felt to watch the other bairns playing, to know I was not welcome? To walk down the street and have people cross to the other side to avoid contact?"

"Bairns can be cruel, Fallon. People often fear what they dinna understand. However, there is no excuse for their ignorance. You should never have listened to them."

"I started to believe what they said about me was true," she blurted out. "My mam told me I was special and had a gift. I saw it as a curse. All I ever wanted was to be accepted, to be normal. When my mother died and my father was killed in battle, I had no one. I saw their deaths before they happened, yet was powerless to stop them. I am destined to spend my life alone. No man will ever want me." She chewed on her bottom lip and glanced away. She'd said too much.

"You were a bairn and canna believe you were responsible for your parents' deaths, for anyone's death." He lifted her hand and pressed her palm to his lips. "Your mother was right. You are special for who you are and not what you see. Never doubt yourself."

A rush of longing washed over her and she withdrew her hand. She didn't want his pity. She didn't want anything from him. Or did she? Yet when Bryce spread his plaid on the ground then lowered himself, taking her with him, she offered no resistance.

He enveloped her in his arms and cradled her at his side. "Fallon." He whispered her name as if in prayer. "I want you. Heaven help me, but I've wanted you since the first time I laid eyes on you at the Scott's stronghold."

Before she could react, Bryce captured her mouth with a kiss that stormed her senses. He tasted of mint and fennel, his tongue teasing as he sampled her slightly parted lips. His roaming hands were strong, yet his caress was gentle. He stared at her with dark, passion-filled eyes, his wolfish grin melting what was left of her reserve.

"Do you want me to stop? Tell me before I lose control."

The kisses he feathered across her nose and cheeks made it impossible for Fallon to think clearly. She steeled herself against his advances, but to no avail. To give in to temptation was wrong, but she couldn't refute the ardency between them.

From the moment they'd met, there had been an unmistakable connection—like they were destined to be together. Something she had never experienced before and feared she might never find again. Bryce told her she was beautiful, desirable. While she'd heard those words before from other suitors, she believed him sincere. When they kissed, all thought and reason dissipated into a euphoric fog. Above all, Bryce accepted her for who she was and her gift of *dà shealladh* did not concern him. When she was with Bryce, her heart raced and her breath caught. When they were apart, he filled her thoughts, despite her effort to put him out of her mind.

Did she dare allow herself to dream of a future together?

"You take my breath away, Fallon. I'm a mortal man and can no longer endure the torture," he groaned in her ear before nipping the sensitive lobe.

"Wha—what if another wild animal or the enemy happens upon us?" She tried to remain strong, but her resolve was fading fast.

"We live in a time of uncertainty and walk a fine line between danger and desire. Nothing worth having is without risk." He hovered over her, his arms supporting the bulk of his weight on either side. His chest muscles bunched, his square jaw tightened, and his neck veins bulged from the strain. The soft glow of moonlight highlighted handsome, rugged features and she caught the tantalizing scent of musk and man.

How could she refuse him . . . deny herself? While not the way she envisioned her first joining, it might be the only time they'd have together. Bryce was heading into battle and she'd had visions of his impending death.

Her mind reeled. Surrendering to her wanton needs was sinful, or so she'd been raised to believe. Her body craved completion, yearned to experience the sensation of him thrusting deep inside her aching core. But Bryce, a restless spirit and adventure seeker, never spoke to her of love or marriage.

Could she give herself freely, aware this night may be the first and last time they share an intimate moment?

"Shall I desist? Tell me now." A possessive growl rumbled from deep in his chest. He slipped his hand beneath her skirt, grazing her inner thigh. Without hesitation, his fingers crept higher, the sensual path setting her ablaze and branding her as his own.

"I won't force myself on you, Fallon. Our union must be something you crave as much as I do."

She gave a hesitant nod. "I want to lie with you."

"Even though I canna make you any promises beyond this night? I care for you, Fallon, but have no idea what the future holds."

She petted his stubble-roughened cheek then buried her hands in his hair. "Aye, I'm certain."

"I wish to please you, m'lady." Bryce's face lit up as he tugged at the laces of her gown then lay open the bodice.

Cool air licked her exposed flesh, but she wasn't certain if the night's chill or the play of his fingers along the valley between her breasts caused her to shiver.

"You're even more ravishing than I imagined." His

voice was hoarse and rasping, his breath warm and moist against her skin.

Her breast grew heavy and she hungered for his touch. She moaned with delight when he stroked the nipple with the pad of his thumb, coaxing the sensitive nub to stand erect. He tugged the throbbing tip between his teeth, nipped, then began to suckle. A billowy cloud of pure rapture enveloped her. Desire curled low in her belly, moist heat erupting between her thighs. Her heart beat wildly and she thought she might faint. She longed for his strong hands to explore and caress every part of her body.

Bryce pushed up her skirt and his deft fingers resumed their exploration. She rocked her head and whimpered with delight. He knew exactly where to stroke, how to elicit the maximum level of pleasure. She never dreamed of being so physically possessed, and her body quickly became a slave to the erotic heat coursing through her veins. She writhed and bucked beneath his talented touch.

A sudden rush of moisture pooled between her thighs. In response, he increased the tempo and pressure. Amidst her moans of pleasure and pleas for mercy, he continued his ministrations, bringing her to places she'd never expected. He fondled and prodded until she was certain she could endure no more, then he dipped his head between her legs, and took her with his mouth.

"Oh . . . Oh, Bryce. Please . . ." She exhaled sharply as a dizzying coil of urgent need unfurled. Her skin heated, about to burst into flames, and her body jerked and quivered. When his gifted tongue encircled the bud of her arousal, her nails dug into his shoulders, and she called out his name. In that glorious moment, she came quickly. But he didn't release her from the exquisite torture. He elevated her buttock, feasting on the honey of her excitement until the last glorious waves of sublime release subsided.

Chapter 9

A vision of loveliness, Fallon's cheeks flushed and her rose-colored lips were swollen from kissing. She languorously stretched, then opened her eyes, peering from beneath thick, dark lashes—a stark contrast to her flawless, ivory complexion. Bryce's breath stalled as he admired her beauty.

"I had no idea something deemed immoral would be so wondrous." Her words mingled with a breathy sigh.

His hand settled over the nest of raven curls at the apex of her thighs. He parted the lush pink lips and dipped his fingers past the glistening feminine folds. She moaned and arched her back, giving him better access. His thumb brushed the hard nub of arousal and her body wept for him. "There is so much more a woman and man can share. You are wet and ready to learn. Will you have me?"

Fallon chewed on her bottom lip—a gesture he noticed she used when nervous or hiding something.

"You appear troubled. Have you changed your mind? If so, you dinna have to do this." He pulled back, but she wrapped her arms around his neck.

"This is my first bedding. I am not sure what to do. I've heard women speak of both pain and pleasure." She failed to hide the tremor in her voice.

He swept a silken loch of hair from her brow then traced her cheek with the tip of his finger. "That makes it all the sweeter, *Leannan*. I promise to be gentle. There will be one brief moment of pain when I break through your maidenhead, but after that, I'm told it never happens again. I will do my utmost to pleasure you." He pressed his lips to hers, hoping to allay her fears and to distract her as he positioned himself between her thighs. "Do you trust me?"

Fallon smiled. "Aye."

Bryce nudged her legs apart and her hips softened. He entered her slowly, pausing at the barrier of her innocence. Despite the overpowering urge to complete their joining, he lay very still, affording her time to adjust to the fullness. But she raised her hips, and he pushed through, buried to the hilt in her hot, lush sheath.

He witnessed a grimace of pain and a tear running down her cheek, but she didn't utter a sound. Instead, her movements matched his tempo, increasing the glorious friction between them.

The tension in his groin intensified and he quickened the pace. Bombarded by divine sensations and captivated by the wonder of the moment, he rocked into her with wild abandon. He was largely endowed by most standards, but she accommodated his size, encasing his erection like a falconer's glove. He pressed deeper, his pleasure mirrored in her expression of rapture and moans of delight.

Fallon's writhing and purrs of enjoyment spurred him on. Her head lolled from side-to-side, and she muttered his name in her delirium as her legs began to shake.

Aware she was close to completion, he slid his hand between them, stroking and fondling until she tossed her head back and her inner muscles rhythmically contracted around him.

On the precipice of his own release, Bryce maintained the momentum. Trapped in a realm of earth-shattering euphoria, the pressure mounted until his loins tightened and he shouted out a war cry then emptied his seed before collapsing on top of her.

When his erratic breaths slowed and heart resumed a normal rhythm, he rolled to one side, taking her with him.

Guilt tugged at his gut and the consequences of his actions weighed on his mind. He'd bedded many women and harbored no regrets. Love and commitment were not an issue. He'd made certain of that. The instant he'd entered Fallon, everything had changed. He'd never felt so possessive, the level of pleasure unfathomable. He knew he could never get enough.

In the past, once his partner found her womanly pleasure, he'd complete the mating ritual by releasing his seed into the bedclothes, eliminating the risk of conception. To his knowledge, he had never fathered a bairn.

He glanced at Fallon, resting quietly at his side. The notion she might harbor his babe in her belly didn't unnerve him the way he'd anticipated. The conjured image of her round with his child, a strapping son to carry on the Fraser legacy or a spirited wee lass with her mother's sapphire eyes, caused his heart to soar.

He considered himself blessed to spend one night with Fallon, and he wished it would never end. The only thing to outshine her physical beauty was her inner radiance and gentle spirit.

Fallon stirred and he pressed a kiss to her brow. He couldn't take his eyes of her, afraid if he did, she'd vanish.

Why should Connor be the only one to experience such bliss?

He cursed beneath his breath. While they may be brothers, he and Connor were different. There'd be no wife and bairns in his future. The fact he'd bedded Fallon on the floor of a cave, with no more regard or consideration than a randy scoundrel shows a tavern wench who lifts her skirt for coin infuriated him. She deserved better.

"Is it morning?" She brought her hand up to stifle a yawn and glanced around the cave.

"The sun has yet to rise and won't for a few more hours. Try to rest." He tucked her securely in the crook of his arm and secured his plaid around her shoulders. Her head and hand rested over his thundering heart.

"I've often wondered about the intimacies between a woman and a man." Her splayed fingers curled in his chest hair before journeying across his abdomen and coming to rest on his manhood.

"How so?" He forced the words despite the sudden dryness in his throat.

Her questioning eyes widened. "My mother died long before she had the chance to explain such things." She skimmed her hand along the length of his burgeoning shaft. "Is it always like this? Does it hurt?"

"Only when I am near you." Overwhelmed with renewed desire, he almost choked on the response. Elated by the promise of another joining, he damned the consequences. But first, he wanted to rid her of her cumbersome gown.

"May I help you with this?" Bryce grasped the hem and slowly raised it to her waist. When she smiled and lifted her arms to assist him, Bryce swiftly peeled the fabric over her head then pulled her onto his lap.

His breath caught as he took in every line and curve of her slender figure in the moonlight. Fallon straddled his abdomen, his arousal pulsing against the soft cheeks of her firm, round buttocks. His hand slip between her thighs and he smiled. Slick and swollen, she was ready to love. Again.

"In the heat of passion, we joined in haste, not how I intended your first time to be." He cupped her breasts and toyed with her nipples as he spoke, causing her to moan and giggle with delight.

"Allow me to enter you again. I promise to show you the wonders you seek." He dropped one hand into her lap and allowed his knuckles to glide along her thigh. Her entire body trembled in response. He wrapped his hands around her waist and lifted her enough to slide his manhood beneath the entrance to her core.

She settled over his engorged flesh. As if trained in erotic pleasures, she slowly lowered herself, enveloping his throbbing rod. He groaned when she began to roll and sway her bottom, sliding up and down in a rhythm that matched his own.

He fought the urge to take control, allowing her to set the pace. But when she raised herself high, rotated her hips, and began to ride him hard and fast, he grasped her buttocks, securing her in place.

He withdrew until only the very top of his manhood remained embedded. He voraciously rubbed the hard nub of her desire with the tip of his shaft, before sinking to the base. Encased in the purest form of ecstasy, a volcano-like pressure filled his core. Ready to erupt, he thrust deep and quickened the pace, encouraging her toward completion once again.

She tossed her head back when her body convulsed and joined him in an orgasm. Sobbing with pleasure, she slumped forward, her forehead resting on his heaving chest, her raven tresses covering her face.

Bryce wrapped his arms around her shoulders and held her closer. Her heart clamored against his chest as she fought to catch her breath. They lay together, legs entwined, basking in the afterglow.

Fallon's eyes fluttered open and she gazed up at Bryce. "Will we be leaving soon?"

"The hour is late and the forest is impassable now that night has settled in. It was by sheer luck that you didn't run off the path and fall to your death from any one of dozen cliffs. Best we wait and return at daybreak."

Fallon placed her hands over her mouth and gasped. "We're not returning tonight?" She could not hide the trepidation in her voice as she sat and peered into the darkness. "We canna stay here. What will the men think?" In truth, she was afraid if they spend the entire night together, she might not be able to let him go.

"Men usually think what suits them, regardless of the truth. Try to get some more rest. I'm sure you must be cold. I'll start a fire." Bryce rose, crossed to the far side of the cave and disappeared into the shadows. He returned a moment later with a small pile of twigs, a few dry logs, and a pelt. He squatted and arranged the tinder on the floor.

"I was surprised you knew about this place. But how did you know where to find those things? Have you been here before?"

"Robert scouted out the entire area before deciding on the perfect location to set up camp and brief all the men as to his findings. The cave has been used for a lookout point in the past. Supplies are often left behind in case the place is needed for a refuge or used again to scout for the enemy."

Within minutes smoke billowed from the wood, followed by flames. He added the logs and some peat to the blaze. "This will take the chill out of the air and provide us with a bit more light." He rocked back on his heels and peered down at her. "You look spent." He spread out the fur and patted the ground beside him. "Move closer. This will be warmer and more comfortable."

Fallon remained sitting, keeping some distance between them. The heat of passion that had brought them together had cooled. While Bryce remained attentive, something was different. Did he regret what happened between them? Did he think her a whore? She wanted to ask, but instead she changed the subject.

"I noticed you were limping when you went to get the wood. Did the beast injure you?"

Bryce shook his head. "He tried his best to gore me, but only caught my shin. I have but a scratch and there is no need to *fash*."

Fallon rose to her knees and pointed to his leg. "Show me."

"There is no need. I'm fine."

"Please dinna dispute with me, Bryce." She leaned forward to get a better view.

Bryce turned so she could examine the wound. He stood before her, his body a finely honed masterpiece. He was truly magnificent. Determined to ignore his nakedness and curb her sinful thoughts, she bit her bottom lip and concentrated her attention on his injury. After tearing a strip of cloth from the hem of her kirtle, she wiped away the clotted blood. "You were very lucky. The tusk broke the skin, but the wound is not deep and should heal quickly." When she realized her fingers rested on his calf, she snatched her hand away and placed it in her lap.

"I told you, the cut is nothing to *fash* over." He stretched out on the pelt and motioned for her to join him. "Come before you catch your death of cold. We still have a few hours to rest before dawn."

Fallon joined him on the pelt, suddenly very aware of her own lack of clothing. She crossed her arms over her chest.

He covered her with his plaid and settled in behind her, her back resting against his chest, her buttocks against his thigh. "Sleep. Tomorrow will be a long day."

Fallon tossed in a fitful sleep. She called out Bryce's name, but he didn't answer. She tried desperately to open her eyes, but the lids were so heavy. When she managed the task, she sat up with her hand clutched to her throat. Her heart pounded in her chest, her pulse racing. She glanced around at her surroundings and began to shiver. The fire had burned down to ashes and a heavy morning mist made everything damp.

"Bryce?" His name rode on a strangled breath. She'd had a nightmare. In truth, it was another vision of Bryce's demise.

She grabbed her gown, tugged it over her head, and fumbled with the laces of the bodice. Her entire body ached, and she was shockingly aware of intimate areas she'd seldom thought about until now.

What have I done?

"Good morning." Bryce spoke to her from the entrance of the cave.

Fallon turned to face him. "Where were you? I was concerned."

"You were sleeping so soundly, I dinna want to wake you. I went to gut the boar and secured it to a tree. I'll send some men to fetch it later. While away, I also gathered some berries. Are you hungry?" He held up a leather pouch.

She studied his stern expression and rigid posture. They'd connected on so many levels when they made love, but something had changed. Along with her gift of second sight, she was cursed with the ability of knowing what people were feeling.

Bryce closed the space between them and offered Fallon a wine skin. "There is a stream nearby and I thought you might be in need of a drink."

She brought the vessel to her lips and drank greedily. Her thirst quenched, she wiped her mouth. "Thank you."

Bryce gave her the fruit. "Once you've broken your fast, we'll be off." Rather than join her, he backed away.

Fallon dumped some berries into her hand and popped them in her mouth. She closed her eyes, savoring the flavor exploding on her tongue.

"Take as long as you need. I'll wait for you outside," Bryce called over his shoulder as he walked toward the entrance of the cave.

"Will you not have something to eat with me?"

"Nay. I ate while picking and am no longer hungry." He didn't turn around.

Fallon climbed to her feet and followed behind him. When he didn't slow his pace, she grasped his upper arm, halting his retreat. "Did I do something to displease you?"

His brow furrowed. "What do you mean?"

"I'm not a fool, Bryce. Your attitude has turned cold and distant."

"You're mistaken. We have been gone a long time and need to return to the Bruce's camp. If you are finished eating, we must make haste."

Fallon shook her head. "This has nothing to do with how long we've been away. We are both grown and dinna need to answer to anyone. You chased after me, begged me to forgive you, and bedded me. Now you're behaving like you can barely stand the sight of me."

Bryce's face blanched. "I wish things could be different between us, but you know I've sworn my oath to Robert and the cause. I—"

"Dinna *fash* yourself. I expect nothing from you that you are not willing to give." He'd hurt her deeply, but she refused to cry. Instead, she swallowed a curse and turned her back, afraid she'd say something she'd later regret. While their time together might have been fleeting, she secretly hoped he'd offer her commitment.

She heard his sharp intake of breath, but stood her ground when he gently touched her shoulder.

"I'm sorry, Fallon. I never meant to hurt you."

"Nay, you were right. We should return to the Bruce's camp immediately." She turned quickly, without making eye contact, and marched toward the opening of the cave.

Chapter 10

"Where in the name of St. Stephen have you two been?" Alasdair shouted as he and Fallon entered the encampment.

Bryce had hoped to avoid a confrontation with Alasdair, but it was obvious that was not going to happen. He stiffened his spine and prepared for the barrage of questions and innuendos that were sure to follow.

"I wasn't aware I had to report my every move to you." He scowled at his older brother. "I found Fallon, we're back, and safe." Bryce strode across the clearing, and Fallon followed a few steps behind.

"There is a very good reason to question you. Fallon dashed into the woods like Hell on fire, you chased after her, and the two of you were gone all night." Alasdair widened his stance. "I was about to organize a search."

"If you must know, by the time I caught up with Fallon, we'd ventured too far into the forest to return safely. I thought it best we seek shelter and travel at first light." He only planned to tell Alasdair what he needed to know and nothing more.

"We also encountered a wild boar. The carcass is hanging in a tree. I'll ask Robert to send some of the men to fetch the beast. Fresh meat will be a welcome treat." Bryce explained, in hopes of changing the subject, but judging by Alasdair's scowl of disapproval, he'd failed at the attempt to redirect the conversation.

Alasdair grunted and continued his inquisition. "Where did you sleep?"

"We stayed in the lookout cave near the stream."

Fallon slid her hands down the front of her gown then backed away. "If you will excuse me, I'd like to find a place to wash." She turned and scurried off.

"Now that she's gone, do you want to tell me the truth?" Alasdair badgered. "What happened last night?"

"Nothing. Even if something did transpire, I would not be explaining to you." Bryce prepared to leave, but a large hand clamped around his upper arm halted his departure.

"You were never a good liar. We had this same conversation with Connor when he bedded Cailin. I thought you had more sense."

"Dinna preach to me." Bryce wrenched free and raised his hand. "I dinna say I bedded her."

"You dinna have to. Fallon is a comely lass and you are known for your way with the ladies. The two of you were gone all night. Any fool can tell what happened just by looking at you. What were you thinking? Until now, you had the brains to keep things simple. No commitments or promises beyond the encounter."

"We've already thrashed the topic of Fallon to death. I know what you are going to say and dinna want to hear it. My plans have not changed. I intend to honor my pledge to Robert and when that is done, I am going to France."

"What if there is a bairn? You're not the sort of man to walk away from responsibility."

Bryce's gut wrenched at his brother's words. He'd succumbed to temptation and was ashamed of his weakness. He wished it were in his power to turn back time and give Fallon back her innocence, but that was a task he could not perform.

"There will be no bairn. But if there were, I would do the honorable thing and provide for Fallon and the babe."

"I remember how you lectured Connor when he got involved with Cailin and I thought you knew better than to let a lass cloud your judgment." Alasdair shook his head and heaved a deep sigh. "Women are trouble and it is better to keep your distance."

"I will admit that I find Fallon attractive, but never did I make improper advances at the Scott's keep or when she came to Fraser castle for Connor and Cailin's wedding. To be honest, once she left, I dinna think our paths would cross again. I was stunned when I awoke to find her tending to my wounds in Galloway. But I left as soon as I was well enough to travel and never acted on my desire. We parted ways and I remained focused on the cause." He threw his hands in the air. "I dinna know why I am wasting my breath explaining something which is none of your affair. Drop it, Alasdair."

Alasdair released a snide laugh. "You may have left her in Galloway, but you ran off and bedded her the first time you had a chance. If I dinna know better, I'd say the rendezvous was arranged."

"When she turned up in camp, I was as surprised to see her as anyone. I dinna plan to spend the night in the cave with her."

"You dinna choose your fate, brother, it picks you."

Tired of a battle of words he had no hope of winning, Bryce made another attempt to change conversation. "Where is Robert? I wish to make arrangements to send Fallon to Turnberry as soon as possible."

"What if the lass refuses to go?"

"She canna accompany us to Loudon Hill. I want her out of harm's way. She will be off once I make the arrangements with Robert." Bryce spun around and in his haste to retreat bumped into Fallon, almost knocking her off her feet.

She straightened her posture and their eyes met. "I dinna wish to go to Turnberry and would like a say in my own fate. I'm a healer and can tend the wounded following the battle."

"You will be as far away from the fighting as possible. I'll make certain of it. Robert has connections in the village.

I'll ask him to arrange a safe place for you to stay. I canna do my duty if burdened with worry about your welfare."

"A burden? Is that how you think of me, after everything I've done for you and your kin? Especially after . . ." Fallon's voice trailed off and she averted her eyes.

Alasdair coughed to clear his throat. "I think I'll leave you two alone."

Ignoring his brother's retreat, Bryce snaked his arm around her waist and pulled her against his chest. "You're wrong. I appreciate all you've done for me and mine. What we shared is very important to me. A beautiful memory I will cherish and carry into battle. But you were aware that I was unable to make any promises about the future."

Fallon twisted out of his embrace. "You made your stand on this issue clear. While I disagree, there is obviously no choice but to concede. Speak to Robert and make the arrangements."

Her willingness to comply without further argument rendered him speechless. He raked his finger through his hair, his gaze following Fallon as she stalked away with her chin held high. He should be pleased, even relieved, but a mix of emotions tugged at his belly. Determined to ignore the pull at his heart and the temptation to follow after her, he went in search of Robert instead. Regardless of his growing affection for Fallon and the lust coursing through his veins, he'd made the right decision. She deserved more than he could ever offer and would be safe in Turnberry.

He spotted Robert on the far side of the encampment conversing with Alasdair and John Kennedy. He headed toward them. "I need to speak to you."

Robert nodded. "Alasdair told me you had an eventful evening."

"Alasdair says too much." Bryce glared at his brother.

"A run-in with a wild boar can be dangerous. You're lucky neither of you were injured. Alasdair also said you wish to send the lass to Turnberry." Robert stroked his bearded chin. "Are you certain this is what you want? Someone to tend to the wounded might prove useful given we are headed into battle."

"Fallon is a gifted healer, but I'll not allow her to remain in harm's way," Bryce replied adamantly.

"She strikes me as resourceful and intelligent. Mayhap she'd like to decide for herself." Robert scanned the camp. "Bring her to me."

Bryce shook his head. "Dinna bother asking. Her departure is not up for discussion. Do you know of a place she'll be safe?"

"I have many supporters in the village willing to grant me a boon. Fergus Carpenter and his wife, Maeve, would be my choice. They own the inn." Robert raised his arm and motioned for one of his men to join them. He retrieved a piece of vellum from a leather satchel and penned a note. When he finished, he handed over the missive. "Take this to Turnberry. Deliver it to the innkeeper and make haste."

The messenger bowed. "I'll leave immediately." He tucked the note in his sporran then trotted toward the horses. Once mounted, he sped out of camp, disappearing into the forest, leaving behind a cloud of dust.

Bryce returned his attention to Robert. "Did you explain everything?"

"I told Fergus to expect you later today and asked him to take her in. He's a good man and willna question my request, so the less said the better. A precaution lest the note fall into the wrong hands."

John Kennedy stepped forward. "Since Fraser is determined to cast the lass aside, I'd be honored to escort her to Turnberry."

Anger slithered like a poisonous serpent through Bryce's veins. He balled his fists at his sides as he approached John.

"I wager you would enjoy being alone with her, but you'll not get the chance. I'm taking Fallon to Turnberry, so dinna trouble yourself any further."

"I only mean to save her the pain of saying goodbye to a fool," John replied.

"I said nay." Bryce narrowed his eyes and raised his fist.

"John," Robert said. "Take Adam and Gordon with you and bring back the boar. Bryce will accompany Fallon." He turned to Bryce and asked, "Do you need some men to go along for protection?"

"That won't be necessary," he answered in a more subdued tone. "Fallon is a fine horsewoman. Two can travel quicker and will attract less attention."

"Mayhap I'll go with you, little brother, and make sure nothing happens on the journey. I'd hate for the lass's reputation to suffer."

Bryce lunged forward and his fist connected with Alasdair's jaw.

"You'll wish you hadn't done that." Alasdair rubbed his chin and climbed to his feet.

Robert stepped between them. "Enough. Tempers are hotter than they should be. I told you before to save the aggression for the battlefield." He placed his hand on Bryce's shoulder. "Find Fallon and be off with you. We'll expect you to return before nightfall."

"Only if they don't get distracted along the way," Alasdair tossed in, but this time his remark didn't elicit a rise.

"The men are waiting in the list, Alasdair. Start the training session and I'll join you in a few minutes. John, tend to the boar." Robert waited until they were out of hearing range before he continued. "I'm certain this was a difficult decision to make. Being separated for the one we love is never easy."

"Alasdair had no right to discuss my personal life or to speak on my behalf."

"Your brother dinna say anything to betray you. He cares about your welfare more than you realize. I've observed the passion between you and Fallon for myself. The way you gaze at her reveals the way you feel, but it also shows in your behavior. You are usually focused, amiable, and take things in stride as they come. Of late, you've been like a cornered wild animal, ready to pounce on anyone who dares speak their mind or gets too close to her."

"If you are referring to Kennedy, he had no right to touch her. I've good reason to challenge his actions."

Robert shook his head. "I've known John for many years. He adores is wife and sons. I believe his intentions toward Fallon are completely honorable. There is no reason for jealousy."

While tempted to argue the point, Bryce refrained commenting further. He offered his hand. "Thank you for your help, Robert. Once I've gathered a few supplies and saddled the horses, we'll be away. The sooner she departs, the better."

"When this is over, you may feel differently. But sending her to Turnberry may be for the best. You need to focus on the impending battle, not the lass." Robert laughed, shook Bryce's wrist, and slapped him on the back. "In spite of what you claim."

Fallon sat on a log, her face buried in her hands. How could she have been so foolish? Did she honestly believe Bryce had feelings for her, might give up the cause in order to make a life together? She knew better than to open her heart up to a man, but she thought Bryce was different.

"My brother is looking for you. He's ready to leave," Alasdair said as he approached her from behind.

Fallon stood and spun around to face him. "He is really bent on sending me away?" She sucked in a deep breath, trying to hide her disappointment.

"Aye. He is finally thinking clearly, with his head and not his . . . er, um . . . Best you not keep him waiting." Alasdair averted his eyes and lumbered past her, but Fallon caught his forearm, stopping his advance.

"You dinna like me very much, do you? Is it the *da shealladh*, or do you think me an unsuitable match for your brother?"

Alasdair grunted and raked his fingers through his hair. "Unlike most Highlanders, I dinna believe in magic or superstition. I make my own luck and govern my own fate." He patted the hilt of the sword hanging at his side.

"Then you must think me unworthy. Please, I'd like to know." She fisted her hands in her skirt to keep them from trembling, but held her head high.

Obviously uncomfortable with the question, Alasdair shifted his bulk from one foot to the other. "You're a comely lass, Fallon. There is no denying that fact. You'd make a fine catch for most men, but Bryce is not looking to complicate his life with a wife or family. He is married to the cause and justifiably so. We've lost many family and friends to the English and traitors like the MacDougalls. He has sworn his oath and sword to the Bruce and means to see this conflict to the end."

"I understand his dedication to the cause and his desire to honor his oath, but I sense there is something more to his reluctance to get involved with a woman."

"I told you his reasons," Alasdair snapped. "Best you accept them and be on your way. The men are waiting for me in the lists and I must go. *God spede t*o you, lass." He bowed and tried to step around her, but she continued to block his path.

"I dinna understand why he canna have both a family and continue to fight for the cause. There is something more troubling him. There are times when he relaxes, lets down his guard and shows a softer, passionate side. But all of a sudden, he changes, closes the door, distances himself."

"My brother is a complicated man. It is not my place to speak on his behalf. If he wants you to know what happened in his past, he will have to tell you himself. He'd see me flayed if I betrayed him." Alasdair grasped Fallon by the shoulders and moved her aside. "Now if you'll excuse me, I must see to the men."

Fallon watched his retreat, more confused than ever.

"There you are," Bryce shouted. "It is time to leave."

As she watched Bryce approach, her heart plummeted. He was determined to send her away and she had no option but to comply with his wishes.

"The horses are saddled and ready. We have a long ride so best we be on our way." He placed his hand in the small of her back and pressed lightly. "We must be off."

"Aye. We would not want you to be away from the camp and the war for too long." She didn't hide the sarcasm in her voice as she moved toward the horses, then mounted her palfrey.

As Bryce secured a sack of provisions on the back of his saddle, she silently prayed he would reconsider and allow her to stay. But she knew once he'd made up his mind to something there was little or no chance of swaying him. It was perhaps the one trait she found infuriating.

Robert approached and stood beside her. "I'm grateful to you for risking your life to warn me of the proposed attacked. For a woman to make the journey on her own shows a great measure of bravery. I also offer my condolences. Your uncle was a true hero. All of Scotland is indebted to him as well." His hand rested on her horse's neck. "You'll be safe in

Turnberry. I'd trust my friend Fergus with my life. He and his wife will treat you well."

"I'm grateful to you, Your Majesty." She spoke to Robert, but her eyes remained on Bryce as he climbed atop his destrier out of earshot.

"Dinna *fash* over young Fraser. He may be a wee bit headstrong and unreasonable at times, but he is a fearless warrior and invaluable to the cause. Alasdair will guard his back."

The ball of emotion rising in Fallon's throat made it impossible to speak. She could not help wondering if they would be forever parted. The premonition she'd had at her uncle's croft flashed in her mind. She'd seen Bryce's death. If only she could convince him to stay with her when they reached the village and not venture into battle.

"Are you ready?" Bryce rode up beside her.

Her heart raced at the sight of him. He sat proud atop a black destrier, his back poker straight, his eyes flashing, and his chin held high.

Bryce was magnificent. No wonder she found him impossible to resist. A breeze ruffled his shoulder-length hair and she caught his intoxicating scent. Her body reacted immediately, with longing so strong, she could hardly stand it. "Best we depart. The sooner we reach our destination, the better." She dug her heels into the horse's flank, urging the animal into a trot.

Bryce caught up and grabbed the bridle of her palfrey, slowing the horse. "You'll run the beast into the ground at this speed. That or she'll stumble and break a leg on this uneven path. I know you are anxious to reach Turnberry, but we need to pace ourselves."

"This wasn't my idea. You are the one sending me away." She bit back a sob and tears ran down her cheeks. With a sweep of her hand, she brushed them away. She wanted Bryce to stay with her by choice, not out of pity.

He reined in his horse, and tugged on the palfrey's bridle again, this time bringing both animals to a halt. He quickly dismounted and wrapped his large hands around her waist. Before she could protest, he lifted her from the saddle.

Fallon's breath lodged in her throat as Bryce let her body slide down the broad plain of his chest. Her knees buckled the second her feet touched the ground, and she inhaled sharply when he enveloped her in his arms.

"I dinna want to push you away. I care for you, Fallon, but I canna rest until you're safe." He brushed her ear with a kiss.

The rasp in his voice and the caress of warm, moist breath against her skin sent a shiver of desire skittering down her spine. She pulled away, and turned her back to him. "You have an odd way of showing you care." She stared into the woods, all the while hoping he'd make a move and declare his love.

"This war with England is bigger than both of us. In a few days, we will confront Aymer de Valance, and I have no idea the outcome."

"You're going to die in battle." Unable to contain herself any longer, she threw herself into his arms and sobbed, soaking the front of his tunic.

Bryce pried her away and tucked his finger under her chin. "All men die. To give your life on the battlefield, fighting for something you believe in, is what a warrior hopes for."

She raised her head with an imploring gaze. "You must listen to me. I witnessed your demise in a vision. Please dinna go with Robert." Her nails dug into his arms.

"I set no store in dreams." He kissed her brow. "You're mistaken. I will be fine."

"Dinna make light of this. I am never mistaken. In my vision, you were walking toward a red-haired woman, a shroud wrapped about your head and body—an omen of death." She dragged her palm across damp cheeks.

"I've heard those legends since I was a lad and never believed them to be true."

"I saw the corpse candles lighting the path to your grave and heard the banshee lamenting. Dinna try to discount my vision, Bryce Fraser. This is going to happen. You will die at the hand of your enemy. If not in this next battle, soon after. I know this to be true."

Bryce held her against his chest. "I promise to be careful and will try and keep my head. Robert needs me . . . Scotland needs me."

"I need you." She nibbled on her lower lip to stop it from quivering.

"You're an amazing woman and deserve more than I can offer. I want you to be happy, Fallon. Some day, you'll forgive me and meet someone who will stay by your side. Love and marriage are not in my future, but when the right man comes along, you will make a wonderful wife and mother."

"I dinna think I will ever marry." She sniffled.

"You will, *Leannan*, and when you do, you will be very happy and forget the heartache from the past. I dinna have to possess your gift of second sight to know this to be true."

Bryce kissed her brow then lifted her into the saddle. "Best we are on our way, before I forget myself and take you here, on a bed of moss." He stroked his finger across the back of her hand, then moved to his horse and mounted quickly.

The thought of making love to Bryce again caused her blood to heat and her heart to hammer in her chest. Nothing would make her happier, but she'd not beg for any man's affection. Bryce had made it clear he was dedicated to the cause. If what Alasdair alluded to was true, he also harbored a painful secret from his past, one that she suspected made it impossible for him to fall in love.

They finished the last hour of their journey in silence and relief washed over her when they finally reached the outskirts of the village.

Bryce slowed his mount and leaned in the saddle toward her. "We need to be as discrete as possible. You never know who might be lurking in the shadows. I will escort you to the inn and make the arrangement before I leave. The less attention we draw the better."

They approached The Skull and Bucket from the back. Bryce dismounted and helped her from her horse. "I'll go inside and make sure everything is safe. Once I've spoken to Fergus, I'll usher you in." He kissed the tip of her nose and disappeared into the shadows.

Heart pounding, she huddled near some barrels, waiting for the signal from Bryce. Fear tugged at her gut. What if someone recognized him and he were arrested?

"Fallon." Bryce whispered her name and motioned with a wave of his hand for her to join him. "Fergus and Maeve are waiting for you inside." When she moved past him, he caught her arm, enveloped her in a tight embrace, and kissed her with a passion that made her chest ache and the parting more difficult. "I willna forget you, Fallon, or our time together. I will carry you with me always. Here." He thumped his breast above his heart and entered the inn.

Chapter 11

"Come with me and I'll show you to your room. After raising six sons, having a lass around will be quite a pleasure. I prayed for a daughter, but the Almighty blessed me with lads." Maeve prattled on cheerfully as she led Fallon down a narrow hall. She halted before a large oak door and slid the key into the lock. "The room is not grand, but the mattress is stuffed with fresh straw, and there is a brazier to take off the morning chill."

Maeve lit several tallow candles, brightening their surroundings. Fresh rushes covered the floor and a bouquet of heather occupied the center of a small wooden table.

Fallon inhaled deeply. The sweet floral fragrance reminded her of the lowland moors outside the walls of Laird Scott's castle. Many a day she'd wandered those fields, picking the delicate blossoms and other assorted wild flowers to use in her healing potions or to scent her bathwater.

She missed her life at Buccleuch. Laird and Lady Scott had accepted her into their home and always made her feel welcome. Now that the last of her family were gone, mayhap she'd return to their stronghold and resume her duties as the clan healer.

"I hope the accommodations meet with your approval." Maeve smiled and touched her arm.

"Aye. I appreciate your kindness, and hope my presence willna cause you any trouble." Fallon stepped deeper into the room.

"Dinna be foolish. Having you here is a pleasure, my dear." Maeve took Fallon's hand, gave it a reassuring pat, then released it again. "Fergus and I are happy to help. As soon as he read the missive from King Robert, he saw the storage room converted into a chamber. My husband is always ready to do what he can for the cause." Maeve crossed to the window then threw open the wooden shutters. "I hope you will be comfortable."

"Everything is wonderful. This chamber is similar to the one I have at the Scott's keep. My mother . . ." She paused and crossed herself. "God rest her soul, was a distant kin of Lady Scott. Mam died when I was ten, and Da sent me to foster at Buccleuch before he went off to battle the English."

"Are you planning to go back?" Maeve's expression grew sullen.

"It was my home for more than eight summers. Now that my uncle and aunt are both gone, there is no reason for me to go back to Galloway. There is naught to keep me from returning to the borderlands."

"What about Bryce? Will you not wait here for him to return for you? A good man is a powerful motivator. You were lucky to find each other."

"I doubt Bryce will come back for me." Fallon lowered her eyes and gazed at the floor. Even though she wished he would.

"To leave before you've had a chance to test the mettle of your relationship would be a shame. Mayhap you should wait to see if he returns before you decide."

"There is no relationship," Fallon answered, more abruptly than she'd intended.

"Given the way Bryce looks at you, I'd say you were wrong. In fact, I'm surprised you're not wed and expecting your first bairn."

"We haven't known each other very long, and the times we've spent together have been brief."

"Fergus and I met at a Samhain festival, and spoke our

vows after only a sennight. Eachan, my oldest son, came along nine months later." Maeve blushed.

Maeve's comment gave Fallon pause for thought. She absently slid her hand over her belly and nibbled on her bottom lip. After the night she and Bryce spent in the cave, she could very well be breeding. Heat rose in her cheeks. Did she carry his babe?

"Bryce has no interest in a wife and family. He is married to the cause, and his home is wherever adventure takes him."

Maeve touched Fallon's forearm. "I find that hard to believe. He may claim no interest, but his actions speak louder. I only spent a short time with the man, but his concern for you and your safety was evident."

"I dinna doubt he cares about my welfare, but he is not prepared to give up his quest to save Scotland or to make a name for himself as a warrior," Fallon replied softly.

"What drives a man can be difficult to understand. In his youth, Fergus was very much like Bryce. He rode with William Wallace and thought only of the cause. That was until he suffered an injury at Sterling. He took an arrow to the leg and was very lucky he dinna lose the limb. His recovery was slow and he could no longer fight, but every time the Scots confront the English, my husband longs to join them."

"At least he's here with you now, and safe," Fallon pointed out.

"Aye, but living with a brooding warrior, a man who once lived to do battle, can be a challenge. Fergus still insists on doing his part, so he makes certain supporters of the Bruce reach their destinations and ensures his enemies are diverted. If his efforts are ever discovered, he'll be hanged. To offer aid to the Bruce is considered a treasonable offence in Longshanks' eyes."

Fallon wandered to the window and peered into the village. "I know all about King Edward's unjust laws. They are the reason my uncle was hanged. We're in Scotland, not England. I don't understand how this travesty of justice is allowed to take place."

"Aye, we're in Scotland, but the country has been under the Saxon thumb for many summers. Edward believes he is sovereign of all he desires, and he dinna gain the name 'Hammer of the Scots' for nothing. And we must not forget about clans like the MacDougalls. The men who supported John Comyn's claim on the throne and oppose the Bruce are as dangerous. A country divided is an easy target for tyrants like Longshanks."

Painfully aware of the MacDougall's connection to the English crown and their oppressive power over the Scottish people, Fallon shuddered at the mention of the clan name. "Did Bryce tell you that I escaped from Dungal and he may be looking for me? Mayhap I should leave before you and Fergus are punished for harboring a fugitive."

"Dinna fash over what might happen." Maeve wrapped an arm around her shoulder. "You are welcome to stay here until Bryce comes for you. He will return. I can feel it in these old bones."

"I hope you're right." Fallon was unable to hide the skepticism in her voice. "But, I would never forgive myself if anything happened to you or your husband because of me."

Maeve reached into the linen pocket attached to her skirt, pulled out a folded scrap plaid, then handed it to Fallon. "I almost forgot. Bryce asked me to give this to you. He also bid me pass along a message. He said he willna rest easy until this is in its rightful place." She rubbed her chin. "I thought his words a bit strange."

Fallon held the item in her hand and hesitated before unfurling the corners of the fabric. She gasped when the contents were revealed. Fighting back tears, and the sudden lump in her throat, she picked up the leather thong and let the emerald-encrusted star dangle in the air.

"How lovely." Maeve touched the talisman and smiled. "Bryce obviously cherishes you very much to give you such a fine gift."

"The pendant belonged to my mam. Passed down from mother to daughter for generations, she believed the star was blessed and held great power. She presented this to me on her deathbed. With her last breath, she bid me wear it for protection." Fallon clutched the treasure to her breast. "I asked Bryce to carry it with him into battle."

"He clearly values your safety more than his own. By wearing the talisman, you'll show your love and support. If the power is as strong as you claim, it will guard you both with the magic binding you together."

Fallon nodded and fastened the strand of leather around her neck. "I fear he wishes to sever any ties we share, not preserve them." She stroked the star with her fingertips.

"I choose to believe in the power of love." Maeve moved toward the door. "I must prepare the evening meal and will call you when the food is ready. In the meantime, think about what I've said, but try to get some rest."

"Thank you again for your kindness, Maeve. I promise not to outstay my welcome."

"You will remain with us as long as necessary." Maeve stepped into the hall and closed the door behind her.

Fallon heaved a weary sigh. After spending the night in Bryce's arms, then the journey to Turnberry, she was physically and emotionally drained. She lowered herself onto the mattress and closed her eyes. She'd rest, but wasn't certain she'd sleep.

Dressed in a quilted linen gambeson beneath a chainmail tunic, Bryce's powerful, trew-clad legs straddled his black destrier. He pressed his booted heels into the horse's flanks, urging him forward as he led a small garrison of warriors into a thick, dense fog.

Despite his inability to see more than a few feet ahead, Bryce continued his search for the enemy. He wove his way along the narrow forest paths, completely unaware that his men dropped off one by one. He soon rode alone. When he came to a stream, he reined in his mount, startled by the wailing of an old hag with stringy red hair as she beat a shroud against a rock.

Bryce dismounted and stormed toward the woman. "Who are you, and why do you screech as if in pain?" He clasped her shoulder, spun her around, and inhaled sharply when he stared into the face of Dungal MacDougall. The blackguard carried a broadsword and his lips curled in a sinister grin.

"Prepare to die." Dungal forced Bryce to kneel before him. He raised the blade above his head then brought it down in a sweeping motion.

"Bryce!"

Fallon shot up in bed, her hand clutching her throat. Perspiration beaded her brow. Her heart clamored in her chest like a beast was trying to claw its way out. Drawing a simple breath was impossible. She squeezed her eyes shut and tried to regain her composure.

Her attempt to reassure herself fell short. She'd foreseen Bryce's death before, but each time the images became more vivid. She heaved a deep sigh. There was no way she could warn him, and even if she could get him to listen, he'd not change his mind about joining the Bruce in battle.

"Are you ailing, lass?" A male voice, followed by a firm rap on the door, caught her attention.

"I'm fine." Fallon dropped her legs over the side of the bed and padded across the room. She opened the door a crack and smiled at Fergus.

"What's all the *palver* about?" he asked. "I heard your outcry clear into the inn."

"I'm sorry if I gave you reason for alarm. I dozed off and must have called out in my sleep."

"Best you temper your shouting. You never know who might hear, or what they may think." The corner of Fergus' lip curled from a frown to a pleasant grin. "Fortunately, no harm was done. Maeve prepared a leg of venison and some turnips for the evening meal. Are you hungry?"

As if answering the question on her behalf, Fallon's stomach growled. "Aye, it has been a while since I had anything to eat. I would welcome a hot meal. Allow me a few minutes to freshen up then I will join you in the kitchen."

Fergus inclined his head. "Make haste. My wife doesna like to be kept waiting. I'd rather face an angry bear than to endure Maeve's ire when her meal grows cold."

Fallon closed the door then moved toward a small basin of water she'd spotted on the table beside the bed. She brushed her hair and straightened her gown before going in search of her hosts.

"Did you rest well?" Maeve gave the contents of an iron pot another stir then wiped her hands on her apron.

"I managed to close my eyes. Can I help?" Fallon paused in the center of the kitchen and glanced around. A platter of roasted meat sat on a shelf by the hearth, the aroma causing her stomach to gurgle in response.

"Nay. The food is ready. Sit yourself down." Maeve pointed to a wooden table with four mismatched chairs.

"Good, I'm starving." Fergus rubbed his belly and laughed. He sat and motioned for Fallon to take the seat beside him. "Join me, lass, so Maeve can serve the meal."

"I canna stay here unless I am allowed to earn my keep. My proficiency in the kitchen may be limited, but I had no complaints about the fare I served my uncle. I am, however, skilled in the garden and noticed yours was overgrown with weeds. Mayhap I can be of assistance there as well."

"I'll simply not allow you to work. You're our guest." Maeve's stern tone and determined stare bespoke her reluctance to bend.

"Then I must leave." Fallon was equally stubborn in her beliefs.

"Let the lass help you, Maeve. You're not so young anymore and often mentioned the chores have become a burden at times."

Maeve's brows knit together and she scowled at her husband. "Insulting me willna gain my favor. If you desire a younger wife, why don't you—"

Fergus stood and rounded the table before his wife finished her tirade. He curled his arm around her waist and kissed her cheek, despite her attempt to pull away. "You know that is not what I meant. You are as beautiful as ever."

Maeve's face flushed and she stopped struggling. "I may have a few more aches and pains than I used to, but I can still dance my way around any lass half my age."

Fallon shifted from one foot to the other, uncomfortable with the tension between her hosts, and searched for something to say. "I'm a healer. Mayhap I can put together a few herbs that will help to relieve some of your discomfort."

Fergus laughed and ran a hand over his left hip. "The lass found a way to make herself useful. I could use a little of that elixir myself."

"I will prepare the brew after we finish our meal. Speaking of which, I do intend to help with other chores as well." Fallon picked up the platter of meat and carried it to the table. "After we've finished this wonderful food, we can discuss a list of things for me to do."

"You are a *thrawn* lass—" Maeve began, but Fergus clutched her upper arm and shook his head. "You are fighting a battle of wits you have no hope of winning. There is no harm in letting the lass help you, as long as she says out of sight. If what Bryce told me is true, she may be in danger should anyone recognize her."

Fallon waited for Maeve to concede before taking her seat at the table. "Thank you. I'll do my best to stay out of the way." She poked her knife into a slice of meat and placed it on her trencher. "This looks delicious. I canna remember the last time I enjoyed such a feast."

Bryce paced, his movements brisk, his posture rigid. No matter how hard he tried, he could not get Fallon off his mind. Despite Robert's reassurances and his faith in Fergus, his gut told him she was in danger. Was sending her to Turnberry a mistake? Had his determination to distance himself and his emotions put her at risk?

He cursed beneath his breath and kicked a small rock in his path.

"Sit and relax, brother. Watching you is making me dizzy. Fallon is safe and you need to regain your focus before the battle." Alasdair added another log to the fire, then picked up a stick and stirred the glowing embers.

"Who said I was thinking about Fallon?" Bryce growled.

"You dinna have to say anything. I know you, little brother, and often what you do or say is totally different from what you are truly thinking or feeling."

Bryce glanced over his shoulder at Alasdair then raked his fingers through his hair. "Leaving Fallon in Turnberry made sense at the time, but I am no longer certain it was a wise choice. What if Dungal finds her?"

"Robert would not send her there if he dinna think she'd be safe. Did you tell her you'd return for her?" Instead of his usual banter, Alasdair spoke with compassion.

"I refuse to make promises I canna keep."

"Canna keep or willna keep?"

"I'm pleased you returned before dusk, Bryce." Robert joined them. "Traveling at night can be treacherous, as you well know." He winked and smiled. "Was Fergus waiting for you when you arrived?"

"Aye. He and his wife were very kind." Bryce faced Robert. "Are we still leaving at daybreak?"

Robert nodded. "We depart at first light. As I mentioned in our last discussion, timing is important. We have tarried here long enough." He sat on a log and picked up a trencher filled with food from the ground. "I've traveled with Alasdair long enough to know he never misses a meal. Is this yours?" He offered the wooden platter to Bryce. "A warrior needs to eat and keep up his strength."

"I'm not hungry." Bryce sat on the opposite side of the fire and lowered his head.

"My brother is brooding over his woman."

"I dinna have a woman."

"Fergus will do everything in his power to protect Fallon. You need to concentrate on the upcoming battle. If you canna do that, mayhap it is best you stay behind." Robert's tone hardened to one of authority. "Every man must have his wits about him and his head on a swivel. This battle is important to the cause. After our success at Glen Trool, winning this confrontation at Loudon Hill will prove to Longshanks that Scotland will never surrender to English tyranny."

"I have no problem staying focused on the battle," Bryce answered. "You sound confident in your strategy to defeat Aymer de Valance. However, we have approximately five hundred men and the English garrison numbers close to two thousand. The odds are not well balanced. Add the MacDougalls and our chance of success diminishes."

"If my plan is executed properly, we canna lose." Robert stood, his chin held high. "Have you ever watched a spider spinning a web?"

Bryce cocked his brow. "A spider? What does that have to do with fighting a battle?"

"While exiled on the Isle of Arran, I spent countless hours observing one's attempt to weave a web on the wall of a cave. No matter how many times he failed, and despite the unlikely odds, the creature kept trying. Eventually it managed to secure a single strand of silk to the stone. Within seconds it began to spin a web, not stopping until the task was completed. Triumphant, the spider waited for his prey. Once entangled in the trap, the victim could not escape."

"Robert, I wish to speak with you." A tall, broad-shouldered young man strode toward them with his hand outstretched.

Robert gripped the man's forearm, giving it a shake. "James, I'm pleased to see you, but I was not expecting to meet up with you until we reached Loudon Hill."

James glanced at Bryce and Alasdair before addressing Robert again. "I need to discuss an urgent matter. Alone."

Robert wrapped his arm around his friend's shoulders. "Anything you need to say can be discussed openly, but if you wish to speak privately so be it." He ushered James away from the fire.

"Who is he?" Bryce craned his neck in an attempt to hear the conversation, but was unable to discern what was being said.

"James Douglas. Some refer to him as Black Douglas. He is the son of Sir William Douglas the Hardy. In the early years of the rebellion, his da rode with Wallace. Sadly, he was captured and executed, their land taken by Longshanks. James was fostering in Paris at the time. The lad had only seen twelve summers when his father died." Alasdair stood and stretched.

Bryce's brow furrowed. "He dinna look old enough to shave, let alone fight. I'm surprised Robert would set store in anything a lad has to report."

"They met last spring, when Robert was on his way to claim the throne. James, now twenty summers, had just returned from a failed appeal to regain his birthright from Edward. With no home and nowhere to go, he offered his sword for the cause." Alasdair threw more wood on the fire. "I made his acquaintance while we were on Arran. He may be young, but he is a bold warrior."

"If he is so valuable and ally, why is it he dinna come over with Robert and his men when they landed in Scotland?"

"James returned to the mainland ahead of us. Since his arrival, he has created a diversion by keeping the English busy, engaging them in skirmishes wherever possible." Alasdair lowered his voice when Robert approached.

"What did the lad want?" Bryce wasted no time inquiring.

"They intercepted a spy from the MacDougall clan on the road outside of Turnberry. After a brief interrogation, the man was eager to tell James anything he wanted to hear." Robert pointed to a grove of trees beyond the clearing.

Bryce narrowed his eyes, adjusting to the darkness. Using the moonlight to focus, he spied a group of men. "Am I to assume the man in chains is the spy?"

"Aye. He was sent to infiltrate our ranks then report his findings, but James and his men intercepted him before he was able to deliver this missive. However, we dinna know how many times he might have slipped out of camp before tonight, or if he was acting alone. Leaving at first light is now more imperative than ever. Alasdair, please inform the men, and Bryce, you come with me."

Alasdair bowed. "I will speak with them right away." He hurried off to do Robert's bidding.

"What will you do with the spy?" Bryce asked as they walked toward James and his comrades.

"What we do with all men who commit treason against their king and country. Hang him."

Chapter 12

Fallon struggled with the weight of a heavy wooden tray. Piled high with clean tankards, she carried it into the taproom and began stacking the tinware on a shelf behind the bar.

"What are you doing?" Fergus lowered his voice so the patrons sitting at a table a few feet away could not overhear.

"You said I could help with the chores."

"Aye, I did." Fergus shook his head. "Since I canna fight you on this, I will concede, and accept your help, but only if you promise to stay out of sight until we are certain you'll be safe. After what happened to your uncle, Bryce fears the English may still be looking for you."

"I give you my word. I dinna want to do anything that might put you and Maeve in jeopardy."

"*Guid*. I'm sure my wife would welcome some help in the kitchen. That is, once she gets accustomed to the idea." Fergus laughed.

Fallon nodded and retuned to the kitchen, mere seconds before the door to the inn opened with such force it struck the wall with a loud crash. When she heard the ruckus, she peered around the doorframe, but was careful to remain hidden.

"Can I help you lads?" Fergus asked as three large warriors lumbered toward a table by the hearth.

Fallon covered her mouth to stifle a gasp. She recognized the plaid often worn by the MacDougall warriors.

"Bring us some ale and make it quick," one of the men growled as he sat down with his companions.

"Get out." A fourth man entered and pointed to the patrons already enjoying their drinks.

Fallon cringed at the sound of Dungal MacDougall's voice. She'd recognize it anywhere. Logic told her to hide, but there was no way to exit the kitchen without being seen. She had to pass by the taproom to go anywhere in the inn and she was certain more of Dungal's men would be milling about outside. Crouched beside the door she'd left open a crack, Fallon watched her nemesis as he surveyed the premises.

Dungal waited for the patrons to leave before joining his men.

"This is Carrick, not Galloway. You are no longer on MacDougall land and have no right to give orders in my inn." Fergus stepped out from behind the bar. "You are not welcome here."

Fallon cringed at Fergus' bold statement and raised her hand to cover her mouth. If he angered Dungal, he was going to get himself killed. What was he thinking?

One of the warriors jumped to his feet and stomped forward. "We are here on the King's business, old man. I'd counsel my tongue if I were you."

"Robert the Bruce is the rightful King of Scotland. Longshanks' arse-kissing minions have no place here." Fergus refused to back down.

"Did you hear what he called us, Dungal?" The warrior drew a sword from the baldric on his back. "I'll gut the bastard where he stands."

Dungal grabbed the man by the arm, halting his advance. "That won't be necessary, brother. Fergus is entitled to his opinion. He rode with William Wallace and supports the Bruce, so there is no question where his loyalties lie."

"What do traitorous dogs know about loyalty? Your ancestors defended Scottish soil and would roll in their graves if they knew you supported the English."

"Are you going to let him talk to you like that?" Dungal's brother lunged forward, but his way was blocked.

"I said sit down, Keith." Dungal growled. He waited for his disgruntled brother to back away then took a menacing step in Fergus' direction. "But he is also subject to the consequences." He slid a dirk from its sheath and flaunted it in Fergus' face. "Is speaking your mind worth losing your tongue?"

Fergus grunted. "I've never been afraid to speak my mind. Especially when what I have to say rings true." He tossed a cleaning rag over his shoulder and turned his back to Dungal. He moved to an ale barrel, tucked a tankard beneath the spigot, filling the vessel to the brim.

Fallon held her breath in anticipation of Dungal's irate reaction, but to her surprise, he threw his head back and laughed.

"You always had more guts than brains." Dungal flung the dirk. Horrified, Fallon watched the blade sail through the air, before sticking into an ale barrel, only a few inches from Fergus' face. "Next time, I willna miss."

Fergus didn't flinch. He filled another tankard, then sauntered past Dungal with a drink in each hand.

Fallon craned her neck, but Dungal obscured her view. She jumped at a tap on the shoulder, her heart rising in her throat.

"Best you find a place to hide," Maeve whispered and motioned with her hand for Fallon to move away from the door. "We dinna want Dungal to find you."

But there wasn't time. Fallon sucked in a sharp breath when Dungal glanced at the kitchen door. Certain he'd seen her, or overheard Maeve, she quickly pulled back her head and muttered a prayer.

"Dungal," a man shouted.

When she heard the stranger's voice, Fallon exhaled the breath she was holding. She must have been mistaken or

Dungal would be upon them by now. Careful to remain out of sight, she resumed her position, watching the interaction going on in the inn.

A short, stout, balding man entered, followed by two burly warriors.

"Bring us more ale," Dungal threw over his shoulder to Fergus as he approached the stranger. "Are there men guarding the door, Aymer?"

"A sufficient number of men surround the inn, and the remainder of the garrison is camped on the edge of the village." He sauntered to the table, took a seat, and glared at Fergus as he placed a tray of filled tankards on the table. "What is he doing here?"

"He runs the inn, but won't be staying." Dungal motioned to one of the guards. "See him out and make sure he dinna disturb us. If he gives you any trouble, kill him."

Seriously outnumbered, Fergus retreated to the storeroom. The sentry followed.

Dungal pointed at two of the three men who had accompanied him. "Do you remember my brother and cousin?"

"I do, but enough with the introductions. Did you locate the rebels?" Aymer brought the tankard to his lips and drank.

"They're gone." Dungal slammed his fist on the table.

"I thought you placed informants in the Bruce's camp? They were supposed to keep you abreast of their activities. How did they get away?"

"There were two men reporting back to me, but last night only one returned. The other was captured outside the village by Bruce sympathizers. I sent a party to check out the encampment at first light, but they found it empty. The fire pit was cold, and their tracks led off in all directions." Dungal downed his ale then dragged the back of his hand across his mouth.

"The ploy to throw the enemy off and to keep them from following has been used for centuries," Aymer pointed out. "My guess is they moved deeper into Bruce territory, hoping to pick up supporters along the way."

"Aye," Dungal agreed. "They eluded us again, but not for long. When we do find them, the battle will be over before it begins. Between your warriors and mine we number over three thousand. At best, the Bruce's force is a mere five hundred strong, most of them untrained crofters."

"Never underestimate the enemy, my friend. Look what happened at Methven. Robert let his guard down and we easily defeated him. He and what was left of his army of rabble were on the run for almost a year." Aymer laughed, then finished his ale. "Good thing I took the precaution of sending a spy of my own. He told me the Bruce is heading to Loudon Hill. A logical choice given it is in the heart of Carrick and a strategic place from which to launch an attack or to make a stand. The Romans used it for the same reason and even built a fort there. The remnants still remain."

"You dinna appear concerned given they've escaped and are headed into Bruce territory." Dungal stroked his chin.

"It is too late to intercept them, but the flat plain around the base of the hill is an excellent place for a confrontation. We canna possibly lose," Aymer replied. "I'll send a messenger issuing a challenge."

"Do you think they will stay and fight, or turn tail and run? I always thought the Bruce was a coward. He proved it when he ran after Methven and in the way he tricked Red Comyn into meeting him at Grey Friar's Abbey, then murdered him."

"Robert will accept. To refuse would make him appear weak, diminishing his chances of ever establishing his reign in Scotland. If he hopes to unite the clans, he has no choice but to face me. Let's go." Aymer stood and motioned for his men to join him.

"Meet me at Loudon Hill two days hence, Dungal. I devised a plan and with any luck this will be the last time we fight the Bruce. Once defeated, he'll hang along with what is left of his men. I suggest you brief your forces and leave as soon as possible." Aymer turned and left the inn.

"You heard the man. Drink up and we'll be off. *Slainte*!" Dungal raised his tankard then downed the contents. "The sooner we arrive, the more time we'll have to prepare for our victory." Dungal leaned closer to his brother. "We'll gather supplies from the village stores before we depart. See that the men are armed and ready to ride."

Fallon watched them leave then backed away from the door. Concerned for Bryce's safety, she began to pace the length of the kitchen. "I must find a way to warn the Bruce."

"You'll do no such thing." Fergus entered the room. "Bryce entrusted me with your safety and you will stay here until he returns."

Maeve dashed across the plank floor and threw herself into her husband's arms. She kissed him repeatedly on the cheek, then drew back, and punched him in the chest. "You old fool! What demon possessed you to behave like a reckless buffoon? You could have been killed."

"I'll not be dictated to in my own inn. Not by the likes of Dungal MacDougall. They are not welcome and I told them so. They're gone now and *guid* riddance to the lot of them." He grasped his wife by the shoulders, kissed her brow, then gently moved her aside. He pointed his finger at Fallon. "And you are not going anywhere, lass. Do you understand?"

"Please. They are in great danger and I must warn them." Fallon resumed her pacing. She had to reach Bryce.

"I'll send a messenger. He'll arrive well before de Valance and the MacDougalls, but dinna *fash*. King Robert was caught in a surprise attack once and he'll not let that happen again. I'd not be surprised if he wanted the blackguards to follow him."

The door to the inn opened and Fergus brought his finger to his lips. He quickly poked his head around the corner and blew out a deep sigh. "Take a seat, lads. I'll be right with you. The first round is on the house. My way of apologizing for the rude way you were tossed out earlier."

"Nothing like a free drink to make a man forget his anger," one of the men called in response to Fergus' offer.

Fergus entered the inn and Maeve approached Fallon. "I know you are concerned about your man, but my husband is right. King Robert willna be fooled again. Now that Dungal is gone and you're safe, why don't you go to your chamber and try to get some rest?"

"Nay. I am too nervous to sleep." Fallon picked up an empty tray. Maeve was right. The danger had passed now that Dungal was on his way to Loudon Hill, but she'd not rest until the messenger reached Bryce with his warning.

"I'll help clean up the mess left by our unwelcome visitors." She was at the door before Maeve could protest and despite Fergus' icy stare of disapproval, she crossed the room. As she placed the last dirty tankard on the tray, she noticed a dirk on the table. She recognized the ornately jeweled hilt immediately. It was the same blade Dungal had held to her throat before her uncle's execution. She slid the weapon onto the tray and was about to head to the kitchen when someone flung the door open.

A dark silhouette blocked the light from outside. "I forgot something."

Fallon shuddered at the familiar cadence of Dungal's voice and dropped the tray, spilling the contents of a tankard onto one of the patron's lap.

"Hey, watch what you're doing." The man sprang to his feet and grabbed her by the arm. "You need to get a serving wench who can handle the duties, Fergus."

Fallon didn't respond, her eyes remaining fixed on the

figure standing in the doorway. "Dungal," she muttered under her breath.

She watched her enemy storm across the floor, the wooden planks creaking with each of his strides. He clutched her other arm and yanked her free of the patron's grip. "Sit and finish your drink or you'll answer to me." He waited for the man to comply before focusing on Fallon. "I never thought I'd run across you again. Good thing I returned for my dirk." Without releasing her, he plucked the weapon off of the floor and slid it into the sheath at his hip.

"I suspect you are the one informed the Bruce we were coming. You lied the first time I questioned you and so did your uncle. I should have cut your throat when I had the chance."

"I dinna know what you are talking about." Fallon tried to wrench free of his grasp. She stared straight ahead, refusing to make eye contact. "I dinna know the Bruce or where to find him. How could I warn him of anything?"

"Still the coy minx." Dungal tightened his hold, his menacing grin darkening to an evil scowl. "You betrayed me once, and no doubt you intend to do so again. I must say, the fact you arrived before us surprises me. Who helped you?"

"What's taking so long?" Dungal's brother and one of his cousins returned. "I was beginning to worry, but see why you dally." His brother joined him. "This is the same lass we met in Galloway, the one who helped Fraser to escape."

"Unhand the lass. She happened along a few days ago, looking for work and lodging. We needed a serving wench, so we took her in. She did nothing to warrant this assault." Fergus spoke up, his voice never wavering.

"She should have been hanged along with her uncle, an oversight I intend to rectify. As for you, the English should have finished you off at Sterling. I grow tired of your interference. Arrest him." Dungal waited until his brother and cousin flanked Fergus and grasped his arms.

"On what charge and by whose authority do you arrest him?" Fallon challenged. "He committed no crime."

"His kind never needs a reason." Fergus struggled unsuccessfully against his captors.

"Housing or aiding a fugitive is a punishable offense, as you are well aware. We also have every reason to suspect Fergus has been conspiring with and offering aid to Robert the Bruce," Dungal replied.

"You murdered my uncle using the same excuse, one that holds no credence on Scottish soil. I'll not see an innocent man put to death on my account."

"Please dinna take him." Maeve crossed the room with a wild cry, then clung to Dungal's arm, but her plea went unanswered. He shook her free with a force that sent her crashing to the floor.

Fergus' back stiffened and his expression turned lethal. As if given the strength of ten men, he broke free of his captors and lunged at Dungal. "I'll kill you with my bare hands if you ever touch my wife again." He raised his fist, then grunted as Dungal's brother struck him hard on the back of the head with the hilt of his sword.

Fallon watched in horror as Fergus tumbled to the floor in a heap. Blood matted his gray hair and trickled down his cheek.

"What do you want me to do with him?" Dungal's brother nudged Fergus with the toe of his boot. Getting no response, he wiped the blood from the grip then sheathed his weapon.

Fallon's heart clenched. This was her fault. Fergus had only been trying to protect her and now he would surely swing from the gallows. No matter how much Maeve begged, Dungal would show no quarter. He'd feel compelled to set an example.

Dungal bent down, fisted his hand in Fergus' hair, and

raised his head. "I warned you," he snorted and released his grip, allowing Fergus' forehead to strike the floor with a loud crack. "Drag him out of here and put him in irons. He'll give you no trouble. Pick two men to accompany you and take him back to the camp. The rest of us will meet you there."

"Nay! Please dinna take him." Maeve made another attempt to intervene, but Fallon grasped her arm and held her in place.

"You canna stop them, Maeve. Fergus would be furious if he knew you tried. I know how much you love him and want to help, but there is nothing you can do." Her voice trailed to a whisper and tightness squeezed her chest as Maeve sank to her knees sobbing. She wanted to offer the older woman comfort, but Dungal's hand wrapped around her upper arm and he yanked her away.

"Now, my little chit, tell me about your visit to the Bruce's camp. Did you go for a roll in the grass with Fraser while there?" He lifted a stray strand of hair from her shoulder and twisted it around his finger.

"Dinna speak to me in such a lewd manner. I dinna go to the Bruce's camp and I roll in the grass with no man."

"A good tumble is exactly what you need. If I raise your skirt, mayhap you'll be more cooperative." Dungal dragged her into his embrace. "Either Fraser is a eunuch, or you are lying." He buried his face in her hair and nipped at her neck.

"I told you before, I'd rather die than permit you touch me." Fallon struggled to break free. She pounded on his chest with clenched fists and tried to knee him in the groin when he refused to release her.

Dungal trapped her wrists and held her at arm's length. "Your death can be arranged, but I have plans for you first."

Maeve slowly climbed to her feet, her face flushed and streaked with tears. "What do you intend to do with her? She is innocent, as is my husband."

"You're wrong, Madame. I can give you a list of her offenses. She will be interrogated at length then accompany me to Loudon Hill as my prisoner."

"What do you hope to gain from this? For her to go with you without an escort is not proper, and arresting her will serve no purpose," Maeve pressed.

"As long as she is in my company, Fraser will think twice about attacking my camp. When the time is right, I will offer to trade her life for his."

"You have no intention of honoring such an agreement, do you?" Fallon fought to hide the tremor of fear in her voice. "Bryce won't fall for your trickery."

"I have no intention of letting either of you go." His sinister laugh filled the inn. "Once Fraser gives himself up, I will present you both for execution."

Chapter 13

Fear and uncertainty gnawed at Fallon's belly as she was unceremoniously taken from the inn. There was no point in fighting or trying to escape—not yet. Dungal's size and brute force were enough to deter an attempt. Being surrounded by the enemy dashed any hope.

Dungal lifted Fallon onto his warhorse, swung his leg over the animal's back, and mounted behind her. He dug in his heels and the powerful destrier sped away, leaving a cloud of dust and a spray of dirt and gravel in their wake.

Heavily muscled arms encircled her waist as he gripped the reins and guided the beast through the winding streets of Turnberry. Certain she'd tumble over the animal's neck at any moment, Fallon furled her fingers in the coarse, black mane, and prayed she'd remain seated.

Within minutes they arrived at the MacDougall camp on the outskirts of the village. Greeted by the shouts from his men, Dungal slid from the saddle, pulling Fallon with him. She spotted Fergus tied to a tree a few feet away. He sat slumped over, eyes closed, with his chin resting on his chest. His age-weathered features were ashen. Without regard for her own safety, Fallon bolted to his side and fell to her knees.

She gently stroked his brow. His skin felt clammy beneath her trembling fingertips. "Fergus. Speak to me. Please." She tapped his cheek with the flat of her hand, but he didn't respond. Her eyes shot in Dungal's direction. "He is badly injured. I must tend to him."

Dungal stomped toward her, clasped her wrist, and hauled her to her feet. "You'll grant him no boons by prolonging his life. Better he die now than to wake up and find the noose around his neck."

"He's a Scot and so are you. Have you no honor or pride in your heritage? Where is your compassion?" A swift backhand sent her tumbling to the ground. She tasted blood and her head spun, but she refused to cry out or cower before this brigand.

"Talk back to me or dart off like that again and you will sample a lot worse." Dungal reached for her arm, but she swatted his hand away.

"I dinna need your help." Fallon rose on wobbly legs, stumbled, but managed to remain upright. With her shoulders squared, she crossed the camp with Dungal shadowing her every move.

They stopped at a large canvas tent and Dungal threw back the flap. "Get in." He waited for Fallon to do his bidding, took a moment to speak to one of his men, then followed her inside.

"Is this where you stay?" Fallon glanced at the dimly lit surroundings for possible means of escape. Unfortunately, the only way out appeared to be through the front opening, and Dungal had that heavily guarded.

"Aye. This is where I sleep when we make camp for an extended period of time, but dinna get accustomed to these comfortable conditions. We usually bed down on a pallet of leaves under the open sky."

A glimmer of hope shot through her mind. Mayhap she'd be able to escape during the journey. Dungal couldn't possibly watch her every minute and when he was distracted, she would make her move.

Dungal strolled closer, but stopped suddenly and spun around as the tent flap opened and his brother entered.

"I dinna believe the rumors being bandied amongst the men. Now I know them to be true. Are you daft?" His brother glared at Fallon.

"Stop babbling, Keith. Speak your mind then get back to work. I want this camp dismantled, and expect to be on our way within the hour," Dungal snapped.

"You canna bring a lass along. She'll be nothing but trouble. I've also heard she brings bad luck." Keith spat on the floor.

"What do you propose I do with her?"

"Hang her for treason along with the old man and be done with the matter. Aymer will be waiting for us at Loudon Hill and we dinna need the added burden," Keith concluded.

"She is coming with us. I'll not have my authority challenged. Should any man step out of line in her regard, I'll personally sever his head from his shoulders." Dungal opened a wooden chest, pulled out a clay jug, then removed the stopper and brought the vessel to his mouth. After imbibing, he offered the flagon to his brother.

Keith waved him off with a sweep of his arm. "What about Fergus? He is in a bad way."

"No thanks to you." Fallon's words spilled out.

"He got what he deserved, as should you, but Dungal's head is up his arse, and he thinks with something other than his brain." Keith grabbed the crotch of his trews and made a lewd gesture.

"Enough." Dungal capped the jug, tossed it into the chest, and slammed the lid closed. The glower on his face spoke volumes. "If you weren't my brother, I'd kill you where you stand. Dispose of Fergus however you see fit. Hang him or run him through. The method of execution is unimportant."

"Fergus is not some mad dog to be put out of its misery. I demand you set him free," Fallon blurted. "He's a good man and was only trying to help me. If someone must die, take my life instead."

"Silence! Dinna give me orders. The decision is made and Fergus will be executed." Dungal glared at his brother. "I expect this to be carried out quickly. Finish him off then prepare to move out." He faced Fallon and pointed to the pallet on the floor. "Sit and dinna give me any reason to tie you up. I have issues to attend to. The door is heavily guarded and if you try to escape, I'll not go easy on you."

His harsh words and the way he glared at her caused the hairs on her neck to bristle. Had he read her thoughts on running away? Rather than challenge him, she bit back the urge and lowered herself to the pallet. The moment Dungal left the tent, she dropped her head, cradling it in her hands. The image of Fergus' death brought tears to her eyes and a sob to her throat, but she managed to choke them away.

Her fate was yet to be determined, and minutes dragged until the guard poked his head inside the tent. "Dungal gave me orders to fetch you." He held back the canvas, allowing her to pass. "He doesna like to be kept waiting."

Following the guard's demands, she stepped outside, pausing long enough for her eyes to adjust to the bright sunlight. Behind her, the tent was collapsed, the musty smelling canvas rolled before being secured to a packhorse. The speed with which the warriors tore down camp astounded her.

"Dinna make any sudden moves. Dungal told me to stop you any way necessary." The guard slid his hand over the hilt of his sword.

"I understand." Fallon's search of the encampment stalled on the tree where Fergus had once been tethered.

Tears burned her eyes and a rush of emotion squeezed her chest. His lifeless body swung from a high branch, a rope around his neck. She crossed herself and offered up a silent prayer, hoping he had not regained consciousness before the execution. Her heart ached for Maeve and guilt hammered at her soul. He'd given his life in an attempt to protect her. A debt she'd never be able to repay.

"The same fate awaits the Bruce and his sympathizers. Best you keep that in mind." Dungal clutched Fallon's arm and dragged her toward his horse. In one swift move she was in the saddle. He hopped on behind her, then kicked his steed into a trot. The men fell in behind them.

"Nayyyyyyyy!" A woman's hysterical cry echoed around them, but no one turned.

"Maeve," Fallon whispered. "She was waiting for us to leave so she could tend to her husband."

"The fool failed to consider the ramifications of his actions. He now leaves behind a grieving widow." Dungal's cynical tone held no hint of remorse.

"You are a heartless bastard, a kin to the Devil, and destined to spend eternity in Hell for your deeds."

"Remember that and we will get along fine. I dinna have time to play games." Dungal molded his chest against her back and growled in her ear. "Fergus was as good as dead, and I granted him a boon. He died a martyr like your uncle."

His hot breath caressed her neck. She shuddered with disgust. Would he honor the threat made to his brother and slay any man who dared to get out of line? Did he include his own actions in the oath? The intimate press of his manhood against her backside and the rub of his muscular thighs against hers indicated otherwise.

Dungal kept a quick and steady pace, stopping only once so she could tend to her needs. They rode for hours, putting a fair bit of distance between them and Turnberry. But as the sun dipped behind the trees, he slowed his steed to a trot, eventually coming to a halt in a small clearing where he dismounted.

She tamped down the urge to dig in her heels and send the horse into a gallop. Despite her skill as a horsewoman, she knew she'd never outride a band of trained warriors.

"We'll make camp here." Dungal tipped his head back, taking in a cloudless sky. "The night will be fair. There'll be no need for tents." He moved to the left side of the horse and lifted her out of the saddle.

Dungal's cousin approached, his eyes trained on Fallon. A suggestive grin curled his lips. "Where will the lass sleep?" He circled around her, sizing her up and down as if she were prize livestock at town auction. "I'd like to take her for a tumble when you're done with her."

"No one tups the chit." Dungal balled his fists at his sides, his face flushed red and contorted with anger. "She will remain untouched. Her virtue—what little is left—will be my reward for a battle well fought. Providing she doesn't do something to warrant it sooner. In any event, I will decide who beds her and when. Do I make myself clear?"

His cousin inclined his head and backed away. "Aye. Very clear." He stormed off, grumbling beneath his breath.

"How dare you insult my honor?" Fallon raised her hand to strike him, but Dungal deflected the blow.

"My informant gave me more than enough reason to question your virtue. He reported what went on between you and Bryce Fraser during your stay at the Bruce's camp." Dungal's lips spread to an evil grin. "If you knew I was in the Bruce's camp, why did you not say so when you abducted me from the inn?"

"Your denial served to prove my point. You are a liar and canna be trusted. My spy also verified that you are not the innocent maiden you pretend to be. A night spent in the forest, performing lewd animal acts, hardly attests to your innocence."

Heat rose in Fallon's cheeks. "Your informant lied. Nothing indecent happened between Bryce Fraser and me. We got lost and it was too dark to travel."

"I dinna care if you are chaste or not. I prefer my women with experience." He fisted his hand in her hair then yanked her head back.

She stared into lust-filled eyes, causing her stomach to tumble. He captured her mouth in a ravenous kiss and forced his tongue past her lips. She bit down hard.

He yelped in pain, but refused to release his hold. He twisted her arm behind her back until she whimpered in pain then ravaged her mouth again.

When he finally let her go, Fallon staggered backward and wiped the smudge of his blood from her lips. "You're a vile creature and I pray you rot in—"

"We've already established my destination." Dungal's sinister laugh rebounded off the rocky cliffs surrounding the glen. "I like a woman with spirit. Breaking you will be an enjoyable task." His wry smirk quickly changed to a menacing glower. "Sit down and dinna give me any trouble. Killing you before I have the chance to sate my needs would be a shame."

Standing atop Loudon Hill, Bryce surveyed the open area below. Made of volcanic rock, the high prominence was nestled amidst smaller hills and grassy moors. The strategic position offered an unimpeded view of the area in all directions and a man could see for several miles. At the foot of the hill was an expansive, flat plain surrounded by boggy marshland.

Here, Robert planned to confront Aymer de Valance. The place where eleven years ago, Wallace defeated the English Lord Fenwick, the man William believed responsible for his father's murder.

When Bryce and his brothers were still lads, his cousin Simon told them about Wallace's victory at Loudon Hill and of other pivotal battles in their war with England. He couldn't wait until he was old enough to wield a sword and join the patriots on the battlefield. Now, he stood on the same ground where his cousin had fought shoulder-to-shoulder with William Wallace and won.

A blend of anger and grief filled him. He missed Simon and wished he were alive to see this battle. Bryce slammed a fisted hand against his open palm. With any luck, he'd have his chance to seek revenge on his behalf.

He joined Robert as he doled out orders to James and Alasdair.

"Take some men onto the plain and have them dig three long trenches. They must be deep enough for the men to hide and wide enough that the English horses canna jump them. Start at the edge of the bog surrounding Loch Gait and work inward, across the flatland."

"Do you want them dug clear across?" James asked.

Robert shook his head. "Nay. You must leave several narrow gaps of solid ground. By doing so, we can slow the English advance and pick them off as they funnel through. Those who try to leap over the trenches will be impaled on our pikes."

"Similar to the tactic used by Wallace at Stirling Bridge," Bryce pointed out.

"Aye. The enemy outnumbers us five to one. If only a few can reach us at a time, our odds greatly improve. I learned a lot from William and men like your cousin Simon." Robert lowered his head and crossed himself.

"We all did." Bryce mimicked Robert's show of respect, a lump forming in his throat.

Alasdair stepped forward. "Best we get started. I will take fifty men and begin the trenches. In a couple of hours, send replacements. By working nonstop we will complete the task well before de Valance arrives."

"He is on his way. One of his men arrived a few minutes ago with a missive from de Valance." John Kennedy moved to the front of the line and offered Robert a piece of vellum with the seal of England binding it closed.

Robert's expression darkened. "How did he get into our camp and where is he now?"

"The messenger arrived under a flag of truce, and I was sure you would want to know immediately. Dinna *fash*. We have him confined and well guarded. We willna permit him to return to de Valance. He already knows too much," John explained.

Robert snatched the missive and opened it. But as he finished reading the note, his rigid features softened into a wry grin. "Aymer has offered a challenge. Little does he know, that is exactly what I hoped he would do. I'll draft a response and send it back. We will meet him two days hence."

While Robert penned the note, Bryce's thoughts drifted back to Fallon. There had been no mention of the MacDougall's whereabouts and the last he'd heard, the blackguard was heading toward Turnberry. He prayed she was safe.

"The plan is a sound one." Alasdair leaned closer to Bryce and nudged him in the ribs with his elbow.

Bryce grunted and shrugged. "What did you say?"

Alasdair tried unsuccessfully to rake his fingers through a matted mane of hair. "This is not a bairn's game we play. Your head is in the clouds and you need to focus on the battle, not your woman."

"You're daft." Anger heated his blood and with his pulse throbbing in his neck and hammering in his ears, Bryce stomped away, lest he let his brother feel the repercussions of his comments. He was fed up with Alasdair's nagging and innuendos.

"Am I the one who is daft? You're the fool who has been sulking around like a lovesick hound." Alasdair grasped Bryce's upper arm and spun him around. "If Fallon is not the cause of your distraction, then tell me what keeps you preoccupied both night and day."

"Let go of my arm," Bryce growled. He glared at Alasdair's hands and fisted his own at his side to keep from lashing out at his brother. To his surprise, Alasdair released him and backed away.

"We will soon be headed into battle, but your mind is elsewhere. I'll wager you dinna hear a word Robert said."

"I heard Robert's plan. His idea is feasible, but I still have some reservations. Everything has fallen into place too easily. But if all goes accordingly, I canna wait to see the shock on de Valance's face when the tide is turned and he is caught in Robert's web. Retaliation for Methven is all I have thought about for the last year."

"The overpowering need for revenge can eat away at a man's soul until there is nothing left. After the battle is over, you can return for Fallon. I imagine you'll be wed not long after and before I know it, I'll be an uncle again." Alasdair slapped Bryce on the back. "Given the virility of Fraser men, Fallon may already be breeding."

"She is not, and I don't intend to return to Turnberry when this battle if over." Bryce cut his brother off. "I will continue in Robert's service until the English are driven out of Scotland. Then I will journey to France as I intended."

"So you keep telling me." Alasdair slid his hands over his belly and laughed.

"What is so humorous?" Bryce asked through gritted teeth as an image of his fist connecting with his brother's jaw rose to his mind's eye.

"You are, little brother. No matter how much you protest or try to deny the truth, your preoccupation with Fallon is evident. I dinna need her gift of second sight to foretell the future. As bleak as settling down with one woman may sound."

James approached. "The messenger has been sent, accepting de Valance's challenge. The English are camped about a mile from here, maybe more. They are not close enough to see the trenches being dug."

"By the time they arrive for the skirmish, we will be ready for them." Robert patted James on the back. "I have faith our time has finally come."

"Do we have any word on the MacDougalls?" A rush of excitement and anticipation coursed through Bryce's veins as it always did before a battle. He relished the idea of facing Dungal again. But concern for Fallon still niggled at his gut, a feeling of foreboding he was unable to shake.

"From what I was told, the MacDougalls are joining de Valance, but have yet to arrive. When they do, it will increase the enemy forces to over three thousand," James replied.

"I have no doubt the MacDougalls will come. Rats always travel in packs," Bryce added, then left the gathering.

Chapter 14

While some of Dungal's men gathered wood and started a cook-fire in the center of the clearing, others piled dried leaves and fresh rushes, covered them with woolen plaids or animal pelts, and arranged the pallets in rows around the perimeter. The task of setting up the camp completed, Dungal left Fallon in the custody of a guard while he and his men imbibed in food and ale.

The rugged sentry towered over her. With his disheveled red hair hanging loosely around his shoulders he reminded her of Alasdair Fraser. He, too, presented the fierce façade of an unapproachable beast, but she'd seen through Alasdair's gruff exterior to the gentle man inside.

"You'll not give me any trouble. Try to run, and I'll cut you down before you take your first step." He slid his hand over the hilt of his sword. "Woman or no, I won't hesitate to use my blade."

"You take your duty seriously. Do you value your honor as a Scotsman as much?" There was no sign of compassion in his eyes, but she hoped if forced to make a choice, he'd opt for the latter.

Dungal had selected well. The guard stood at attention, staring straight ahead, and did not utter a word in his own defense. His expression was unreadable.

The spicy aroma of roasted meat wafting in the air caused her stomach to growl, providing a stark reminder she'd had nothing to eat or drink since breaking her morning fast. She licked her parched lips, imagining a dipper of cool water to sate her thirst, but quickly pushed the thought to the back of her mind. She refused to ask her captors for anything.

Dungal staggered toward her. "Leave us. I'll watch the chit while you eat." He dismissed the guard, and waited for him to saunter away before dragging Fallon to her feet. Amidst the bawdy comments and shouts of encouragement from his friends to take her where they stood, he snaked his arm around her waist. "Shall I do as they request?" he groaned in her ear.

She'd rather be struck dead than to suffer the humiliation of spending one minute wrapped in his arms. The notion of being physically claimed by her enemy made her skin crawl. Convinced if she showed him any sign of weakness he'd follow through with his threats, she steeled herself against his advances. "You told the men I was not to be touched. Have you forgotten, or do you not abide by your own demands?"

"I set the rules, m'lady, and I can change them." He nuzzled his beard-roughened chin against her neck.

"So it appears." She stiffened in his arms.

A chuckle rumbled deep in his chest, but his stern expression remained unyielding. "In all my days, I've never met a woman as outspoken or as irritating. Yet I find your tenacity intriguing." He tightened his embrace. "I should have killed you when I had the chance, but like a burr under a horse's blanket, you hold my attention and pique my curiosity. You are either a very clever temptress or a fool."

"I am neither, sir. Before she died, my mam taught me to stand up for myself and to speak my mind, even against overbearing men. I demand you release me at once." She tried to wriggle free, then pressed her palms to his chest and shoved. He may think her bold, but if he knew how terrified she was that he'd rape her, he might complete the deed. She pushed him again, but he remained steadfast.

Dungal grabbed her hands and twisted her arms behind her back until she released a whimper of submission. "You are my prisoner. Best you remember your place." He let go of her wrists and pinched her cheeks between his thumb and forefinger, forcing her to look him in the eye. "Dinna delude yourself, woman. I can, and will, have you whenever I see fit to do so." He released his grip, and she stumbled backward.

Fallon bit back the urge to further express her disgust at the idea of bedding Dungal, deciding it was better to hold her tongue rather than anger him further. In his drunken state, there was no telling how he might react.

"I am weary from the journey and need to rest." She lowered herself to the ground.

"Is that so?" Dungal raised his brow. "You may share my pallet if you wish, or spend the night tied to the tree. The choice is yours." Dungal crossed his arms over his chest and awaited an answer.

"I dinna consider those suitable options."

"You are fortunate that I gave you any choice at all. Nonetheless, they are the only two you have. Either you select one, or I will do it for you."

"I pick the tree."

"Suit yourself. After we win the battle, you will no longer have a say in where you sleep—or with whom," Dungal sneered as he summoned the guard. "Tie her to the tree and when you're done, take her slippers as an added precaution."

Twilight faded into night and the forest grew dark with ominous shadows shrouding the clearing. Except for the low drone of a conversation going on at the distant edges of the camp, the crackle of burning wood, and the warriors' snoring, all was quiet.

Fallon shifted her position, trying to get comfortable, but with her back against a hard tree trunk, her efforts proved futile. Dew-laced fog swirled around her, dampening her clothing and hair. She tucked her bare feet beneath her gown and shivered. A plaid or pelt would shield her from the elements, but she would rather freeze than ask Dungal for anything.

She'd need her wits about her if she had any chance of getting away, albeit at this moment the possibility appeared bleak. Determined to make the most of her precarious situation, she inhaled deeply, allowing the scent of pine to calm her senses. Exhausted, she closed her eyes and drifted off.

"Do you plan to slumber the day away?"

The deep voice startled her. When someone nudged her with the toe of his boot, Fallon opened her heavy eyelids and found herself staring into the face of Dungal's brother squatting beside her.

Keith straightened his posture. "You haven't eaten since yesterday and I'd wager you're famished and thirsty. I brought you something." He raised a wineskin to her mouth.

Fallon stared at him in disbelief. Until now, he'd been gruff and unaccommodating.

"Dinna glare at me as if I am trying to poison you. It's ale. Drink." He brought the vessel to her lips again. "If you dinna want it—"

Fallon drank greedily then pulled her head away. "Thank you."

His act of kindness surprised her. Fallon glanced around the camp, but amidst a flurry of activity, Dungal was not present. "I'm not sure your brother will approve." She accepted another sip of ale.

"Dungal isn't here. He had an important matter to tend to and left me in charge." Keith raised his chin and puffed out his chest with pride.

"Where did he go?" she couldn't help but to inquire. Her uncle's wise words sprang to mind. *Always keep your enemy close, so you know what they are about.*

"You'd do best not to *fash* over things which are none of

your concern. Dungal will return soon enough." Keith stood and capped the wineskin. "Are you hungry?"

Fallon gave a hesitant nod. "Aye. I would appreciate something to eat."

Keith trotted off, but unlike Dungal, he did not ask anyone to stand guard. Fallon searched the surrounding area, hoping to find a suitable means of escape. She tugged at the ropes binding her hands behind her back, but the knot tightened. She blew out a deep sigh of frustration. Unless she convinced Keith to untie her, there was no way she could flee.

"It's not fancy fare, but will fill your belly." Keith carried a trencher and eating knife. He squatted beside her, stabbed a small portion of meat, and held the morsel to her lips.

Fallon accepted a piece of venison and then another. The spicy flavor exploded in her mouth. She closed her eyes savoring each bite, forgetting for a moment she was being held captive. The oatcake that followed was dry and not as tasty, but Keith was right, it did allay her hunger. She swallowed the last mouthful then coughed to clear her throat. "I must tend to my needs."

Keith grunted. "I, um, I dinna know where to take you," he stammered, his face turning a deep crimson. "Mayhap we should wait until Dungal returns."

"Your brother may be an arrogant, insufferable . . ." She refrained from further comment on Dungal's despicable character. "But he granted my request when the need presented itself. It will take but a minute and the thicket at the edge of the camp will do fine." She inclined her head in the direction.

As he took a minute to ponder the request, her mind raced with possibilities. Was he softening to her? Guilt niggled at her belly. If she managed to flee, he'd be left to face Dungal's wrath. After showing her a gesture of kindness, she hated to deceive him, but she had to try. Keith was different in many ways from his older brother, but desperate times called for her to use whatever tactics were necessary to get away. "Please, I would not ask if it wasn't urgent."

Keith raked his fingers through his hair. "I guess there is no choice but to trust you." He bent and untied her bonds, releasing her from the tree. "Get up." He cupped her elbow and helped her to stand.

Fallon rubbed her raw, swollen wrists and rotated her shoulder to work out the stiffness. "Thank you. I am again indebted to you for your kindness." The words left a sour taste in her mouth, but she had to win his confidence. Her legs were numb from sitting, but after a few steps the feeling returned.

"Wait. Dinna go any farther."

The deep rumble of Keith's voice stopped her in her tracks. She glanced over her shoulder.

"Give me your hands or I'll tie you to the tree again." The rope dangled from his fist as he closed the gap between them. "I am not the buffoon Dungal believes I am. If you dinna cooperate, you can sit and wait for my brother to return."

Fallon slowly raised her hand. There was no point in challenging and her compliance might win him over. "I never believed you were. Dungal is the fool."

Keith shrugged. "That may be, but he is my brother and laird of the clan. It is my duty to serve him. If I let him down, he'll see me flayed."

"Even if what he does is wrong?"

Keith grunted again, but did not respond to her question. He tied the rope around her wrists then led her to the thicket. "Hurry and do what you need to do," Keith mumbled under his breath as he placed his hand on the small of her back and urged her to move.

Fallon planted her feet and refused to budge. "I canna hold my skirts with my hands bound. If you'll untie me for just a moment, I promise to be quick."

"Dungal will skin me alive if I cut you loose. I won't go against his orders. You'll have to manage."

"Your brother took my slippers. We are in the middle of a dense forest. What harm can it do if you untie me for a few minutes? Surely Dungal would understand a woman's need for privacy," she concluded, and dropped her chin, hoping he'd be embarrassed enough at her implications to comply. Her heart leapt when he cupped her hands and the cold blade of his dirk brushed her skin.

"Dinna make me regret my decision." He cut the rope. "Do what you must and make haste."

"Will you step away or at the least turn your back?" she asked while offering him a pleading pout.

She was pressing her luck, but she stood a better chance of getting away if he wasn't watching.

Keith grumbled something indiscernible, threw up his hands, and turned around. "Make haste. You have but a minute."

Fallon stepped into the bushes, then bolted without glancing behind her. The moment of remorse at duping Keith was brief. This was war, and despite his compassion, he was duty-bound to Dungal and her enemy.

Keith let out a string of ribald curses that she was certain resonated for miles then shouted for warriors to join him in the chase.

She started out on a well-worn path, but if she had any hope of eluding capture, she needed to find a less conspicuous route. She could never outrun highly trained men in a sprint, especially if they hunted her down on horseback. Leaving the marked trail might prolong her journey, but it gave her a fighting chance.

Making her way through bracken and branches, stumbling over rough rocky terrain, she headed east, in the direction of Loudon Hill.

Her heart hammered and her chest constricted, begging for air. The painful stitch in her side worsened with each step, but she kept up the pace. Her feet were bloody and laced with cuts and bruises from the stones and twigs on the forest floor. Taking her slippers was a strategic coup for Dungal, but while it slowed her down, it would not deter her from her goal.

She heard Keith and the others in pursuit and judging by the closeness of the approaching voices, they were gaining ground. To linger in one spot was not prudent. However, with her feet in their current state, things could only get worse.

She paused for a moment and sucked in a gulp of air. In desperate need of a rest, she was frantically searching for a place to hide when an idea came to her. She quickly scaled a nearby tree, climbing to a large curved branch. From her perch she could see for miles and the thick foliage kept her hidden from view.

"I found a scrap from her gown, but her tracks end here," a male voice echoed. "She must have doubled back."

She covered her mouth, stifling a gasp. Keith and five warriors stood directly below. Even the slightest movement would alert them to her presence.

"I canna believe we lost her." Keith bent over at the waist, planted his hands on his knees, and drew in a slow breath. "Dungal is going to kill me."

"I dinna want to be present when he finds out she's gone." One of the men let out a long, slow whistle as he sat on the ground then rested his back against the base of the tree. "She scurries like a hare, and I'm spent. I'll rest here for a while if you want to go on without me."

Fallon couldn't breathe and panic squeezed her lungs. Her heart raced and remaining still seemed to be an impossible task. But she had to try. If she made any noise or rustled the leaves and the man raised his eyes, she'd be discovered.

"Get up." Keith kicked the man's boot. "If we dinna locate her before Dungal returns, you will be the target of his ire as much as me. And you're right when you say he'll not be pleased about this turn of events."

The man's face paled and he lumbered to his feet. "I'm suddenly refreshed." He brushed the dirt and dried leaves from his tunic then trotted into the woods with Keith and the others on his heels.

A temporary reprieve did not mean she was free—far from it. But in case they returned, she decided to wait several minutes before climbing down. When she felt it was safe to do so, she lowered herself to the ground, but not before tearing strips of fabric from the bottom of her kirtle and wrapping them around her feet. The makeshift bandages provided meager protection for her throbbing soles, but offered some relief and would hopefully prevent further injury.

Despite her discomfort, she took off running again. She had no idea how close she was to Loudon Hill, but she knew it was east of the camp, and she willed herself to forge ahead.

Keep going. You can do this. Bryce needs you.

The deeper into the woods she moved, the farther away the voices sounded. Relief washed over her and she paused to catch her breath. Had she managed to get away?

A tree branch snapped, and her head shot up. She felt certain she'd been discovered. Winded, and unable to take another step, she closed her eyes and waited with baited breath for Keith to pounce.

Steely determination coursed through her veins. She'd not give up without a fight. A thick hardwood stick lay at her feet and she snatched it up, along with a palm-sized rock, her pulse pounding and her breath coming in ragged pants. She widened her stance, braced herself, and prepared to face her fate.

A red doe and her fawn stepped onto the path and passed a few feet from where she stood. With a soft cry of relief, Fallon dropped the stone and sank to her knees.

Her hope of escape renewed, she climbed to her feet and moved through the woods with speed and vigor. Certain she must be getting closer to her destination, she decided to return to the path. She scurried up a small embankment, only to come to a dead halt when she reached the road. In her effort to avoid her pursuers, she had somehow doubled back and had almost run full circle. How could fate be so unkind?

There was no point wallowing in self-pity and she had no time to waste. Fergus had been captured before he'd had a chance to send a messenger to warn the Bruce. It was now up to her. Reoriented, she took off running along the path, in the direction she had originally intended to go.

It had been a while since she'd heard Keith's voice and the forest around her was silent. Had she managed to elude capture? She blew out a shuddering breath and slowed her pace to brisk walk.

The sound of an approaching rider caused her heart to lurch. As the echo of hooves pounding against the ground got closer, she frantically searched for a place to hide. But it was too late. The rider rounded a bend in the path and came to an abrupt halt directly in front of her.

"Going somewhere?" Dungal slid from his destrier and stomped toward her.

Tears pricked the back of her eyes and her shoulders slumped forward as she faced her enemy.

"Where in damnation is my brother? He better provide me with a good explanation as to how you managed to escape. I should never have left that buffoon in charge."

She wanted to dash again, but her legs felt like anvils. Before she took a single step, he was on her. He buried his fingers in her hair and snapped her head back. "What have you to say for yourself? Tell me why I shouldn't kill you right now. Or mayhap sate my needs. This time, no one is around to hear you scream or to interrupt."

"Over here!" someone shouted.

Keith and his companions stumbled onto the path, all looking the worse for wear.

"Dungal." Keith stopped in the middle of the trail. "Let me explain. I—"

Dungal placed his hands between her shoulders and shoved, forcing her to her knees. He faced his brother. "There is no excuse for your incompetence. Leaving you in charge was obviously a huge mistake. I'm gone for a few hours and come back to find my unfettered prisoner darting through the woods with a band of idiots chasing her."

Dungal pulled a rope from behind his saddle and approached her. "Give me your hands." When she didn't comply, he lunged forward and grabbed her wrists then tied the rope around them. "Stand," he growled and dragged her to her feet. He glared at his brother. "We join Aymer at daybreak so best you return to camp. That is if we still have a camp to go back to." He whistled and his horse trotted forward. He hoisted Fallon onto the saddle and mounted behind her. "I will be briefing the men on the battle plans before we leave. I'd suggest you start walking, brother."

Chapter 15

Six hundred strong, the Scottish patriots assembled atop Loudon Hill. Dressed in their heavy quilted gambesons, steel and leather skullcaps, they prepared for battle. Bryce joined Alasdair, John Kennedy, James Douglas, and a few other Scottish nobles, including Robert's brother, Edward, as the Bruce prepared to address his army.

Robert stood before them and raised his hand. The boisterous crowd immediately grew quiet. "Today we face our enemy, Aymer de Valance, second Earl of Pembroke. For some of you, this will be your first skirmish with the blackguard, but for many, this is an opportunity to seek revenge for the losses we suffered at Falkirk, Methven, and for the years of English tyranny we have been forced to endure. Your bravery and dedication to the fight for freedom will long be remembered. Scotland's sons and daughters will forever be indebted to you. Before we enter into combat, join me in prayer." He dropped to one knee, bowed his head, and began to speak in Latin.

After the benediction was completed, Robert's expression hardened. "Fight well and hard, as if today was the last day of your lives. Fail to win, and de Valance will have you hanged for treason. Keep that in mind as you face the enemy." Robert rose and lifted his sword. "With the Lord's help, success is in our grasp!"

"Aye, Bruce!" The men, primarily spearmen, hoisted their weapons and targes, echoing their leader's enthusiasm. The few bowmen present did the same.

Following Robert's speech, Bryce stood on the rocky ledge overlooking the plain below. He tried to focus his mind on the upcoming battle, but thoughts of Fallon flooded his mind.

It was as if she called out to him. He'd swear he could hear the soft lilt of her voice, feel the beat of her heart in rhythm with his own. He could smell the sweet lavender scent of her hair and the spicy tang of her arousal when they made love. He could see her beautiful face and reached out to touch her, but she wasn't there.

"Are you ready to kill some English?" Alasdair joined him.

Bryce inclined his head. "Today is a good day to fight and, if need be, a good day to die. Aymer de Valance appears to agree." He pointed at the sea of English soldiers, some on heavy horse, the rest on foot. They spread out in rows across the flat grassland in an age-old pattern typically used for battle. "I must admit they are an impressive sight in their polished armor, chainmail, and stark white hauberks."

Brightly colored pennons flapped in the breeze and armor-clad warhorses restlessly danced beneath their Saxon riders.

"They must number at least three thousand." Alasdair cupped Bryce's shoulder. "I wish you'd heeded my request, little brother, and were on your way back to Fraser Castle."

Bryce slid his hand over Alasdair's. "I couldn't let you hog all the glory again. Besides, someone needs to watch your back."

"I can fend for myself and would rest easier if I knew you were out of danger. I can still speak to Robert and tell him you are not strong enough to fight after your injury at Loch Ryan. He'd understand."

"You've been like a mother hen, protecting both Connor and me since Da was killed. I appreciate your concern, but this is something I must do."

Alasdair pulled Bryce into an embrace. There was no witty banter or sarcasm, just a genuine show of affection between brothers. A bond no mortal man could sever.

"Do you think the MacDougalls are among them?" Bryce asked.

"I'm certain of it. We will have our revenge, brother. Not just for the losses suffered in battle, but for the slaughter of our parents and brothers," Alasdair replied.

"I'll not rest easy until Longshanks is in his grave, Dungal is brought to justice, and Robert sits on his rightful throne." Bryce turned to face James and John as they approached.

"The men are ready. Will you and Bryce lead the first line of attack?" John glanced from one brother to the other.

With a spear in hand and Bryce at his side, Alasdair shouted to the group of patriots assembled and awaiting his orders. "*God spede* and keep your heads on a swivel." He crossed himself, spun around, and led them in a charge down the slope.

After a short sprint, they reached the bottom of the hill and manned the first trench. There, they waited for the English to launch their assault.

Following a volley of arrows, the ground vibrated under the thundering hooves of heavy horse. Bryce wrapped his hand around the shaft of his pike, hoisted his targe, and drew in a slow, deep breath to steady his nerves. He'd been on countless battlefields, but had never grown accustomed to the unsavory mix of heart-stopping excitement and gut-wrenching anxiety. "May the Almighty be with us." He raised his weapon as the first warhorse attempted to hurdle the trench.

Horses became impaled, along with their riders. The shatter of spears on armor and the bloodcurdling cries of wounded men and beasts echoed across the moor.

"Robert's plan is working." Alasdair yanked a claymore

from the baldric on his back and swung it in a sweeping arch, felling the English soldier racing toward Bryce.

"Thank you, brother." Bryce inhaled sharply, then quickly spun around, his sword connecting with that of an English knight approaching from the other direction. No match for his skill and determination, his attacker soon lay facedown in a pool of blood.

Bryce sheathed his blade, picked up a pike, and spoke to Alasdair. "The blackguards who dinna die in the trenches and manage to filter through the small gaps of land face an even bigger challenge with our spearmen and bowmen."

"The enemy is in a state of chaos. This is the perfect time to press forward." Alasdair swung his claymore over his head to rally the men. He shouted out a war cry then led them onto the plain, boldly confronting the unorganized English forces as they advanced.

In the confusion of battle, Bryce lost sight of his brother. He prayed the Lord would look after him and continued the fight. The skirmish was fierce, but brief. Despite being outnumbered, the patriots forced the English back.

Atop a black charger, Robert approached at full gallop. "We are victorious. De Valance retreated and fled the field, along with the remainder of his army." His words were drowned out by the cheers from his men.

"How many warriors did we lose?" Bryce's stomach clenched with worry as he surveyed the area in search of Alasdair.

"We suffered few casualties compared to the English." Robert struggled to keep his spirited mount under control. "The men fought with valor and have reason to be proud."

Relieved to see Alasdair walking toward him, Bryce raced to his side and threw his arms around his brother's broad shoulders. "I'm glad you're well and uninjured."

"And I'm pleased to see your pretty head remains where

it belongs." Alasdair laughed and tousled Bryce's hair as one would a wee bairn.

"As am I. War is always a terrible waste, but it's a necessary evil." Bryce glanced around at the carnage. He squatted down, then rolled over the body of a felled Scot warrior and stared into lifeless eyes.

"Our casualties were light. The English dinna fare as well." Alasdair softened his voice.

"Tell that to Brian." Bryce slowly rose to his feet, brought his sword to his nose, and snapped his heels together in a show of respect for his fallen comrade.

"There is nothing you can do for him. We must be away. Robert will send men to bury the dead and aid the wounded." Alasdair motioned for Bryce to follow him.

"I come anon. Give me a few minutes." Bryce watched his brother trot up Loudon Hill before dropping to his knees. He buried his face in his hands and wept for those who'd lost their lives in the battle. Not usually this sentimental, he found his thoughts strayed once again to Fallon. He prayed she was safe and that he'd made the right decision to leave her in Turnberry. But once again an uneasy feeling of trepidation tugged at his gut, and he feared the worst.

He'd felt a strong connection with Fallon since the day they met. But until this moment, he didn't realize how much he cared about her. Was Alasdair right? Had he let her breach the wall he'd so carefully built round his heart? Despite his effort to keep his distance and remain focused, was he falling in love with her?

Bryce cursed. After what happened to Ashlen, he'd sworn never to love. His heart could not take the pain again and he wasn't worth of a woman's adoration and trust.

He slowly rose, and after a final salute to the lost souls who littered the battlefield, he raced up the hill.

"Where is your brother, Alasdair? He dinna return after

the battle. Have you seen him?" Concern resonated in John Kennedy's voice.

"I'm here. Did anyone encounter the MacDougalls?" Bryce crested the hill and strode toward the gathering of men.

"Aye. They attacked the trench near the bog. Many of their clansmen fell. The rest turned tail and ran off." James Douglas joined the group.

"What of Dungal? Did he escape?" Bryce impatiently shifted his weight from one foot to the other in anticipation of the response.

"He was seen fleeing on horseback with a wounded man slung across the back end of his horse."

Bryce slammed his balled fist against the open palm of his other hand. "Damnation, I'd hoped to meet him on the field or at least hear he was dead."

James patted Bryce on the shoulder. "You still may have your chance to meet him in battle. They made camp five or six miles from here."

Bryce shook his head and raised his hands in question. "What makes you think they will return to their camp? If they do, I doubt they'll remain there for any length of time? My guess is that they would return to Galloway as quickly as possible."

"They will go to their camp to tend their wounded. With our own to care for, they won't be expecting us to follow right away," James replied.

"Then we best make haste. I won't rest until Dungal is punished for his treachery." Bryce moved toward the horses, prepared to give chase, but stopped when he saw Robert approaching.

"I want him punished as much as you do. Mayhap, more so now than ever before." Robert spoke with conviction.

"Something is amiss." Alasdair stepped forward.

"Aye. One of Dungal's wounded men was captured and taken prisoner. Before he died, he boasted about a hanging that took place a few days ago in Turnberry." Robert bowed his head.

Feeling as though he'd been gut-kicked and momentarily forgetting respect for his king, Bryce grabbed Robert by the shoulders. "Fallon?" *Dear Lord, let her be alive.* He swallowed hard. "Tell me who was hanged."

"Fergus."

Fallon fidgeted, certain she'd go insane if word of the battle did not reach them soon. She remained tied to the tree, and the man left to guard her would not speak to her, let alone answer her questions or her request to tend to her needs. Attempts to clear her mind of worry proved futile. She feared for Bryce's safety and prayed he had survived the confrontation unscathed.

The rumble of hooves broke the silence. Fallon craned her neck, uncertain if it was her nemesis or someone coming to save her. She was a healer, her life dedicated to aiding the ill and relieving their suffering. Until today, she had never prayed for a man to die. She made an exception in Dungal's case.

The guard drew his sword and broadened his stance. He stood between Fallon and the direction from which the sound came. Had she not been so frightened, she might have laughed at the man's foolish bravado against unknown odds. She had to give him credit. He would die loyal to his leader if the need arose.

The guard lowered his weapon and bolted toward the path leading into the clearing. Several MacDougall men rode past him, many carrying wounded and dismembered victims of the battle.

There was no sign of Dungal or his brother. Dare she hope he had met with his demise? If he was dead, she couldn't help but wonder what would happen to her at the hands of his men? Would they let her go, or would they ravage her and later slit her throat?

She bit down on her lower lip in an effort to suppress the growing terror squeezing her chest, and inclined her head when Dungal entered the camp and slid from the saddle.

"Over here! My brother is in need of assistance." Dungal rounded his horse and lifted Keith's body from across the rump of his steed.

Several of his clansmen ran to his aid. Together, they carried Keith to a spot beneath a tall oak tree and positioned him on his side. "Fetch the wench, and dinna tarry," Dungal growled.

The guard cut the ropes binding her to the tree and dragged Fallon to her feet. "Dungal wants you. Dinna give me any trouble."

Fallon nodded and accompanied the man.

Dungal squatted and focused his attention on his brother.

"Dinna die on me. I'll not allow it." Dungal tore open Keith's bloody tunic to reveal a jagged chest wound with a metal tip protruding from it. The arrow had entered through his back, but had not gone all the way through.

Fallon gasped at the sight. She'd tended many wounded men in her days with Clan Scott, but her gut told her Keith's injuries were grave, and if he died, she'd be blamed.

"Don't stand there staring at him. You're supposed to be a healer. Do something to assist." Dungal leaned close to Keith's ear. "Hold on, brother."

Keith moaned, but did not wake when Fallon knelt beside him and peeled back his shirt. "If I am to assess the full extent of his injuries, I'll need something to cut away the fabric." She held out her hand, waiting for Dungal to respond. She wanted to ask about the outcome of the battle, about Bryce, but she didn't dare.

Dungal took a moment to ponder her request then pulled his dirk from its sheath. "If you do anything foolish, or my brother dies, you willna live long enough to tell about it." He gently stroked his brother's cheek, but his eyes remained fixed on Fallon's every move.

She turned the dagger over in her hand. It would be so easy to lunge forward and kill Dungal, but it wasn't in her to take a life, even to save her own.

The concern Dungal showed for his brother took her by surprise. The last thing she'd expected was compassion and even a small showing of affection. She honestly believed him to have a heart of stone. His brother's injury had obviously unnerved him, which, she concluded, made him more dangerous than before.

Fallon sliced open the fabric. "We must extract the arrow and seal the wound. Have you any whiskey?" She carefully removed what was left of Keith's tunic and tossed it aside.

"Bring me the jug from my chest and anything else the lass requests." Dungal issued his orders to one of his men and returned his attention to his brother when he began to thrash and cry out. He placed his hands on Keith's shoulders, but he was no match for a mountain of a man made delirious with pain.

"You must keep him quiet." Fallon examined the spot where the arrow entered Keith's back then reassessed the exit wound on his chest.

"Can you help him?" Dungal's voice cracked with emotion when he spoke.

"The steel tip pierced the skin of his chest, but the arrow head has not gone all the way through. To try and draw it out the way it entered would do more damage and kill him. Before we can remove the arrow, you will need to snap off the feathers about an inch up the shaft."

Dungal's face blanched. "Then what do you propose to do? I dinna see how that would make a difference. The arrow will still be lodged in his body."

"Once the end is cleared, I'll require two strong men to assist me. One on either side of him to thrust him back against the tree. The metal tip will be forced the rest of the way through his flesh when the shaft strikes the trunk and the arrow can then be pulled out." Fallon swept a strand of hair from her sweat-dampened brow. "It is the only way." She glanced up at another man. "Take two daggers and heat them in the coals. The wound will need to be sealed."

"You heard her. Heat the blades and be quick about it," Dungal shouted at the man as he trotted off, nearly colliding with the one sent to retrieve the whiskey. He looked at Fallon. "You've done this before?"

"Aye." Fallon opened the flagon. "I'll need the two of you to hold him steady while I clean the wounds."

Dungal positioned his brother according to Fallon's instructions then snatched the spirits from her hand and took a drink before handing it back to her. He placed his hands on Keith's shoulder and ordered his friend to do the same.

Keith bucked and shouted in agony when Fallon poured the liquid over his chest. He'd been the only person to show her any kindness since her abduction and she hated to cause him additional pain, but the cleansing was necessary.

"One of you must restrain him while the other breaks off the feather end of the arrow. Do it quickly, he has already lost a lot of blood."

Dungal pulled Keith to a sitting position, then reached behind his brother, grasped the arrow, and snapped off the end. He nodded to the man assisting him. "When I count to three, shove him against the tree with all the force you can muster."

The man nodded and wiped the beads of sweat from his forehead with the back of his hand.

With one on either side, the two men pushed in unison, the shaft striking the trunk, and freeing the tip. "Easy, brother," Dungal cautioned when Keith struck out wildly in response to the sudden pain. But in his weakened state, the blow was ineffective.

The heated daggers arrived and Fallon prepared to seal the torn flesh. "Hold him securely. This will hurt." She wasted no time completing the task. Bile rose in her throat. The familiar odor of seared flesh and hair assaulted her senses, bringing memories of Bryce's recent near-death encounter to the forefront of her mind.

"I'm finished. It is now up to the Almighty if he lives or dies." Fallon wiped her hands on her skirt.

"Pray he survives." Dungal laid his brother on a pallet of leaves and covered him with a woolen plaid. He faced Fallon. "There are others who need tending. See to them at once." He dismissed her with a wave of his hand. As she rose to do his bidding, Dungal grabbed her wrist. He glanced around the group of bystanders and motioned to the man who had guarded her during the battle. "Dinna let her out of your sight. If she does anything you consider questionable, kill her."

By the time the heat of the afternoon gave way to the cooler evening breeze, she had treated the wounds of at least thirty men. Some would survive, but the fate of others remained uncertain. The guard followed as she made her way to a tree at the edge of the clearing and slid to the ground, resting her back on the trunk. Exhausted, she blew out a ragged sigh.

"You did a fine job, lass. Would you like something to eat and drink?" The guard spoke with a tone of admiration rather than distain.

Fallon shook her head. "Nay, I am too tired to eat." She closed her eyes, reveling in the moment of peace and silence.

But her respite was short-lived when Dungal's cousin rode into the camp shouting.

Dungal sprang to his feet. "I'm pleased to see you survived. I heard you were taken prisoner."

His cousin leapt from his horse. "I was captured but during the post-battle confusion, I managed to escape. Not before overhearing a discussion between some of the Bruce's men. There is reason to believe he is planning to search the area for traitors and survivors. Those found alive will be shown no quarter. Best we prepare to move out as soon as possible."

"We made sure the camp was not too close to Loudon Hill. Does the Bruce lead the search?" Dungal glanced over his shoulder at his brother. "The wounded are too weak to travel. We have no option but to remain here, at least until the morrow."

"Nay. I heard Bryce Fraser and his brother will lead one party of warriors and John Kennedy another," the man replied. "Fraser in particular was very interested in your location."

Fallon's heart leapt at the messenger's words. Bryce was alive and so were Alasdair and John.

Dungal cursed then marched toward Fallon, grabbed her wrist, and hauled her to her feet. "So he lives to be a thorn in my side." Before she could respond, Dungal tore the pendant from her neck, the leather thong snapping under the pressure. He wrapped the talisman in a small scrap of MacDougall plaid and summoned a messenger. "Take this to the Bruce's camp. Deliver it to Bryce Fraser, no one else." Dungal wrote a note and put it with the pendant. "Make haste. I want to deter them before they leave the camp."

Dungal glared at her. "Fraser will know who owns the item and once he reads the message, I'm certain he willna follow us. Not if he values this one's life as I believe he does."

Fallon brought her hand to her throat where her pendant once hung and raised her chin. "He'll come and he will show you the same mercy you did Fergus and my uncle."

"Mayhap I will offer your life for his."

"You aren't thinking of letting her go, are you?" His cousin moved to within an inch of where Fallon stood, ogling her from top to bottom. "You promised to give me a go at her after you've had your fill."

"Once the fool surrenders himself, I will offer them both over to Longshanks to deal with as he sees fit."

Chapter 16

Bryce stormed toward Robert. "Is the rumor true? We are not going after de Valance and MacDougall? In light of what happened in Turnberry, I canna understand your lack of initiative in pursuing them." After hearing about Fergus' execution, his concern for Fallon mounted. While there had been nothing said to indicate she was in danger, he still felt it in his gut.

Robert dismissed the man he was speaking to with a curt nod then faced Bryce. "We won the battle today, but not the war. My decisions have nothing to do with complacency. Each move we make must be carefully planned, or we risk losing the ground already gained. This victory is a huge step on the way to securing Scotland. We canna ignore the entire picture in order to appease personal grudges." Robert placed his hand on Bryce's shoulder. "I understand the desire for revenge and your frustration. Seeing Dungal hang would give me great pleasure. But at what expense?"

"Dungal sided with de Valance against his fellow Scotsmen at Methven, Dahl Righ, and again today. He boasts about his affiliation with Longshanks, flaunts his self-appointed authority, persecuting innocent women and children. He hanged Fallon's uncle and now Fergus. If that's not enough, he handed your brothers over to be executed after the ambush at Loch Ryan, for god's sake! What more reason can I give?" Bryce was quickly losing his patience, the unsavory churn of dread building in his stomach. With the hatred he harbored for Dungal threatening to consume him, he took a step back and tried to catch his breath.

"Robert is right. Rather than rushing off without a solid plan, taking the time to regroup makes more sense." Alasdair joined them with James Douglas in tow. "The enemy suffered heavy casualties and will need to tend to their wounded. We can use a day to care for our own injured and to prepare for our next confrontation."

"Do you always listen in on other people's conversations?" Bryce snapped.

"You could be heard shouting halfway across the camp, little brother. I'm certain Dungal caught wind of all you had to say, and he is five or six miles away."

"What of de Valance? Are they together or did they part ways after the battle?" Bryce lowered his voice, but his ire remained on edge.

James joined the group. "Dungal fled south. He is likely headed back to Galloway to regroup. Aymer retreated in the direction of Bothwell Castle." He pointed to the east. "My father and I visited that stronghold several times when I was a lad. The donjon is well fortified, so retaliation will be difficult if he remains behind the walls. I agree with Alasdair and Robert. We need time to map our strategy."

"Robert!" John Kennedy shouted as he sprinted toward them. "A messenger arrived with a missive from the MacDougall."

"Bring him to me at once, and I'll listen to what he has to say."

"He said his message is for Bryce," John informed them.

"The only news I want to hear is that Dungal is dead and buried." Bryce spat on the ground.

"Bring the envoy here at once." Robert issued his orders before addressing Bryce. "You must speak to the man. It is imperative we ascertain what Dungal is up to."

"No good if you ask me," Alasdair interjected and clasped his brother's shoulder.

John returned a few minutes later with one of the MacDougall clansmen. "Bow and show your respect." He shoved the man forward, causing him to stumble, then fall to his knees. "Deliver the message to King Robert and make it fast."

A sneer tugged at the man's lips. "I see no king before me. However, I do see a scoundrel and a murderer. But that matters not. My orders are to speak to Bryce Fraser and no one else. If he'll not meet with me, I can return to my clan. He'll only have himself to blame for the consequences." The messenger stood and brushed the dirt from his trews.

"I'm Fraser." Bryce stepped forward.

"Dungal bid me speak to you and no one else. He sent you a wee gift and a note, but I'll not give it to you unless you agree to meet with me in private." He patted his sporran, a cynical grin tugging at his lips. "If you dinna want it."

Alasdair tackled the man and tugged the pouch from around his waist. He opened it and pulled out the scrap of plaid.

Bryce grabbed the item from Alasdair's hand. The moment the fabric touched his skin, his throat tightened and he struggled to catch his breath. He cursed as he unfolded the tattered corners then closed his fist around what was inside.

"You look like a banshee crossed your path." Alasdair peered over his brother's shoulder. "What did he send?"

Bryce opened his hand and picked up the leather thong, broken where it would normally hang around a person's neck. He let the star dangle, the emerald facets catching the sunlight.

"You've seen this before?" Alasdair asked.

Bryce nodded. "This belongs to Fallon, a gift from her mother. She gave it to me when we were at her uncle's croft and bid me wear if for protection. I asked Maeve to give the pendant back to her when I left her in Turnberry."

Alasdair grabbed the note, broke the seal, and read the contents before handing it back to Bryce.

"What does the missive say?" Robert asked.

Alasdair hesitated and dragged his hand across his chin before he spoke. "Dungal holds Fallon captive and threatens to kill her if we dare follow. He also states he will consider an exchange. Bryce's life for hers."

Bryce crumpled the note in his hand. "Bastards!" He lunged forward, his fingers encircling the messenger's throat with a vise-like grip.

The man's eyes bulged from their sockets and his face turned blue. Gasping for air and clawing frantically at Bryce's hands, the messenger launched a fruitless attempt to break away.

"Stop. You're killing him." John tried to pry Bryce's hands free, but he tightened his grip. "At least let us question him first."

"One less MacDougall is fine with me. I've had my fill of the lot of them." Bryce forced the man's back against a nearby tree and continued his chokehold until Alasdair intervened.

"Go easy, brother. Your issue is with Dungal, not the messenger. Release him. His death will serve no purpose." Alasdair lifted Bryce's fingers from the man's neck.

Bryce backed away as the man slid to the ground, clutching his throat. "You tell Dungal I will come for her. When I do, I'll show him no mercy." He turned abruptly and stomped toward his horse. "Never mind. I'll tell him myself."

"I'll not grant you leave," Robert shouted after him.

"Try and stop me."

"I'm your king. You've sworn your fealty to me, and I order you to stand fast. Try to run off and you'll be arrested and hanged for treason."

"Do as you wish, but I'll not allow Fallon to spend one minute with that spineless blackguard than is necessary." He fisted his hands in the horse's mane and prepared to mount.

Alasdair caught Bryce from behind, lifted him off the ground, and trapped his arms at his side. "You're upset and understandably so, but stop and think before you react. This is not the way to save Fallon. If anything, you'll get her killed. Do as Robert says and stand down."

"You read Dungal's note. If I offer to swap my life for hers, he'll release Fallon." Bryce struggled to free himself, but to no avail. He had never been a match for his brother's size and brute strength. "Let me go, you big ox. Fallon needs me. She is in danger, and I'm to blame. I willna let her down, I canna let her down. Why did I leave her in Turnberry?"

"Second guessing yourself will do no good. You canna predict the future, anymore than you can change the past. You must think this through." Alasdair softened his voice, but his restraining embrace held firm. "Surrendering yourself over to Dungal won't guarantee Fallon's release. He canna be trusted."

"I have to try." Bryce stopped fighting and slumped into his brother's arms. "Why does the Almighty see fit to put decent people in harm's way? Fallon is an unselfish, gentle, giving woman, yet he allows a vile bastard like Dungal to breathe the same air and to take her captive. I shudder to think what has befallen her while in his clutches." Memories of his past flooded his mind.

Alasdair released his hold on Bryce and stepped away. "I dinna believe the Lord deliberately puts good people in danger."

"Doesn't He?" Bryce whipped around with renewed anger. "He allows the English to raid our villages, to commit murder, and to violate our women. Or did what happened to our mother and our youngest brother slip your mind? Mam was with child and Evan had only seen eight summers when they were butchered by the English swine. Where was the Almighty's mercy and wisdom then?"

Bryce paused long enough to draw in a gulp of air. "Mayhap the events at Berwick on Tweed escaped your memory as well. Our father and oldest brother cut down before our eyes, along with nearly eight thousand other innocents put to sword on that dreadful day. What about Ashlen?" His voice wavered when he said her name.

Alasdair's jaw clenched. "I will never forget the events of those days. The memories are forever etched in my mind. We will find a way to rescue Fallon, but not until we have devised a sound plan of recourse. Can you at least give me that?"

"I'll award you a few minutes, but no more. Fallon's life might depend on our speed." He glared over Alasdair's shoulder at Robert. "I intend to go after her, regardless of the consequences. Her welfare may be of little concern to you and her death willna influence the outcome of the war, but she is important to me. I'll not sit idly by and allow that blackguard to harm the woman who might someday be the mother of my bairns." He let the words slip out before he could hold his tongue.

Alasdair's jaw dropped open. "Are my ears deceiving me, or did you just say you wanted Fallon to bear your babes? Sounds like a man in love to me. Now I'm sure you've lost your mind."

Bryce didn't answer. Instead, he dragged his hand across the back of his neck, and turned away. In his anger, he'd allowed his true feelings for Fallon to rise to the surface, and God willing, he'd have the chance to make amends for being such a fool. But he had to find her before it was too late. He stiffened his posture and glared at his brother.

"We are wasting precious time. I am going after Fallon with or without your help. The Lord had best protect anyone who attempts to stop me," Bryce challenged.

"I've got your back, brother, if any man tries," Alasdair announced.

"I'll stand by you as well." John stepped forward.

"And I." James pulled his sword from its sheath and waved the weapon in the air.

"I'm not an unreasonable man or the heartless bastard you think I am. Threats of imprisonment and execution dinna deter you, so there is no choice but to concede. However—" Robert raised his hand. "I intend to engage the English three days hence and there are preparations to make. I canna spare all of my best warriors."

"I will go alone if need be." Bryce balled his fists at his side and began to pace. "Too many lives have already been forfeited and I'll not permit Fallon's death to be added to the list."

Robert ran his hand over his chin before he responded. "Select ten men to accompany you. Alasdair may go, but I need John and James to remain behind. God willing, you'll eliminate some of the blackguard's men along the way. Take any longer than two days, and we'll be gone by the time you get back."

Bryce gave a curt nod. "Our endeavor will be fruitful, and Fallon will be with us when we return. If there is justice to be had, I'll present Dungal's head to you on a pike."

"Be off with you, and may the Almighty guide your path." Robert turned and strode away.

"I'll ask for volunteers and bid them join you immediately." James trotted off to gather the men.

"While he is doing that, I'll arrange for supplies." John followed in James' footsteps.

Bryce moved to his horse, but rather than mounting, he rested his forehead on the animal's neck. "Do you think this a fool's errand? I dinna even know if she is still alive."

"What does your gut tell you, brother?" Alasdair placed his hand on Bryce's back.

"She's alive. I canna explain how I know, I just do. But I am also certain if we dinna find her soon, it will be too late." Bryce swung his leg over the horse's back and pulled himself into the saddle. "I'll ride ahead and you can join me when the others arrive." He pressed his heel to the horse's flank, but Alasdair grabbed the reins and held the beast steady.

"Either you wait for the men and supplies, Bryce, or you dinna go at all. If I have to tie you to yonder tree, I will. Ever since the lass came back into your life, you've been distracted. You are not usually so careless. It goes to show that women are more trouble than they are worth. We depart together. A few minutes canna make that much difference."

"I hope you're right, brother. I hope you're right."

The journey was short, their horses swift. As they neared the last reported location of the MacDougall's camp, Bryce slowed his horse, and ordered the men to keep their voices low, their conversation to a minimum.

Uneasiness tugged at Bryce's stomach. The fact they had traveled this far without a challenge was both odd and unsettling.

"The Bruce's informant gave us directions, but we have yet to come across a camp or anyone guarding the path. Something is amiss." Unable to stand the uncertainty, Bryce kicked his horse into a gallop, leaving his brother and the other warriors behind in a cloud of dust.

Alasdair's curse carried on the breeze, but Bryce refused to slow his pace, or to turn around. With reckless disregard for his own safety, he sped along the trail, coming to an abrupt halt when he entered what he assumed had been Dungal's encampment.

He slid from the saddle and stood in the middle of the deserted clearing. A spattering of hot embers glowed in the fire pit, but the exact time of their departure was difficult to determine.

The echo of thundering hooves approaching fast caused Bryce to draw his sword and spin around in the direction of the noise. Was it Alasdair, or was this a trap? Prepared to fight, he widened his stance, then inhaled a fortifying breath.

Bryce narrowed his eyes, his gaze fixed, his reflexes keen. Relief washed over him and he sheathed his blade when Alasdair and their companions entered the clearing.

"Have you totally lost all of your God-given senses?" Alasdair shouted. "You could have been riding into an ambush. Hell, Bryce, I could be scraping what was left of you off the ground had Dungal been lying in wait."

"They're gone." Bryce threw his hands up in frustration and stomped toward his brother.

Alasdair jumped from the saddle. "How long ago did they leave? This could be a ruse. The blackguards might be waiting in the bushes, prepared to strike at any moment." He glanced over his shoulder and scanned the periphery of the clearing.

"The cook-fire is still smoldering, but has burned down to ash. My guess is they broke camp several hours ago. Likely while we were dallying. I should have gone with my gut and left immediately."

"You canna be certain." Alasdair scratched his head. "I was positive they'd still be here. They had wounded who needed tending and rest. Most would assume this spot was located far enough from the battleground to be secure."

"Dungal is not like most men." Bryce motioned for everyone to dismount. "Search the area. We need to determine when they left and in which direction."

The men scoured the surrounding area, while Alasdair and Bryce approached what appeared to be a row of freshly dug graves.

Bryce lowered his head and crossed his chest. "It appears many of the wounded dinna live long enough to make the journey." A knot formed in his stomach. Was Fallon buried in one of these mounds of unhallowed ground?

As if he knew Bryce's thoughts, Alasdair spoke. "You must believe Fallon is alive. If what the messenger told James during the interrogation is true, Dungal forbid his men to touch her. He plans to hold her hostage until you come for her."

"He also said Dungal intended to claim her as his prize following the battle." Nausea churned in Bryce's belly and his pulse pounded in his ears. He had to find Fallon before Dungal had a chance to make good on his threats, if he hadn't already. He'd experienced these feelings of fear and uncertainty before and they mounted with each passing minute.

Bryce turned when one of the men approached. "Did you find anything?"

"Aye. Horse tracks lead out of camp in all directions, but the majority of them depart from the south end of the clearing. We also noted the imprint of cart wheels in the mud."

Bryce and Alasdair accompanied the man to the southern edge of the clearing.

Alasdair squatted and examined the tracks. "They are heading toward Galloway as we suspected. Mayhap they've gone to Dunstaffnage Castle in Argyll. It has been a MacDougall stronghold for many years. Their action is a logical choice given their losses and casualties."

"It also stands to reason that Dungal would try to return to his own land and kin." Bryce climbed onto his horse's back and shouted to his companions. "Mount up and head south. If we make haste, we can overtake the bastards before nightfall."

Chapter 17

"My brother remains unconscious. You claim to be a healer. Do something." Dungal paced beside the pallet.

"I warned you he was too weak to travel, but you insisted on moving the camp. With the constant jarring of the cart over bumpy roads, I'm stunned his wound dinna open and start to bleed again." Fallon lifted the linen dressing to examine the injury. "Fortunately, there is no festering, but I'd not be moving him again. At least until he is stronger."

"I'm certain you would like it if we stayed here and waited for Bryce Fraser to find us. Fortunately, I make the decisions for my men, not you. Keith has always been as strong as an ox. If he dies, I'll know who to blame." Dungal stared at the ground and rubbed his temples.

"He's your brother and concern is natural, but I have done all I can for him. His fate is in the hands of the Almighty."

"The arrow was meant for me," Dungal blurted out. "The damned fool stepped in the way, taking it in my stead." His voice cracked with raw emotion he'd manage to hide until now.

"You owe your brother your life." Fallon was taken aback by his momentary show of compassion, but refused to believe the sentiment would last.

"I am beholden to no one," Dungal snapped.

Keith wheezed and coughed, rolling his head from side-to-side.

"A fever is brewing." Fallon dipped a rag in cool water then placed it on Keith's brow. "I noticed the men were setting up your tent. I take that to mean we are spending the night in this spot." She didn't wait for him to answer. "Mayhap we could move Keith inside for the night. Keeping him warm and dry will be beneficial to his recovery. I'll also need some herbs. Will you allow me to gather them?"

"After your attempt to escape, you canna possibly think I would let you out of my sight to go pick wild flowers."

"How I acquire them is not important, as long as I get what is necessary to make my tonic. Your brother lost a lot of blood and must drink to replenish. An herbal tea will also ease the pain and aid in healing." She pointed to the thick ropes around her ankles. "You keep me tied to a tree when I am not tending the wounded. The rest of the time, you have me hobbled like a horse."

"You were bound when I left you in my brother's care, but that dinna stop you from escaping. Besides, what guarantee do I have that you won't poison him?"

She shrugged. "I suppose that is a chance you must take. You ordered me to care for him."

Dungal glanced at his brother then at her. "Tell me what you need. I will send one of my men to gather the items."

Fallon slid her hands down the front of her gown. "Have you something I can write on?"

"A verbal list will suffice."

"Very well. Instruct your man to collect foxcote, tansy, comfrey, willow bark, and henbane. I also require some clean water and a pot for boiling. Once I've taken care of Keith, I will check on the others who were injured." Treating the enemy might be considered treason by some, but she forced herself to view them as men who needed her help and nothing more.

"I'll see it done." Dungal summoned one of his clansmen and repeated her list. "Fetch these things at once." He returned his attentions to Fallon and cocked a brow. "You can write?"

"Aye. I can read and write. Despite the fact I was born a lass, my parents believed it was important for me to learn all I could."

"You are full of surprises, lass. Most women possess neither the interest nor the need for such skills, and I agree, the less they know the better."

"You are as crude and archaic as the men who believe woman hold no value and consider them nothing more than chattel."

"Women are good for two things—bedding and bartering. If we dinna need them for breeding and pleasure, we could do away with them all together." Dungal lifted a strand of her hair and rubbed the lock between his fingers. "The educated women I've met are usually of noble blood. With your raven locks and mysterious sapphire eyes, you put me more in mind of a gypsy."

"I have no royal ties. My parents were both born in Scotland and were proud of their heritage." Fallon inclined her head and raised her chin. "Unlike some people I've had the misfortune of meeting." She had nothing to lose by speaking her mind. "I canna understand how you can turn your back on your country and betray your heritage."

"Scotland is and will always be my homeland. I dinna turn my back on my country. I chose to oppose a murderer and a scoundrel. Robert the Bruce is no more the King of Scotland than I am." He spat on the ground. "He killed John Comyn, my kinsman, and the only man who stood in his way. For that crime, he will never be accepted by all of the clans. Those who remain loyal to the heirs of King John Balliol will always contest the Bruce's claim to the throne."

"You may have reason to oppose the Bruce's right to govern Scotland, yet you kill innocent people and persecute your countrymen in the name of the English King. The same man who has kept his oppressive thumb on this country for so many years."

"When the Bruce is defeated, I will take my stand against the English. For now, it serves me well to keep them at my side. Best you curb your tongue," Dungal growled and grabbed her chin between his fingers.

"I speak the truth and am not afraid to do so."

Dungal laughed. "Nothing appears to frighten you, does it? Your spirit and temerity intrigue me."

"I have nothing to fear but the wrath of God and what might happen if I dinna live in the kind and decent way He intended."

"Mayhap you should worry about what I have in mind for you when I finally get you alone. I have no doubt you'll be a wildcat when bedded." Dungal grabbed the crotch of his trews and thrust his hips. "It's been a while since I rutted with a whore."

Rather than cower, Fallon met his stare with equal intensity. "I'm no whore, and I dinna dread something that is never destined to happen. Bryce will come for me, and you'll not have a chance to do anything more than to beg for your life."

Anger flared in his dark eyes. "I grow tired of your belligerence." Dungal's glower spoke volumes. "Dinna challenge me, or you'll regret the result. When I am finished with you, the name Bryce Fraser will be stripped from your mind like the clothes from your back."

"I would rather be hanged. You will never be half the man Bryce is in thought or deed. You—"

Dungal's fingers snaked around her throat, cutting off her air. "I could snap your neck like a twig if I so choose. But I think the time has come for me to teach you a well-deserved lesson in obedience and servitude." Dungal tossed her over his shoulder and carried her across the camp.

"Put me down!" With her feet tethered, she was unable to kick, but that didn't stop her from flailing in his arms or from pounding her fists on his back. She'd not go easily.

"*Haud yer wheest* or I'll cut out your tongue." Dungal tightened his grasp. "Get out of my way," he growled at a man who stood in their path. He threw back the flap of his tent, placed her feet on the ground, then shoved her inside. "I am not to be disturbed."

Bryce crouched in the bracken and watched the activity going on in the MacDougall encampment. His heart leapt at the sight of Fallon engaged in a verbal battle with Dungal, but rage clawed at his chest when the blackguard carried her to his tent.

Fallon was in danger, but he had to keep his wits about him. Drawing on every ounce of self-control, he refrained from rushing headlong into the midst of his enemy with his sword drawn, demanding her release.

He had to do something to help her, but the wrong decision might get her killed and put the entire rescue party in jeopardy. His strength of will waning, he reluctantly backed away and rejoined his comrades.

"Did you spot Fallon?" Alasdair kept his voice low, even though they were well out of their enemy's earshot.

"Aye. Dungal holds her prisoner in a tent at the north end of the clearing. I say we storm the camp now." On edge, Bryce tensely shifted his weight and clenched his hands into tight fists.

"I know you're anxious, brother, but if we hope to free Fallon, we must exercise caution. How many men does Dungal have? I fear if we dinna make haste, the bastard will violate her." Memories of Ashlen flashed before his mind's eye, her screams echoing in his head.

Alasdair was the voice of reason. But Bryce's concern for Fallon threatened to override all logic. "There are fifty, mayhap sixty armed warriors. Less than I expected. They suffered more casualties in the battle than we thought, or he has sent some of clansmen on to Galloway ahead of them."

Alasdair's brow furrowed. "Either way, they outnumber us five to one."

"Aye, but one Scot is better than a dozen ordinary men," Bryce responded quickly.

"That would be so if we were confronting the English. Don't forget we are dealing with the MacDougalls, a Scottish clan who have struck fear in the hearts of those who oppose them for centuries. Fallon is also Dungal's captive, which complicates things."

"I dinna need you to remind me." The mention of Dungal's name in conjunction with Fallon's caused Bryce's blood to boil. "What do you suggest we do? We canna stand by and let him have his way with her."

"Darkness will be upon us within the hour. I propose we wait and—"

"We canna delay that long. There is no telling what might happen to Fallon if we wait. If you won't help me, I will go after her alone." Bryce threw his hands in the air and began to roam like a cornered animal. "For all we know, he might be ravaging her as we speak."

"Then we are already too late to stop the vile deed. But we can still save her life." Alasdair placed his hand on Bryce's shoulder. "Calm yourself and hear me out, brother, before you run off and get yourself killed. Once I've stationed the men in the forest, I will ride to the edge of the encampment and shout out a war cry. The MacDougalls won't be able to resist the challenge. When they give chase, I will lead them into the woods to be picked off by our waiting archers. The light of full moon will prove beneficial to the task."

"What will I be doing while you lead this fool's mission?"

"You'll take up a position in the brush behind the tent and when the time is right, cut through the back and rescue

Fallon. We will kill as many of Dungal's men as possible and keep the rest busy so you and Fallon can escape."

Bryce shook his head in frustration. "I just hope we are not too late."

"Take off your gown." The expression on Dungal's face was lethal and his words ripped through Fallon like a blade.

"I willna." She brought her hand to her throat.

"You heard me. Do as I instructed."

"And if I refuse?" She raised her chin in defiance.

"Then I will do it for you." Dungal took a menacing step forward. "Take it off now, or I will rip it from your body and take you where you stand."

In spite of her desire to resist, Fallon reached for the laces of her gown with shaky fingers. Better to buy herself some time rather than to anger him further and invite the inevitable. Dungal would not go easy on her.

"Now!"

Fallon pulled the gown over her head and dropped it onto the floor beside her. A fine linen kirtle was all that kept her from standing naked before him. Heat rose in her cheeks and she refused to look him in the eye. She jumped when he grabbed her wrists, secured them with a rope, then tied the ends to the rafter of the tent.

Without saying a word, Dungal went to his trunk, pulled out a clay jug, and drank deeply. He dragged the back of his hand across his mouth then retrieved a tin cup and filled it to the brim.

He returned to her side and held her head steady. "Drink." He pressed the rim of the small tankard to her mouth. "The whiskey will relax you and make you more agreeable."

Fallon sputtered. "I have no taste for spirits, and I'll agree to naught." She pursed her lips, the liquid dribbling down her chin.

"Why must you torment me? I cared for your brother and the wounded as you requested, I've committed no crime, yet you continue to hold me captive."

"Dinna *fash*. I'll not keep you much longer. Once I take Bryce Fraser into custody and have sated my needs with you, I plan to turn you both over to Longshanks."

Stretched above her head, her wrists and arms ached, the circulation cut off by the ropes that bit into her flesh. Already well into his cups, and beginning to stumble on his feet, Dungal downed the contents of the tankard for the third time. At this rate, she could only hope he'd be too drunk to follow through with his threat to bed her.

"You can make this easy on yourself and come to me willingly, or I can take you with force. The choice is yours." Dungal removed his tunic and loosened the cord at the top of his trews.

"Please me," he said, "and I will request that King Edward forgo the ritual of purification by pain routinely done prior to the execution of traitors."

Her eyes widened, but she said nothing.

Grinning, Dungal added, "Have you ever attended a hanging? The more you struggle, the tighter the noose becomes. Robbed of air, your lungs burn until you are certain your chest is about to burst." He paused to pour another drink before he continued.

"However, if the Almighty is merciful, your neck will snap when you drop from the gallows. Being hanged is a terrible way to die." Dungal concluded his macabre tirade, and pinched her chin between his finger and thumb, forcing her to look at him. "Beg me to bed you, and mayhap I'll ask the king to give you to me for service rendered. I'm sure you could bear me many fine sons. For Fraser to go to his death knowing you warm my bed and grow round with my bairn is a fitting punishment."

Fallon lowered her head and her gaze trailed the ground. The thought of a slow and agonizing death sent chills down her spine. Longshanks' reputation for heartless and cruel forms of punishment was well known, but despite her fear, she refused to surrender. She would endure the torture Dungal described, and if the Almighty deemed it so, go willingly to her grave. But she'd not go willingly to his bed.

"Bryce won't allow that to happen. He will come for me."

"If Fraser tries to save you, he will meet the same fate as your uncle." Dungal's sinister laugh made her cringe. "First, I'll enjoy making him watch as I repeatedly fill you with my seed," he hissed and moved so close that his hot, whiskey-tainted breath brushed her cheek. "Then I'll see him hanged, drawn, and quartered."

"The only reason you wish to bed me is because you know I love Bryce and despise you with every fiber of my being." She could not believe what she'd just said, but it was too late to take it back.

"I beg to differ, my dear. You are indeed a bewitching creature. I grow hard thinking about burying myself deep within you." He ran the pad of his thumb over her lips then dropped his hand and cupped her woman's mound. "I'd wager the wetness of your arousal is as thick and sweet as honey. I canna wait to spread your legs and taste for myself."

"You're a filthy, vulgar swine. How dare you speak to me of such lewd things?"

"I plan to do more than just speak of them. You may even find you enjoy it." Dungal nonchalantly blew on his fingernails and then brushed them across his bare chest.

"I will never give myself to you." She spat in his face. His response was a swift backhanded slap that left her hovering on the edge of consciousness.

"If I decide to keep you for my personal enjoyment, that

attitude is something a few good beatings will rectify soon enough."

With one hand, he cupped her breast and squeezed. With his other hand fisted in her hair, he snapped her head back and his mouth came down on hers in a harsh, rapacious kiss. He licked the blood from her split lower lip and glared at her like an animal prepared to devour his prey. "Like it or not, you will comply or I will teach you to obey."

"You'll have to kill me first." Tears welled in her eyes, but she managed to blink them away. She'd not give in to his demands. Were her hands and feet not bound, she'd fight with every ounce of strength she could muster.

"That's bold talk given the fact that you are my prisoner. Your death can easily be arranged, but not until I am fully sated." Dungal picked up his tankard, drank to the last drop, and slammed it down on a wooden trunk. Drawing his dirk from its sheath, he methodically ran his finger along the blade. An evil smirk tugged at his lips as he raised the weapon above her head.

Fallon prayed that he would plunge the weapon into her heart and end this torture here and now. Instead, he cut the ropes he'd used to tie her to the rafters of the tent, releasing her arms. To her amazement, he severed the bonds on her feet as well.

She dropped to her knees and tried to crawl away, but he twisted her hair around his fist then dragged her kicking and clawing toward the pallet in the corner of the tent. He forced her to lie down, using the weight of his body to hold her in place. With bated breath, she braced for what was about to happen next.

With the dirk clenched between his teeth, Dungal clasped her wrists with one hand and jerked them above her head before slitting the front of her kirtle.

"You're lovelier than I imagined," he groaned as he peeled back the fabric, exposing her naked flesh. He fondled her breasts, roughly rolling the nipple between his fingers, and then lowered his head, nipping at her neck. "The time has come for you to learn your lesson." His mouth crashed down upon hers.

Fear squeezed her chest and nausea rolled in her belly, but she refused to beg him for mercy. Instead, she glared up at him. "When Bryce comes, I hope he lops off your ballocks before he runs you through."

"Silence!" Dungal growled. "You will lay there and allow me to breed you or so help me, I will beat you into submission."

From his vantage point, Bryce heard their entire conversation. Like a volcano ready to erupt, rage welled from deep in his gut. He fought the urge to tear into the tent and run the bastard through. But to do so would only put Fallon in more danger. He had to wait until the members of the rescue party were in their places, leaving him no choice but to listen and hope that if he was too late to stop the bedding, he'd be in time to her life.

He'd seen too much death and suffering in his travels to remain a religious man, but out of desperation, he lowered his head in prayer.

"Lord, if you're there, please keep Fallon strong. Make her understand that whatever he does to her doesn't matter. Keep her alive and I'll do whatever bidding you see fit."

An ear-piercing war cry cut through the air as Alasdair broached the edge of the encampment. Bryce sprang into action.

"What the Hell is going on out there? I told those imbeciles that I was not to be disturbed," Dungal growled. "I best go and see what's amiss."

Bryce quickly made his way to the back of the tent and waited, giving Dungal sufficient time to check things out and hopefully leaving Fallon unattended. Relief washed over him when he saw the shadow of a figure at the rear of the tent move toward the front. So far, the plan to distract Dungal appeared to be working.

"What goes on out here?" Dungal bellowed.

"I'm sorry to disturb you, cousin," a man at the front of the tent said, "but someone entered the south end of the camp."

Satisfied Dungal was occupied, Bryce swiftly used his dirk to cut a hole large enough to climb through.

"Do you know who it was?" Dungal asked.

"It could be a spy sent by the Bruce to determine our location or mayhap a drunken thief. We willna know until we catch the bastard," the man replied.

"Was he alone?"

"I have no idea, but several of our men went after him. Do you wish more to follow?"

"Do what is necessary to capture the bugger. Make haste and dinna disturb me again. There's a flower to be picked, and I grow tired of waiting."

"Take a dozen men, follow the blackguard, and bring him back for questioning. The rest of you are to stand guard. Dungal is not to be bothered again this night," the man shouted.

While Dungal issued orders to his men, Bryce seized the opportunity to climb through the opening he'd cut in the back of the tent. His eyes met with Fallon's and he brought his finger to his lips as a warning for her to remain silent as he moved with stealth to her side.

Fallon threw her arms around his neck and kissed him repeatedly. "I knew you'd come for me," she whispered.

Dungal lowered the tent flap, turned, and rubbed his groin. "Now, where were we? My ballocks ache and I know how to relieve them." His smug grin quickly faded when he stared at the gaping hole at the back of his tent and him crouching over Fallon. "Halt!"

Bryce ignored Dungal's command, dragged Fallon to her feet, and shoved her toward freedom. "Go!" he ordered aloud and then whispered in her ear, "Run to the east as fast as you can. No matter what happens, dinna turn back. My brother and other members of our rescue party will see you to safety." His instructions given, Bryce positioned himself between Fallon and Dungal, and drew his sword. "You'll not live long enough to harm another lass. After I lop off your ballocks, I'll run you through."

Dungal laughed and picked up his blade. "We'll see who ends up a gelding," he scoffed. "Once I've done away with you, I'll track down the little whore. By the time I'm finished with her, she'll beg to die. I'll gladly do the honors. Unless I decide to offer her to my men first."

Fallon clutched her torn kirtle together with one trembling hand and grabbed her gown and slippers with the other. She turned to leave, but hesitated. "I canna go without you, Bryce," she sobbed.

"How touching," Dungal scoffed.

"Go now, Fallon!" Bryce shouted as Dungal lunged forward in an attempt to stop her.

She nodded and began to climb through the opening, but as two men's swords collided, she paused and looked back. "Bryce," she gasped.

"Be gone, Fallon," Bryce ordered, the momentary distractions affording Dungal the chance to knock him off balance. He tumbled backward and the bastard snatched his weapon. Fear swept through him as he stared up at his nemesis. Not for himself, but for Fallon, who once again hesitated. "Run!"

"Prepare to die. This time, I'll do the task properly," Dungal growled.

Chapter 18

Tears flowing freely down Fallon's face as she slipped through the hole. Bryce had lost his weapon because of her. Her premonition of his death at Dungal's hand appeared about to come true and there was nothing she could do to stop it. She clutched at her throat. The last thing she'd seen was a self-aggrandizing grin on Dungal's face as he hovered over Bryce, his blade raised in the air.

She fought the overwhelming urge to go back, but that would be exactly what Dungal wanted. She tugged her gown over her head and donned her slippers before darting into the forest. She had no idea where she was headed, but Bryce had assured her Alasdair waited.

Go east and dinna look back.

Bryce's words echoed in her mind, and her chest tightened. He'd risked all to save her, traded his life for hers, and she might never see him again. A myriad of concerns for Bryce flooded her mind, threatening to override her good senses. Bryce had ordered her to leave, but if she located Alasdair quickly, he might be able to assist his brother.

Her heart pounded a warrior's beat and the surge of energy coursing through her veins gave her the strength to forge on. With the stealth and determination of a wildcat hunting its prey and the full moon to light the way, she raced along an overgrown path. The smell of the MacDougall's cook-fires and the sounds of angry men shouting faded deeper into the distance with each step.

After her narrow escape, she wondered if the other members of the rescue party had made it to safety. Did

Alasdair survive, or had he been captured? Was Bryce alive? Her mind raced with questions. Mayhap Dungal was only a few steps behind her.

A strong arm snaked around her waist and a calloused hand covered her mouth. "Dinna make a sound." The brute raised her off the ground and yanked her against a solid wall of muscle, leaving her with both feet dangling in the air.

Was he friend of foe? He hadn't announced his intent, so she assumed the latter. She bit down on his hand and kicked back with her heel, connecting with his groin.

He dropped her immediately, then doubled over, a string of curses flowing from his mouth.

Fallon scrambled out of his reach, but in her haste to get away, bumped into another man blocking the trail.

She staggered backward, staring into the eyes of someone else she did not recognize. He stomped forward, and she took a step back, all the while searching for a means of escape.

"Watch her. She bites like a viper and kicks like a horse," the first man cautioned as he tried to stand upright.

Before either of her assailants could speak again, Fallon headed for the edge of the woods, taking refuge behind a large boulder. She picked up a sharp branch, wielding it like a sword. "Dinna come any closer. I'll not surrender, and I refuse to go back to Dungal while there is breath left in my body."

The second man laughed. "I applaud your bravery, but dinna think you pose much of a threat with a stick. Be a good lass and come here."

The two men closed in, but stopped when a third person approached. "What in damnation is going on?" he bellowed as he strode out of the shadows.

Fallon's heart raced and her breath lodged in her throat. Her odds of outsmarting two warriors were slim, but she didn't stand a chance against three. Panic squeezed her chest.

"You were supposed to find the lass and bring her to me, not frighten her to death." The third man threw his hands in the air and continued toward her.

The timber of his voice was vaguely familiar. However, it was not enough to let down her guard. She narrowed her eyes, the breath she held escaping in a whoosh when she saw Alasdair's face appear in the moonlight.

He reached for her. "Dinna fear, lass, these two idiots are here to help you, not to harm. Come to me, and we will be away."

She dropped the branch and moved forward, but her head began to spin. Before she could steady herself, everything went black.

When her eyes fluttered open, she looked up at a rugged face etched with concern peering down at her. She rested on the ground with her head on Alasdair's knee.

"You gave us a scare." Alasdair inclined his head and issued orders to one of his companions. "Fetch me a plaid and a flask of whiskey. Dinna tarry." He focused his attention on Fallon. "Take a few deep breaths and calm yourself. You're safe now, lass." He brushed a lock of hair from her forehead.

For a gruff man of his size, Alasdair's touch was much gentler than she'd anticipated. "I'm fine. Please let me up."

"I'll decide what is best for you. You'll be allowed to rise when I'm sure you've had sufficient time to recover from your fright." Alasdair accepted a plaid from one of the men and covered her. He took the flask of whiskey and pulled out the stopper. "Drink," he demanded huskily and brought the vessel to her mouth.

She pushed his hand away and turned her head. "I said I am fine. I dinna want any whiskey, but I must speak to you about Bryce."

"My brother will meet us when he is done with Dungal." Alasdair's reply was simple and direct. He made a second fruitless attempt to give her a drink.

"You dinna understand." Fallon tried to stand, but when her head spun and her stomach clenched, she slowly sank to her knees. "What happened to me?"

"You fainted and look ready to do so again." Alasdair ran his hand over his stubbled chin.

"I never fainted in my life. But I've eaten very little in the last few days, so that might explain my weakness." She made another attempt to rise and this time succeeded, despite her wobbly legs.

"You must listen to me." She stared at him in frustration. "Bryce needs your help. That is, if you are not too late."

She quickly crossed her chest. "He managed to free me, but Dungal returned before we could escape together. Bryce insisted I leave while he stayed behind to face Dungal and his men alone. He is sorely outnumbered, and the last I witnessed, Dungal had forced him to the ground and relieved him of his sword."

"My brother knew the risk before he entered Dungal's tent, but it was our only hope of saving you. He was clear we were to find you and wait in this spot. That is exactly what we'll do."

Fallon's mouth dropped open in utter disbelief. "We canna just leave him to Dungal and his men. You must try to assist him."

Her plea fell on deaf ears. Alasdair hoisted her into his arms before she could protest further and carried her down the path.

Her attempt to struggle failed. Alasdair ignored her badgering and strode toward a small clearing. Frogs croaked and the reflection of the moon wavered on the rippling surface of a nearby pond.

"We wait here." He plunked her down on a log then handed her the plaid he'd slung over his shoulder while carrying her.

"I dinna need coddling." She pushed the length of fabric from her lap, stood, and planted her hands firmly on her hips. "I canna believe you refused to lend Bryce your support. He's your brother and would surely not desert you in the face of such odds."

"My brother must possess the patience of a saint to tolerate your constant nagging and demands. If you were my woman, I'd put an end to the nattering in a hurry."

Fallon harrumphed with indignation. "I'm not your woman. I belong to no man and answer to no one but the Almighty."

The man she'd bitten laughed, then quickly held out his hand as evidence. "I'd not rile her if I were you."

"Had you announced yourself and your purpose, I would not have retaliated so aggressively. But you came at me from behind. How was I to know if you intended to help or harm me?"

"She has a point." The second man slapped the first man on the back. "We handled the situation poorly. Good thing she dinna carry a dirk or sword. We'd both be flayed." He threw back his head and laughed.

Fallon balled her fists in her skirt. She could not believe Alasdair's complacency or that of his men. "What is the matter with you? Bryce is in danger. He may already be dead." Tears welled in her eyes, but she scrubbed them away with the back of her hand. "If you won't to do anything to help him, give me a sword and I'll go myself." She made no effort to hide the urgency or determination in her voice. "I never should have left Dungal's tent without Bryce. If he dies, I'll not forgive myself." Unable to contain her regret, she buried her face in her hands.

"Calm yourself. You're going nowhere. Bryce entrusted me with your care, and I won't let him down. Rushing off and putting yourself in danger would only make things worse." Alasdair gently touched her shoulder, but she shrugged him away. "We'll wait a little longer, but if he doesna arrive in the next hour, we must head back to the Bruce's camp."

"I'll not leave without Bryce. You may go if you choose, but I'll not accompany you. Once you've departed, I will return for him."

"I understand your concern, but Bryce would want you to wait here. If he fails to return, it is my duty to see you to safety."

"Do you have such little faith in me, brother?"

Fallon's heart leapt at the sound of Bryce's voice. She spun around and flung herself into his arms. Allowing the tears to flow, she frantically kissed his neck, his jaw, and his lips. "I thought Dungal killed you." She sobbed, soaking the front of his tunic and holding on with a death grip to the fabric. "I canna believe you're alive. Thank God, you're here."

"Believe, *luaidth.*" He dropped his head and captured her lips with a kiss that stole her breath and rattled her to the very core.

Her moment of bliss ended when she noticed the blood stains on his tunic. "You're wounded." She gasped. "Show me where."

"The blood belongs to Dungal. After you left, he drew down on me with his sword, but not before I rolled out of the way, pulled the dirk from my boot, and plunged it into his chest. You were right when you gave the weapon to me at your uncle's croft and predicted it would save my life again." He pulled her closer and kissed her soundly, then held her at arm's length, his face suddenly contorted with concern.

"Did Dungal . . .?" He choked on the words, but he had to know. "Did he harm you? Did the bastard violate you?" He spat out the words. "Tell me I wasna too late to stop him."

"Aye. You arrived in time. Dungal was about to ravage me, but he dinna have the chance."

"Thank you, God." Bryce looked skyward, then hauled

her against his chest and kissed her like a drowning man struggling for his last breath.

"I hate to break up this happy reunion, but we best be on our way." Alasdair placed his hand on Bryce's shoulder. "Was Dungal dead when you left him?"

"Would that I had killed him." Bryce released his hold on Fallon. "Unfortunately, two of his clansmen entered the tent and I was unable to finish him off. With any luck, the wound I delivered will be enough."

"Even more reason to be off. I am sure the MacDougalls will give chase, and we've already lost two men in the skirmish."

Bryce glanced around the clearing at the men. "Blair and Derek were killed?"

Alasdair nodded. "Aye, both died quickly."

"Their sacrifice willna be forgotten." Bryce bowed his head.

Fallon's heart plummeted. She'd cost two men their lives. "I'm sorry," she whispered.

"You have no reason to apologize. Dungal took you prisoner, and it was not your fault the men were killed. They volunteered for this mission, and while it is sad they perished, they died a warrior's death, in a battle against an enemy they despised." Bryce slid his arm around Fallon's shoulders and held her tightly. "You are not to blame."

"This is not the time to discuss who is responsible. We must depart for the Bruce's camp." Alasdair led a horse forward.

Bryce lifted Fallon into the saddle then climbed up behind her. Unlike the disgust she'd experienced when Dungal had done the same thing, she felt a warm rush of longing, a surge of excitement brewing in her belly and beyond when Bryce encircled her hips with his powerful thighs.

With a sharp kick of Bryce's booted foot, the horse lunged forward.

Chapter 19

They rode nonstop for three hours, arriving at the Bruce's camp before midnight.

"Your journey appears to have been successful. Is the lass not well?" Robert greeted them and grabbed the reins of Bryce's horse.

"She's exhausted and fell asleep a few miles back. I dinna have the heart to wake her." He glanced down at Fallon, snuggled in his arms, her hand fisted in his tunic. The sight of her made his heart thump so hard, he wondered if Robert could hear it.

Robert held Fallon while Bryce dismounted. "You have two less men than you had when you started out."

"Outnumbered six to one, I'm surprised we dinna lose more." Bryce gathered Fallon into his arms and carried her toward a fallen tree. "When do we leave for our next encounter with the English?"

"At daybreak. You've arrived in time to get a good night's sleep." Robert cocked a brow. "Unless you have other plans."

Fallon stirred, then brought her hand up to her mouth and yawned. "Have we arrived?" She yawned again and glanced around the clearing, her eyes meeting with Robert's.

Bryce set her on her feet and she quickly combed her fingers through her hair. She smoothed her hands down the front of her disheveled gown then offered a curtsy of respect to the Scottish King. "I must look a fright."

"On the contrary, you put me in mind of my Elizabeth on our wedding night. She was about your age when we married. I was a widower. My first wife died after giving birth to my daughter, Marjorie. I was not certain I wanted to remarry right away, but the lass needed a mother, and it was my responsibility as clan chief to provide a male heir if possible. Love and duty have a way of conquering many obstacles." Robert lowered his head. "Both are being held prisoner by Longshanks. Something I soon hope to rectify."

"I'll pray they are safe," Fallon said.

Robert coughed to clear his throat. He glanced from Fallon to Bryce. "You're welcome to use my tent for your wedding night if you so desire."

Bryce shifted his weight and ran his hand across the back of his neck. "I'm sure Fallon would welcome a warm place to sleep for the night. I can fetch a plaid and bed down with the men."

Robert's brow knit together. "I assumed given the circumstances, you'd be sharing a tent."

"I dinna know what he means." Fallon looked to Bryce for answers.

"If I spoke out of turn, please accept my apology. Mayhap we should give the two of you some time alone to speak." Robert gave a curt nod and motioned for Alasdair to join him.

"What was Robert talking about?" Fallon gripped Bryce's forearm, but he didn't turn around. "Please tell me."

"He assumed we would want to spend the night together," Bryce finally answered, but didn't elaborate any further. His pulse raced and his stomach twisted. He didn't want to upset Fallon, but he could not bring himself to say what she wanted to hear. Despite his strong feelings for her, he could never enter into a relationship. It wouldn't be fair to either of them. He'd almost cost Fallon her life once and he refused to take that risk again.

"I see." Fallon withdrew her hand and stepped away. "I suppose that is a ridiculous assumption given your dedication to the cause and determination not to fall in love. I was foolish to believe—"

"To believe what, Fallon?" His resolve wavering, Bryce spun around to face her. "You are a beautiful, desirable woman. Any man would be proud to call you his own."

"Except you." She wrapped her arms around her waist, her eyes downcast. "You've made yourself clear on more than one occasion that you have no interest in anything beyond the present."

"It has nothing to do with you. The problem lies in *me*. If I were to take a wife, you would be my choice. But I canna fall in love. It would not be fair to you. Besides, I'm not worthy." He couldn't hide the emotion in his voice when he spoke.

"You once asked me to share my inner thoughts with you, Bryce, to tell you why I felt the need to do everything alone. I am asking you to grant me the same boon. Tell me why you've built a protective wall of stone around your heart?"

Silence stretched between them for so long, Fallon didn't think Bryce was going to answer. Then he ran a shaky hand through his hair and stared at a distant point somewhere behind her.

"I was sixteen summers, a lanky, moonstruck lad who, despite the horror I had already witnessed in my life, still believed in love and romance. My brothers told me I was being a fool and begging for trouble. But I wouldn't listen to them. I was enamored of the smithy's daughter. She was thirteen summers and her father thought her too young to marry. He forbid us to see each other, but we continued to meet in secret, swore our eternal love before the Almighty, and promised to marry when we were old enough." He stopped speaking to clear his throat.

Fallon stepped forward and placed her hand on his arm. "Please go on."

He glanced at her, then stared again at the spot that seemed so far away. "Ashlen was a beautiful lass. Her flaxen hair reminded me of summer wheat, her face like that of an angel. Sometimes when I close my eyes at night, I can still hear the sweet lilt of her voice. But as the years go by, it happens less and less. But I'll never forget it." His heart twisted in his chest. "Nor will I forget the sound of her screams when English soldiers raided the village and dragged us away."

Fallon moved closer and brushed her hand along his cheek. "And you blame yourself?"

Bryce ducked away and began to pace. "I am to blame. Don't you understand? Had we not been meeting in secret, she'd have been at home with her parents."

"You were bairns."

"Aye, but that is no excuse. When they got us to their camp, she called to me for help and I didn't do anything to save her. She begged the soldiers for mercy, but they just laughed. They held me and made me watch as the first man violated her. By the time the third began his assault, she'd grown quiet and had stopped struggling, the life and spirit gone from her eyes."

He rubbed a shaky hand across his brow. "I tried to fight them, but there were too many. When I did manage to twist free, one of the men struck me in the head with the hilt of his sword and I dinna remember anything after that."

Tears ran down his cheeks, but he scrubbed them away and turned his back. He could not believe he was sharing his inner torment with Fallon. Until now, he'd refused to discuss that day with anyone. Yet the words poured out of his mouth like a river over a waterfall.

He blew out a ragged sigh, then continued. "When I woke up, they were gone. I frantically searched for Ashlen, but could not find her. Then I heard her mother wailing. I raced to her side. Ashlen lay on the ground at the edge of a crofter's field. She'd been stripped naked and her head was twisted at an unnatural angle. The bastards broke her neck." Bryce buried his face in his hands. "She was so young and had had her whole life ahead of her. I wished they'd killed me in her stead."

Fallon caressed his shoulder, but he shrugged away.

"What happened to Ashlen was not your fault," Fallon said softly. "The English ravaged many women and young lasses on their campaigns. No one was able to stop them. Especially a lad who himself was being held against his will by the blackguards."

He didn't want her pity, but he had to make her understand. He'd never spoken about that day, but it had eaten away at him for eight years.

"I had my chance at love, Fallon, and dinna meet the challenge. I failed miserably and let Ashlen down. The day they lowered her into the ground, I vowed not to fall in love again. I promised her there would never be another."

"If what you say about Ashlen is true, she loved you very much. She would never want you to blame yourself. Nor would she want you to live your life alone."

"I'm not worthy of love. I canna." He grabbed her by the arms and shook her. "No matter how attracted I am to a woman. And I am so drawn to you, it drives me insane." He tugged her into a tight embrace, pressed his lips to the top of her head, then stepped away. "May the Almighty help me. No matter how hard I try, I canna get you out of my mind or my heart. But don't you see? I must. I let you down, too. Just like I did Ashlen."

Fallon stepped toward him with her hand outstretched, but he backed away. "I did everything I could to ensure your safety. When you showed up before the battle, I was furious. But not at you. I was angry at John for bringing you to the camp, but I was also afraid, terrified, that history was about to repeat itself. When we got word that Dungal had taken you prisoner, I almost went out of my mind. Hearing he planned to violate you, then kill you if I dinna do as he demanded, was like reliving the day Ashlen died all over again."

Before she could respond, he strode away. He needed time to get his emotions in check, to regain his composure.

"I dinna usually tell a man how to run his life. Heaven knows I have enough troubles in my own, but it is clear to me that you and young Fallon are meant to be together." Robert joined Bryce by the fire a while later.

"I canna argue about Fallon's many qualities. She is a wonderful woman, but I am not looking for a wife."

"So you claim." Robert cocked his head to the side then continued. "But your actions say differently." He patted Bryce on the shoulder.

"Fallon helped me when I was injured and came to warn us of the pending attack. When Dungal took her prisoner, I felt duty-bound to rescue her. But there is nothing more, and never can be," Bryce answered, but did not make eye contact with Robert. If he did, he was certain his friend would know he was a liar.

"I'm sure you have your reasons for pushing her away, Bryce, but life has a way of taking twists and turns we are not anticipating. Time lost canna be regained."

"You dinna understand. And you're right. I do have my reasons. I mean no disrespect, but would appreciate some time alone." He gazed into the fire, hoping Robert would honor his wishes, drop the topic, and give him some space. Heaven help him, but Alasdair nagged him enough for ten men.

"Mayhap I am not privy to everything you hold in your heart, but hear me out. Once I've said my piece, I will give you the solitude you desire."

Bryce nodded, but didn't reply. He picked up a stick and stirred the embers.

"I've been away from my wife and family for so long, I scarcely remember what they look like. I'd do anything to see them. To know they are safe and not in the hands of the enemy," Robert began.

Bryce lowered his head. "I'm sorry about your wife and daughter. I pray they are returned to you soon and in good health."

"There is a very real possibility that will never happen. Are you willing to throw away your chance for happiness? You canna change the past, but you can have some control over the future. If this war has taught me anything, life is too short to throw away opportunities. We never know what tomorrow has in store for us."

"Exactly. And if I die in the next battle or the next, I'll not leave behind a wife and mayhap a child to mourn me."

"Is it for your bride you fear, or yourself?"

"What is that supposed to mean?" Bryce snapped.

"I dinna know everything that has happened in your past. Some things a man must keep to himself. But it is clear that you are as much afraid of risking your heart as you are of leaving behind a family in the event of your death." Robert placed his hand on Bryce's shoulder. "Think long and hard, my friend, before you make a final decision that will affect the rest of your life. I am powerless at this moment to rescue my family, but you can do something to save the bond between you and Fallon."

Bryce pressed fingers to his temples and rubbed. After an extended pause in the conversation, he spoke. "The war brings with it so many uncertainties. I could not in good conscience ask Fallon to marry me, knowing I had to depart right away to do battle, and mayhap leave her a widow. Besides, I gave you my oath and pledged my sword to the cause. And my life if need be."

"Should you decide to ask for Fallon's hand, I willna expect you to remain with us. You have done more than your share to help the cause. Returning to the Highlands and taking care of you new bride would be your priority."

"I canna forsake my oath. My word is my bond and—"

Robert held his hand in the air to silence him. "Nay. I will release you from your pledge. If you wish to return to the fighting at a later time, you will be welcome. I told Connor the same thing when he married Cailin."

Bryce grew quiet. He had a lot to consider. Could he let go of the past and risk his heart again?

"Think about what I've said." Robert began to walk away then paused. "But dinna wait too long to making your decision. Brooding aside, there are far better things you could be doing with your time."

Fallon craned her neck and stared in the direction Bryce had gone, praying he'd come back. What was she to do? She had to find a way to reach Bryce, but how? He'd obviously suffered a great loss and could not move beyond his grief. To add to an already burdened conscience, he was blaming himself for her abduction. For a young man, he'd seen his fair share of sorrow and death. Her heart ached for him.

"When I'm wrong, I say so." Alasdair approached from behind.

Fallon turned to face him. "Wrong?" She had no idea what Alasdair was talking about. Yet his somber expression indicated he considered the issue serious.

"Aye. I dinna think Bryce should get involved with you, with any lass and did my best to dissuade him. I've always believed women are good for two things, tupping and bearing bairns. A man has more important things to think about than marriage and family. Losing his head to a woman spells nothing but trouble for a warrior."

"And you've changed your mind?"

"Nay. But I've learned there are men like Connor and Bryce who need that type of commitment, or they'll spend their lives feeling incomplete."

"What about you, Alasdair? Are you not a man who deserves a loving wife and family?"

He grunted and averted his gaze. "I'm a warrior and have no need in my life for such things. But my brothers are different."

She heard the uncertainty in his voice. "What is it about yourself that makes you different from your brothers?"

"I'm not a smart or bonny man, and the lassies dinna flock to me the way they do Connor and Bryce. I have never felt comfortable around a woman and dinna know what to say. I either end up blurting out something foolish or nothing at all. I prefer not to engage in the conversation in the first place. Most consider me a buffoon, and best they continue to do so."

"I think you are wrong. Mayhap if given a chance to get to know you, to see the gentler side you've shown me, they would change their minds." She lightly touched his arm, but he yanked it away.

"Well, that is not likely to happen. I dinna want a woman. I'm content with my life the way it is."

"Why are men so stubborn and blind? You sound like Bryce. Cailin told me Connor was equally reluctant to admit he needed a woman in his life." She shook her head. "Unfortunately, Bryce has suffered a great loss and canna move beyond his guilt. He seems to think that everything bad that happens in life is his fault."

"He told you about Ashlen?"

"Aye." She nodded. "But he was a lad and while I dinna doubt he loved her, it was not his fault she died. I don't know how to reach him or how to make him understand he is not responsible for her death or for my abduction."

"He has carried that burden for many years. When our mam and youngest brother were killed, Bryce took their loss very hard. He tried to put on a brave front and mimic our father's stoic attitude, but he still had the heart of a lad who had barely seen eleven summers. When Ashlen was killed, the fact her father blamed him for her death dinna help."

"But he was a bairn. A lad of sixteen summers canna possibly expect to fight off a band of highly trained English soldiers single-handedly."

"Connor and I have both tried to reason with him, but he refused to listen. We lived with our cousin Simon at the time. He spoke to Ashlen's father on Bryce's behalf, but nothing came of it. The day she died, my brother became focused on the cause and dedicated his life to it. He's had many a lass willing to warm his bed, but he would commit to none of them. He has not wavered until he met you."

"What makes you think I can change his mind?"

"There has been an obvious connection between you since the day you met at the Scott's castle. When we left and you were not there to say goodbye, I could tell it bothered him greatly. Even if he would never admit it."

"I was assisting with the birth of a bairn and was unable to be there when Connor and Cailin departed for Fraser Castle." While she spoke the truth, she kept the fact that she didn't want to say goodbye to Bryce a secret. She'd felt an overwhelming attraction to him the first time she saw him, but she had her own demons of the past to deal with.

"Do you love my brother?" Alasdair asked boldly.

"I—I," she stammered, uncertain how to answer Alasdair's question. She felt the heat rising in her cheeks and lowered her gaze.

While she loved Bryce, she didn't know how to compete with *taibhs* from the past or how to rid herself of the uncertainty she felt about falling in love. Everyone she loved had died and while Bryce set no store in prophecy, she had seen his death in a vision. She didn't want to be responsible for his demise simply because she selfishly wanted his love and to be loved.

"How I feel about Bryce dinna matter. He has his mind set and his reasons for not wanting a woman in his life. I canna see a way to change how he feels."

"If you love him, tell him," Alasdair said bluntly.

"It is not that simple."

"Things are only as complicated as you make them, Fallon. I admit that Bryce is a stubborn man. It runs in the family." He laughed, then continued. "Sometimes he dinna see what is best for him unless it jumps up and bites him in the arse. As much as I hate to admit it, the two of you were meant to be together."

Fallon chewed on her bottom lip, contemplating what Alasdair said. She'd always hoped Bryce would realize they belonged together, but she'd also feared falling in love for her own reasons. She'd lived most of her life alone, an outcast, feared because she possessed second sight. She had built her own protective walls to keep people out. Her heart clenched, afraid to believe she might find happiness with a man she adored more than life itself, afraid to love.

"Could I have a moment alone to speak with Fallon?" Bryce approached and she turned to face him.

"About time you came to your senses," Alasdair said and thumped Bryce on the back.

Bryce scowled at his brother. "I thought you had no use for women or marriage."

"Och, so we're talking marriage now, are we?" Alasdair laughed.

"If she'll have me." Bryce dropped to one knee and brought Fallon's hand to his lips.

Fallon stared at him in disbelief. Was she dreaming? She shook her head to be sure. "You want to marry me? Have you forgotten your plans to travel and finding your fortune? What about—"

He rose and silenced her with a quick kiss. "I'm certain with you for a wife my life will never be dull or lacking adventure. As for my fortune . . . I canna think of a more valuable treasure than having you as my bride. *Tha gaol agam ort.*"

"But you told me you could never fall in love, that you would never take a bride. What prompted you to change your mind?"

"A wise man talked some sense into me. He made me understand that while I canna change the past, I must try to move forward and take control of my future. He also made me realize time is fleeting and we dinna always get a second chance. You were right when you said Ashlen would not blame me for what happened or wish me to live alone."

"We've been telling you that for years," Alasdair said, but got no response from Bryce or Fallon. They were too busy looking at each other to pay him any mind.

Bryce took Fallon's hand and continued. "I was a fool and blind to the truth. I tried to distance myself. I dinna want to fall in love. But when I learned that Dungal had taken you prisoner, it became clear how much you meant to me. I was so afraid I'd lost you, and might never have the chance to tell you I was wrong for leaving you in Turnberry . . . for leaving you at all. I promise to make amends starting now if you'll give me that chance." He brought her hand to his lips. "Will you accept me as your husband, Fallon?"

She didn't know how to respond. She loved Bryce with all her heart and wanted to marry him. But the fact remained, she believed her love was a curse of death. With downcast eyes, she tried to back away, but he refused to let go.

"Are you not pleased by my offer of marriage? Am I presuming too much?"

She detected the nervous tremor in his voice when he spoke and inclined her chin. "Becoming your bride would make me very happy."

"Then marry me, Fallon."

"I canna."

Alasdair threw his hands in the air. "The two of you are making me dizzy. Best you decide what you want and then see to it." He turned and stormed off.

"I have to admit, I am confused. I thought you wanted us to be together." Bryce's voice softened to a whisper.

"I do . . . or I thought I did." She nibbled on her bottom lip and averted her eyes.

Bryce slid his fingers beneath her chin and raised it. "Talk to me, Fallon."

She wrapped her arms around her waist and turned her back. Her mind reeled and the tug on her heart was too much to bear. "I canna marry you. If I do, you will die. My love is a curse. I saw your death—"

Bryce spun her around and kissed her before she could finish, then lifted his head and laughed.

"I dinna see what you find so humorous."

"I feared your refusal to marry me was because you dinna love me. But the visions are what bother you. I told you I set no story in superstition."

"But I saw your death. I saw Dungal kill you."

"Aye, but as you can see, I am very much alive. Mayhap it was your love that saved me."

Taken aback by his remark, she was rendered speechless. What on earth was he saying?

"Don't you see, Fallon? We both had things in our past that kept us from falling in love. Riddled with guilt over the deaths of others, deaths we had no control over, we were ready to deny our happiness and throw it all away. But it wasna until we met and our love was put to the test, that we both learned the past was not our fault." He drew her against his chest and tucked her head beneath his chin.

She heard his heart pounding in unison with hers and smiled. She found the slow even raise and fall of his chest soothing. "I'm not sure I understand."

"A series of tragedies happened to us when we were both bairns. But you were right. We were too young and innocent to be held responsible for the deaths of those we loved. Loving them dinna kill them. You saw my death in a vision and until now, you have never been wrong. That in itself is an omen of good fortune. You saw Dungal destroy me in your dream, but my love for you gave me the courage and determination to fight. In turn, I destroyed Dungal."

Fallon gazed up at him and smiled. "I never looked at it like this before now."

"In a way, we saved each other. It was your dagger that kept me from bleeding to death when I was wounded. It saved me again when I faced the boar, and in my final confrontation with Dungal." Bryce reached into his sporran and pulled out the swatch of MacDougall plaid. He opened it, lifted her talisman, and tied it around her neck. "This kept you safe when you were in Dungal's clutches and it brought me to you when I was sure I'd never see you again."

"If you'd dispense with the idle chatter, you can get on with more important things." Alasdair retuned and nodded toward Robert's tent.

"Ignore my brother's crudeness. He never did learn any manners." Bryce scowled at Alasdair before returning his attention to Fallon. "You dinna answer my question. Will you, Fallon MacCrery, of the Clan MacCrery, agree to be my wife?"

"We've not read the banns. Nor do we have a priest present." Her heart hammered in her chest and her voice trembled when she spoke.

"Robert can declare us married and forego the reading of the banns. We can have a proper ceremony when we return to Fraser Castle if that is what you wish and all of our family can attend."

"What about your duty to Robert? Can you turn your back on the cause? I willna be the reason you give up your dreams."

"Robert has insisted that if we decide to marry, we return to Fraser Castle and start our new life together. He has released me from my pledge." Bryce smiled and tucked a wisp of hair behind her ear.

"It appears you have given this a great deal of deliberation." Fallon stroked his cheek. "Are you certain this is what you want?"

"I love you, Fallon, and was a fool not to realize how much until now."

His words gave her heart a jolt. Fallon offered a hesitant nod and smiled. Bryce loved her enough to forego his quest to make a name for himself, was prepared to give up his fight for the cause, to put his past heartache behind him. How could she deny him?

"Aye. I agree to marry you."

Chapter 20

Before she had a chance to say another word, Bryce scooped her into his arms and carried her toward the tent, amidst the cheers from the men. "Fetch Robert," he called over his shoulder to Alasdair. "We've already wasted enough time." He could hardly contain his excitement.

Fallon nuzzled her nose against his chest, her fist curled in his tunic. "You suddenly appear to be in a hurry."

"I canna wait to get you alone. Not only will I make you my wife, but I promise you a night to remember."

Robert joined them outside the tent. "Alasdair tells me you wish to take me up on my offer." He shot Bryce a knowing glance and a wry smile.

"Aye. I wish to make Fallon my bride." He set her down, brought her hand to his lips, then held it in the air. "I wish to declare before the King of Scotland and all those present that I take Fallon MacCrery as my wife."

"What have you to say, lass? Do you accept Bryce as your husband?" Robert waited for Fallon to answer.

"Think long and hard, lass. You dinna know what you are in for," Alasdair added and laughed. "There is still time to change your mind."

Bryce shifted his weight and anxiously awaited her reply. When she hesitated, his chest tightened. Had she changed her mind?

She gazed up and him and smiled. "Aye. I do wish to marry him," she answered softly. "Nothing would make me happier."

"Then it shall be done." Robert took their hands and wrapped length of plaid around their wrists, binding them together. After he recited several prayers in both Scots and Gaelic, he smiled and patted Bryce on the shoulder. "You have chosen well. I wish you much happiness and many strong sons."

Onlookers raised their swords in the air, then shouted, "Aye, Fraser!" along with some bawdy comments that made Fallon's face flush red.

"Go ahead and kiss her," Robert prompted. "The hour grows late and you have more important things to tend to."

Bryce kissed her with purpose, lifted her again, then entered the tent.

The soft glow of tallow candles added a romantic ambiance to their surroundings. A jug of mead and a trencher containing bread and cheese sat on a small table beside an overstuffed pallet in the corner.

"It appears Robert was expecting us." Fallon smiled and kissed Bryce on the cheek.

"This is not how I envisioned our wedding night, but it is a far cry better than the place we first joined." Guilt tugged at his gut when he recalled the selfish way he'd taken her innocence.

He set her down, then took both her hands and kissed her knuckles. "I'm ashamed of the way I behaved that night in the cave. But you are so ravishing and my body burns with desire every time you're near. You came to me a virgin, yet I acted like a randy lad, taking you on the cold stone, with little regard for the fact you were a maiden." He let go of her hands and shook his head. "In truth, I dinna want to be attracted to you. Mayhap a small part of me even hoped you'd hate me for being such an insensitive brute, that you'd be glad to be rid of me. I'm afraid you've married a fool."

Fallon caressed his cheek. "I'd not trade my memories of our first night together for anything."

Bryce encircled her waist, pulled her into his arms, and dropped his head. She opened her mouth, meeting the sweep of his tongue with equal enthusiasm, and the fire in his groin burned hotter.

"You taste like Heaven. I don't think I will ever tire of kissing you." He moaned the words into her mouth as he deepened his sensual exploration. His hands tugged at the neckline of her gown, but she covered them with her own.

"Let me do it." She fumbled with the laces, and soon the creamy flesh of her throat and breasts were exposed for his perusal. She let her gown slide over her shoulders and down her body, coming to rest in a pool of fabric at her feet.

She stood naked before him, rendering him breathless, just as she had the first time he'd laid eyes on her at the Scott's castle and the first time they'd joined. But tonight she belonged to him, and he intended to show her how much he loved her.

He eased her onto the pallet, tugged the tunic over his head, and removed his trews.

She rose to her knees, her eyes sparkling with mischief. Her fingers lightly floated over his burgeoning shaft.

His body responded with a lustful vengeance. He clutched her hand to stay her ministrations, but she'd not be denied. She lowered her head, touching the tip of his arousal with a brush of her soft, pink tongue, the erotic act sending a shiver of pure ecstasy up his spine.

He swallowed hard. This night was Fallon's and he meant to see her sated before seeking his own pleasure. "Do that again, our encounter will be over before it begins." He almost choked on the words.

She smiled up at him. "I've heard that a woman can drive a man to madness with the flick of her tongue. Is this true?" Before he had a chance to respond, she parted her lips and took him into her mouth, one agonizing inch at a time.

He threw back his head and growled like a feral beast, the threat of releasing his seed a very real possibility. But sublime bliss outweighed logic. He threaded his fingers through her hair, holding her head in place for a few glorious minutes before backing away.

"Tonight is our wedding night, and I want to make it special." He placed his hands on her shoulders and eased her back until she lay on the pallet. "Trust me and I promise I willna disappoint you."

Fallon was truly the loveliest woman he had ever met. He drank in her beauty while his body burned with desire and his mind reeled with possibilities. He stifled the overwhelming urge to take her hard and fast. He intended to spend the night exploring her silky skin, memorizing each sensual curve and dimple.

She languorously stretched before him. "Make love to me, Bryce." She reached for his aching rod, but he caught her hand and brought it to his lips instead.

"You are so exquisite. I'm not sure where to begin." He brushed her lips with a kiss. "Here . . ." He kissed her again. "Or here." He lowered his head, then quickly drew a nipple between his teeth and tugged. "Mayhap, I should start here." He cupped her other breast with his hand, causing her to arch her back and moan aloud. "What suits your fancy, m'lady?"

"I'm confident you will think of something, m'lord." Her words mingled with a breathy sigh.

Her dark lashes fluttered against her pale cheeks, and her sultry voice caused his heart to quicken. Her pouty lips were swollen from kissing, but he needed to sample them again.

He captured her mouth in an all-encompassing kiss. While he tasted her desire and her surrender, his hands skimmed along her ribs and across her flat stomach, coming to rest in a nest of soft, dark curls at the apex of her thighs.

She whimpered when he put his mouth to her woman's mound and began to nibble and suckle. Her body answered with a surge of wetness, and the scent of her arousal urged him on.

Her hips relaxed, giving him better access to the soft, pink folds that guarded the entrance to her most intimate place. His mouth watered at the thought of her sweet nectar, of plunging his tongue deep, and watching her writhe with pleasure.

With each lap of Bryce's tongue, every skillful stroke of his fingers, Fallon drifted deeper into a euphoric fog. He repeatedly brought her to the edge of rapture then eased off so he could build the tension again.

She closed her eyes, savoring the firestorm of sensations raging through her body, heating her blood, and igniting her soul. The moment he dipped his head between her thighs and circled the bud of pleasure with his tongue, she thought she might melt into a pool of ecstasy.

He lapped hungrily, alternating the speed and pressure until she found herself on the precipice of release. Her legs began to quiver and when he quickened the pace, she threw back her head and called out his name as she tumbled into an abyss of pure bliss. He continued to fondle and stroke until the last ripples faded and her erratic breathing slowed.

"That was incredible." She found it hard to speak.

"This is only the beginning, *Luaidth*. The best is yet to come." Bryce trailed kisses across her belly and paused to nip at her breast before settling his stiffened member in the hollow between her legs. He traced her lips with his fingertips. "Are you ready to truly become my wife?"

"Aye, husband. I want you more than anything." Even though they had already made love, this time felt like the first. Ignoring the nervousness twisting her stomach, she wrapped her arms around his neck and pulled him closer than she believed two people could ever be.

Wonder prompted her smile. She loved Bryce and had prayed they'd find a way to be together, but now it was actually happening, and it was amazing.

He kissed her, gently at first and then with purpose. His mouth moved over hers, and she tasted her own tangy essence, caught the strangely intoxicating scent of her climax. For the second time, her body responded with urgent need. Moist heat surged between her thighs.

"You are so wet and ready to love." He groaned and pressed the thick tip of his manhood against the entrance of her core.

She sucked in her breath and her body tensed when he slid to the hilt in one smooth move.

"Are you all right, Fallon?" He lay very still and raised his head.

Unlike their first joining, there was no pain. She smiled and released a shuddering breath. "Aye. Everything is wonderful."

"Try to relax. I won't do anything not meant to give you pleasure," he whispered in her ear then started moving slowly. As she mimicked his actions, he altered the tempo, pressing deeper into her body with each thrust.

Beads of sweat misted his forehead and soaked his chest. The muscles of his arms and thighs strained and bunched as he continued his fervent ride toward their mutual release.

The pressure began building in her core yet again. Her body bucked beneath his powerful form, and together they let the waves of rapture carry them to the height of completion and beyond.

After shouting out a war cry and releasing his seed, he collapsed on top of her, his heart pounding in unison with her own. He rolled to the side, taking her with him. Cradled in the crook of his arm, she rested her hand on his heaving chest and her fingers furled in dark, sodden curls. "You kept your promise." She snuggled closer.

"Rest for a bit. The night is still young, and I have many things to show you."

To her utter delight, he honored that pledge several times.

Dawn came too early. Huddled in Bryce's arms, Fallon let her mind wander. A smile of contentment tugged at her lips. She closed her eyes, wishing that when she opened them, it would still be night, and that Bryce would make love to her again.

A king-sanctioned union, they were legally wed by declaration according to Scottish law, yet she found it difficult to believe her dream had come true. Joy filled her as she thought about their future together. Bryce accepted her for who she was and didn't fear her gift of second sight. For the first time in her life, she felt truly blessed.

Their first few hours as man and wife had been incredible. Her hand slid over her belly. After a night of fervent passion, did she carry his babe?

"Do you think my son will be born when the snow flies?" Bryce's voice was thick and hoarse from lack of sleep. He covered her hand with his and smiled. "I'd like to have five bairns, mayhap more. What do you think?"

She looked at him and smiled. "Best we consider one first." She managed to force the words past a sudden sob building in her throat.

Bryce frowned and lifted her chin, forcing her to look at him. "Why are you upset? Are you not happy?"

"I need to be certain marriage is what you truly want. It is not too late to change your mind, or to ask Robert to repudiate his declaration of marriage."

Bryce pulled her into a tight embrace. "I am so fortunate to have you for a wife. Did I not prove that to you last night?" He brushed aside a stray curl and pressed his lips to her brow. "I know I dinna make it easy on you, but I hoped by consenting to marry me you had forgiven me, and were ready to move ahead. Are you having second thoughts?" Bryce's expression darkened and he tightened his hold on her.

"Nay." She stroked his cheek. "I could never imagine being with anyone else. But I also know how duty-bound you are and that by giving up the cause, you also relinquish your chance to seek amends for the deaths of your parents and friends. I want to be certain you can you live with that decision?" Her voice trailed off and tears threatened again.

"After my parents and brothers were killed, I thought the Lord had forsaken me. When Ashlen died, I was certain of it. I carried that grief for so many years that I almost missed out on the most important thing in my life. You. Things changed the minute we met. No matter how hard I tried to fight temptation and deny what was in my heart, the battle was over before it began. I love you, Fallon, and when my son is born, I will adore him, too." He cupped her belly again.

"Daughter," Fallon whispered.

He cocked his brow. "A lass?"

"I had a vision my first babe would be a daughter. Will you be terribly disappointed?"

Bryce tossed his head back and laughed. "I would be the proudest da in Scotland. Especially if she is half as beautiful and feisty as her mam." Before she could respond, he rolled her beneath him, kissed her, then raised his head. "In case she has yet to be conceived, I think it best we try again." A devilish grin brightened his face.

"The time has come to pack up the camp. If the two of you wish to break your fast before we leave, I'd suggest you make haste," Alasdair shouted from outside their tent.

Bryce heaved a deep sigh and kissed the tip of Fallon's nose. He wished the night could go on forever, but unfortunately good things must end. Best we get dressed before they pull the walls down around us." He rose and handed Fallon her gown and kirtle. He quickly donned his clothes and tugged on his boots. "I'll meet you outside."

Alasdair was waiting for them in the clearing. "There are oatcakes and porridge if you're hungry. I'm sure you worked up quite an appetite." He slapped Bryce on the back then doubled over laughing.

Bryce grunted at his brother's crudeness, but did not allow his remarks to rile him. Not today. He was married to Fallon, had spent an incredible night making love to her, and was happier than he deserved to be. He would not let anyone spoil the mood.

"Have you seen Robert? I need to speak to him." Bryce scanned the campsite for the Bruce.

"I'm here. What did you wish to talk to me about?" Robert approached.

"After we've eaten, Fallon and I will be on our way." Bryce slid his arm around her shoulders and brought her to his side.

Robert extended his arm and Bryce clasped his wrist. "You'll need to take along some men for protection. I will ask for volunteers to accompany you. The MacDougalls were driven back and you are heading north, not south, but you canna be too careful." Robert turned to Alasdair. "Pick a dozen men from those who offer their service to escort you and your brother to Fraser Castle. Also select a suitable mount for Fallon."

Alasdair glanced from Bryce to his king. "I will gladly select the men and horse, but I willna be going to Fraser Castle. I intend to stay with you, Robert, and will continue the fight to drive the English out of Scotland."

Bryce's brows knit together. "We will sorely miss you on the journey, and I am sure Connor will be disappointed if you dinna return with us. But you know your mind, brother, and must do what suits you. Promise you will come home to us soon."

Alasdair took a stepped backward and sniffled, his voice strained with emotion when he spoke. "I will be home in time for the birth of your first babe. Tell Connor and Cailin I am well, and give Andrew a hug from his uncle." He reached into his sporran and pulled out a small, carved wooden ball. "Give this to the lad?"

Bryce took the toy. He'd noticed Alasdair carving the ball while sitting around the fire at night. "I'll hold you to your word and will tell Andrew you made this for him. Are you certain we canna convince you to come with us?"

Alasdair shook his head. "Nay. My place is here and yours is with your wife. I must admit, I never thought I would say those words to you, but am pleased you chose Fallon for your bride."

Bryce swallowed against the lump of emotion growing in his throat. Despite their frequent bickering, they cared about each other. His heart twisted in his chest. Leaving his older brother to fight alone was one of the hardest things he had ever done.

Fallon moved toward Alasdair, stood on tiptoe, and kissed his cheek. "Take care of yourself, brother. Come home safe and soon."

Alasdair nodded. "I will, but now I must gather the men who will travel with you." He trotted off.

"He'll be all right." She placed her hand on Bryce's forearm.

"He'd better be, or I'll never forgive him." Bryce hauled her into his arms and kissed her. "Time to leave, *mo goal.*"

She gazed up at him and smiled. "I love you, Bryce. Let's go home."

Epilogue

July 1308, Castle Fraser, Beauly Scotland

The sun hung high in the sky and a warm breeze ruffled Elise's raven curls. Fallon kissed her sleeping daughter's brow then laid her on the plaid she'd spread out on the ground. "Sleep, my wee one. Your da will be back from the hunt very soon and I'm sure he'll want to see his little princess. I've never seen a man dote on a bairn the way he does on you." Fallon smiled. Her life was perfect.

"Andrew Simon Fraser! Come back, you little scamp!" Cailin raced after her son. "When I get my hands on you—" She came to an abrupt halt, pressed her hand to her lower back, and doubled over at the waist, her breath coming in sharp pants.

"Nay!" The toddler giggled and raced to where Fallon sat beneath the shade tree and climbed into her lap.

"Mamma mad." He popped his thumb into his mouth and buried his face in Fallon's gown.

"Are you all right, Cailin?" Fallon tousled Andrew's auburn hair. "You must be kinder to your mam. She is going to give you a little brother any day now and canna keep up with you the way she used to." She peered up at her sister-by-marriage. "He is a handful."

"He's his father's son. Always on the go and giving me grief." Cailin laughed and lowered herself to the ground beside Fallon. "I'm sorry. I hope he dinna wake Elise."

"She is a very sound sleeper. Not much disturbs her." Fallon gazed at her babe and covered her tiny shoulders with a knitted shawl. "She is growing so fast. I can hardly remember the day she was born."

"How could you forget?" Cailin shook her head. "We were in the middle of the worst snow storm I'd ever seen. You labored for two long days before the babe decided to finally come. She entered the world early, feet first, and you almost died."

"Aye, but I survived and she is the joy of my life." She tore her eyes from her daughter and looked at Cailin. "Andrew's delivery was not easy for you, either. I remember how surprised you were when your birthwater broke during your wedding dance. I'll not forget the look of shock on Connor's face or his anger when we told him he could not be in the chamber during his son's birth." She reached out and touched Cailin's swollen belly. "You labored long and hard, yet you are about to do it again. Are you afraid?"

Cailin patted her belly and gave her head a shake. "Giving birth is always frightening, but you are right, the risk and pain is well worth it. She reached for her son and tugged him into her lap. "Andrew did everything so early. He walked before he was one summer old and has never stopped. He started to talk not long after that. I hope our next one stays a babe a little longer."

"Da, Da!" Andrew jumped to his feet, scurried to his father, and scrambled up his leg.

Connor hugged his son and spun him around in a circle. "Have you been a good lad for your mam?" He carried the toddler across the grass and put him down beside his mother. "Are you well, lass?" He bent over and kissed his wife.

Bryce approached and laughed when Andrew darted after a butterfly and Connor gave chase. "And how are my ladies?" he asked, then squatted and kissed Fallon."

"We are well. Did you have a good hunt?" Fallon smiled at her husband.

"Aye. We killed two bucks and a wild boar. There will be plenty of meat to get us through the first part of the winter. We plan to go out again before we leave-"

"Leave?" Chest suddenly tight, Fallon stood and touched Bryce's forearm. "Where are you going?"

Bryce shifted his weight and glanced away. "We received a missive from Alasdair."

"Is he all right? Will he coming home? He promised to return to Fraser Castle before Elise was born and has yet to do so."

"Robert has been engaging the English across the Highlands since last fall. He has retaken many of the castles under English rule and those that once belonged to the supporters of King John Balliol. He is planning to return to Galloway and is preparing for a major battle with the MacDougalls and McCanns. He has called for support."

Fallon wrapped her arms around Bryce's waist and pressed her cheek to his chest. "You and Connor are going to join them, aren't you?"

"Aye. We canna turn our back on our countrymen while Alasdair is fighting on behalf of the Fraser Clan."

"I understand. Will your brother return to Fraser Castle or meet you in Galloway?"

"Since he has been fighting in the northern part of Scotland for so long, he has decided to accept an invitation to visit the Clan Sinclair. The laird was a dear friend of our da and his oldest son, Jayden, and Alasdair played together as lads. My brother spent many a summer there before our parents were killed."

"Your brother deserves a chance to rest and to have a wee bit of fun. He is always so somber and gruff. Mayhap he will someday settle down with a lass of his own. I pray he finds the kind of happiness we have." Fallon kissed Bryce's cheek.

Bryce shook his head and chuckled. "Why do women feel the need to see all men betrothed? You know my brother. He has no use for a woman in his life."

"People can change. Mayhap he has not found the right lass and when he does—"

He brought his fingers to her lips. "Hell will freeze over before Alasdair marries so there is no point wishing for things that willna happen."

"When do you depart for Galloway?" Fallon asked as she fought to rein in the knot of dread squeezing her chest. She didn't want him to go, but would never try to stand in his way.

"We'll wait until after Cailin has her babe. According to Alasdair's missive, Robert doesna plan to launch his attack until the end of summer. We have plenty of time to join them." He glanced down at Cailin. "I'm sorry you found out this way. I know Connor wanted to tell you about this himself."

Cailin shook her head. "I knew this day would come. It was just a matter of time." With Bryce's help, she climbed to her feet.

Bryce gathered Fallon in his arms. "I know I promised to stay with you and Elise—"

"You must do what is in your heart. I remember you once said that to Alasdair. Your brother needs you. Your king needs you. I would never try to stop you from doing your duty. Elise and I will be waiting and praying for your return."

"You never cease to amaze me. I best go help Connor catch Andrew before he reaches the stream." He pressed his lips to her brow then trotted off to find his brother.

"Will you ask Connor to stay?" Fallon chewed on her bottom lip as she watched Bryce disappear over the hill.

"I know better than to try. I am fortunate Connor has not returned to the cause before now. When we met, it was his whole life. He gave it up to care for Andrew and me, but I always knew in my heart it wouldn't last."

"Aye. Bryce was destined to return to the fight as well." Fallon sat on the plaid beside her daughter.

"Did you see it in a vision?" Cailin asked. She held her chin high, but failed to hide the nervous tremor in her voice. "Tell me. I want to know good or bad."

Fallon took Cailin's hand and gave it a comforting squeeze. "I have not had a premonition since the day Bryce rescued me from Dungal. Mayhap the curse is lifted. But like you, I know my husband and his sense of duty."

"Do you think Elise will inherit your gift of second sight?"

Fallon lightly stroked her daughter's brow. "It is possible. They say *da shealladh* is passed from mother to daughter, but I hope not. I would never wish it upon any bairn."

"Do you plan to tell Bryce about the new babe before he leaves?" Cailin slid her hand over Fallon's shoulder.

Fallon caressed her belly. "Nay. God willing, I'll share our good news when he returns."

The Fraser brother's saga continues with
Highland Homecoming.

CPSIA information can be obtained at www.ICGtesting.com
Printed in the USA
LVOW10s1144051113

359969LV00004B/19/P